THE SUMMER FIELDS

An inspiring journey of self-discovery

Jess Crichton is a bright, conscientious girl whose self-inflicted failure at school only makes her more determined to make something of herself.

In her first job she meets people very different from herself and her life seems to be on course. But there are lessons to be learned, and Jess's initial experiences with the opposite sex do not bode well. Until she travels to Skye, and her mind is opened to new horizons...

THE SUMMER FIELDS

THE SUMMER FIELDS

Frances Paige

Severn House Large Print
London & New York

This first large print edition published in Great Britain 2002 by
SEVERN HOUSE LARGE PRINT BOOKS LTD of
9-15, High Street, Sutton, Surrey, SM1 1DF.
First world regular print edition published 2001 by
Severn House Publishers, London and New York.
This first large print edition published in the USA 2002 by
SEVERN HOUSE PUBLISHERS INC., of
595 Madison Avenue, New York, NY 10022

British Library Cataloguing in Publication Data

Paige, Frances
   The summer fields. - Large print ed.
   1.   Glasgow (Scotland) - Social life and customs - 20th century -
        Fiction
   2.   Love stories
   3.   Large type books
   I.   Title
   823.9'14 [F]

   ISBN 0-7278-7125-0

Except where actual historical events and characters are being described
for the storyline of this novel, all situations in this publication are
fictitious and any resemblance to living persons is purely coincidental.

Printed and bound in Great Britain by
MPG Books Ltd, Bodmin, Cornwall.

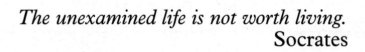

The unexamined life is not worth living.
Socrates

One

1928
The two sisters reacted differently to the flat they all moved into in the West End of Glasgow.

It just managed to escape being in Anderston, which was on a lower social scale. Not, of course, that they understood such refinements.

'Opposite a school,' Peggy said. 'That will suit Jess and James at least.'

Maggie Crichton, their mother, looked at Jess. 'You're no' saying much. Are *you* pleased?'

'It's all right.' She had scarcely recovered from the upheaval in their lives – their mother's decision to give up 'the premises', as she called them, after their father's death. And seeing she wanted more, Jess added, 'It's near a park. I like that. And I took James to see St Andrew's Hall yesterday. It's got stone men all round it.'

'Stone men!' Mrs Crichton threw up her eyes as if that was a further example of her younger daughter's strangeness.

Actually Jess would have liked to say, 'Anything's better than the East End,' but she knew her mother would have bridled at that. She had once said it was ugly, and her mother had said what a word to use and she should thank her lucky stars that she was kept like an egg in a cake.

The business her father had built up there before he died proved, however, a valuable tool for impressing her new acquaintance, Mrs Thompson, the janitor's wife from the school across the road who had been quick to offer help when they were in the process of settling in.

One of the few good memories of 'the premises' Jess had was of her father coming into the girls' bedroom, white-faced but happy, and saying, 'You've got a new wee brother.'

She had burst into tears of relief because she had thought her mother's screams and groans meant she was dying, her fear not helped by Peggy who had said, with a smug face, 'She's no' dying. They aw do that.'

Her father had come over to Jess and taken her in his arms and said it was all right now, and when she met his eyes they were full of love for her. 'A wee brother,' he had said, stroking her hair. 'James.'

But for the rest, especially the antagonism they had suffered after the death of Danny, the milk-boy, she was glad to leave the mean streets, the dirty closes chalked with crude drawings and even cruder words, glad to be rid of the ever-present feeling of shame when she saw the bare feet of some of the boys in her class – in winter swollen red with chilblains – their tattered jerseys hanging over their wrists in seaweed strands. The Crichtons had been considered capitalists in a Red Labour district, especially in the Depression years of the twenties. Anyhow, here they were in the flat the Grays – friends of their father's – had fixed up for them, with a new school across the road. And there was that lovely Kelvingrove Park where she could take James, with its green grass, trees with birds in them, and if the flowers were not for picking, at least they were there.

Peggy liked it. She was already working in a grocer's round the corner through the good offices of Mrs Thompson, and had been introduced by the other assistants to the delights of the city, the cinema cafés, the 'pictures' and the Aladdin's caves of the big Sauchiehall Street shops.

The school turned out to be a sad disappointment to Jess. There was a definite defeatist air about the place – it was running down, or being allowed to run down, and the teachers were lackadaisical, like leftovers from earlier and better times.

Miss Mackie sat at her desk absorbed, it seemed, in inserting the screwed-up point of her handkerchief into her nostrils, especially in foggy weather. Miss Durie, a fluttery old maid, sat companionably on one of the desks with her feet up on the one in front. She seemed unaware of the tittering as the boys pushed to get near enough to see the display of blue silk Directoire knickers, and the hope of a gleam of white thigh.

The apathy of the teachers spread to the pupils. When during an interval Jess asked a girl what the thumping in the attic was, she said, 'Come up and see!' The sight that met Jess's eyes after they had run up the stairs took her breath away.

Girls were dancing madly in circles which Jess recognised as bearing some resemblance to eightsome reels; others were whirling in pairs, hands clasped, arms outstretched, backs bent backwards, hair flying. They 'hooched' and shouted, some sang in time, and the wooden floor shook with the dancing and sent up clouds of dust.

'Will they no' get a row?' she asked.

'Ach,' Chrissie said, 'these auld besoms doonstairs couldny care less, they're just passing the time till they get their pensions. Come on and we'll burl each other!'

She was surprised, after a little reluctance, at how easy it was to break rules, and even to get an illicit thrill in breaking them. The

12

East End school had been run on firm lines because of the amount of truancy. That and any insolence were punished in the only way the headmaster recognised – severe belting with a leather strap whose ends, they said, he toasted in the fire to make them harder. That it hurt was evident in how the boys jumped about blowing on their hands and then tucking them under their arms. Some wept. Jess had kept her head down in case it might be her turn next.

Insubordination became easy because of the example set her. She slacked in class, lounged in her seat the way the other pupils did, giggled with them and presented scanty and badly written homework. She was a quick learner in that as in everything else.

The sewing mistress who came once a week knew Jess. She had taught at her other school, and welcomed her with pleasant surprise. 'What are you doing here, Jess?'

'We shifted here because of the Strike, Miss. And then there was Danny...'

'Yes, I was sorry to read about that. Your mother would miss your father then. A true gentleman.' She looked kindly at her. 'Well, what have we here?'

'It's the dress I was making at the other school, Miss Pollock.' It looked more like a crumpled rag.

She examined the botched pink linen. 'You haven't got much further with this, Jess

Crichton.' Her tone changed. 'You could have ironed it at least. It looks like something the cat brought in.' There was a titter from the girls. 'I suggest you take out the basting stitches and iron in the pleats again. I'll expect an improvement next week.'

'Yes, Miss.' She walked back to her seat, sullen and resentful. She had been made to look like a fool in front of the class.

It was a fortnight before Miss Pollock came again, and the class had been under the care of Miss Mackie, who had cheerfully confessed she knew nothing about sewing. Jess had re-basted and ironed the pleats, and managed to get two further spots of blood on the white collar. She knew the whole thing was a mess.

During this time her periods had started, and she felt odd, not herself. Her fingers were clumsy. The dull ache in the pit of her stomach was new to her. Peggy scoffed. 'You've taken ages! Mine came at eleven – you're nearly fourteen! You know you can't have weans unless it comes.'

Who wanted weans? All the women in the East End had big families and then couldn't look after them. And the fathers drank. Her mother said they were lazy, wouldn't know how to do a good day's work if they were given the chance.

Miss Pollock's disappointment in her still rankled when she took the dress to her for inspection. She presented it silently, her eyes downcast, her shoulders hunched. The dull ache was still there. She was a different person since 'it' had come, as if one part of her was a woman, and the rest of her, like now, was awkward and miserable.

Miss Pollock was examining the dress with a steady gaze. She put her finger on the two spots of blood, shook her head impatiently, then handed the dress back to Jess.

'This will all have to come out. See!' She stretched her inch-tape across the pleats. 'These are all a different size. What's happened to you, Jess Crichton? You used to do such good work. You seem like a different person!' She waited for a reply. Jess stood, head down, still silent.

'All right.' Miss Pollock's lips were tight. 'Go back to your seat and unpick it.'

'I'm not picking it out.' She didn't know where the words came from. She heard a loud gasp behind her. She stood, clutching the pink dress, and wished she could faint.

Miss Pollock didn't look angry. Only puzzled. Her brows were knitted. She waited, a long time, then said, 'Very well. Go back to your seat and stay there till you feel better. I'm going to forget what you said. Next, please?' She looked up at the class.

The girls' looks as Jess walked back between the desks were admiring, but fearful. They hadn't as yet gone in for outright

15

rebellion, only a disregard of rules which barely existed. This was a new departure, and from a least likely source – the new girl.

She had her fourteenth birthday, feeling ill and depressed. Mrs Thompson suggested a doctor but her mother said there would be no doctor coming to their house for pure laziness. She spoke severely to Jess when Mrs Thompson had gone.

'A thought you were goin' to be the scholar. Ah, well. A should have known better. Your sister's working and a'm no' goin' to keep a big lump like you lounging about doin' nothin'. You can tell them you're leavin' and you'd better start lookin' for a job.'

She'd agreed. She had made a fool of herself. Besides, if she left she wouldn't have to face Miss Pollock.

The teacher hadn't mentioned the episode of the dress again, indeed she had given her a traycloth to embroider with lazy daisies instead, but it didn't help. She suffered from burning shame. What would her father have thought of her?

Peggy laughed and said she was making a fuss about nothing. Wait till she saw the fun she could have 'up the town'.

She told James she was leaving one summer Sunday when she took him to the Park, but at six he had no opinions. The only boy in a feminine household, he had learned to

16

distance himself already.

'And I've got a job,' she said, 'in a Nautical Instruments office. Ten shillings a week.'

'That's a lot of money, Jess, isn't it?'

'It's usual for an office girl, but I've got to go to College and learn to be a shorthand typist.' Peggy had said Jess had been born lucky, sitting on her backside all day while she herself was on her feet from morning to night.

'Well you shouldn't gallivant up the town every night,' she'd said, but their mother had told them to stop quarrelling and do something useful.

'Will it be in a building like St Andrew's Hall?' James asked. 'This College?'

'Glasgow's full of big buildings,' she told him. 'I'll take you some day.'

She liked the Park, the people strolling about in the sunshine, the lawns and beds of flowers, the river running through it, the children playing in the paddling pool.

They walked uphill to see Lord Roberts' statue and James, pointing to a spired building on the hill, asked, 'What's that, Jess?'

'It's Glasgow University. Gilmorehill, it's called. You'll maybe go there when you're big.'

'Is it only for boys?'

'No, girls too, if they're clever enough.' You've missed the boat, she told herself, through your own stupidity. So you'd better 'stick in' – her mother's favourite expression – now.

'Race you to the foot!' James said.

The wind blew through her hair as she ran, being careful not to outdistance James. Soon, she thought, I shall have to walk circumspectly, an office girl in the city. She hadn't meant it this way. She'd had plans, scarcely formulated, but she'd always felt there would be something different for her. Well, she had only herself to blame. Her childhood was over.

Two

1931

'I'm hanged if I'd trail round the town deliverin' letters,' Peggy said.

Each morning Muriel, the typist at James MacIntyre and Son, gave Jess a bundle of letters to deliver by hand. Muriel was a cheerful young woman with brown curly hair, a little beak of a nose and a chirping voice which reminded Jess of a canary they'd had at the last flat.

'It's Mr MacIntyre's orders,' Jess said. 'I can't say I'm not going to do it.' Memories of Miss Pollock flashed through her mind. It still bit deep.

'He sounds like a mean skinflint,' her mother pronounced, 'but she's right. She's paid to do what she's told. We'll go to Bayne & Duckett's, then. They've got a sale on. And we might as well have a look at the shops for your wedding outfit.'

Muriel was getting married to Richard, now a chartered accountant, a rugby player for the 'Accies' – Jess understood this meant

former pupils of the Glasgow Academy –
and she had invited Jess to the wedding.

Mrs Crichton had accepted the challenge.
'They may be toffs, her folk, but you'll be
turned out like the rest of them if it costs me
my last penny.'

'Trust you,' Peggy had said when she saw
the outfit. Jess had grown used to her criti-
cism. They had little in common. Both went
their own ways – Jess to conscientious
studying at the Secretarial College, Peggy to
her own fun and games with the two shop
girls, Jenny and Dora, and, Jess suspected,
'fellas'.

The three years she had spent in the city
had changed her, outwardly at least. She
was first in all her examinations at the
College, and she had copied the students
there in her neat dressing and attention to
detail. She was slender, still shy, but she was
a typical business girl. She knew her way
about the city, she admired its gracious
buildings, felt pleased that the office where
she worked was in St Vincent Place in a
classical Greek building. She could find
copies of it in all parts of the city – the
Greek Thomson church in St Vincent
Street, Blythswood Square where the
notorious Madeleine Smith had lived.

'Of course it was her!' Peggy said. 'Easy as
pie. A basement window, in he goes, then
when her rich Daddy wants her to marry

someone of his choice she had to find a way to get rid of the Italian lover!'

It was 'not proven', Jess had pointed out but Peggy had poured scorn on that too. 'The judges would be in wi' the toffs, mark my words.' Peggy had strong opinions and stuck to them. Jess admired her.

She was to take Muriel's place when she left. Mr MacIntyre, a portly gentleman with a large red face generally topped with a bowler, told her he hoped she appreciated her good luck since there were so many unemployed people in Glasgow. 'Even this firm...' he'd said, then had stopped. In spite of his jolly appearance he looked perpetually worried.

'Where do you think you're going?' Peggy had laughed at Jess standing at the mirror in their bedroom in full panoply. 'Buckingham Palace?' To meet the sartorial requirements of Muriel's wedding Mrs Crichton had spared no expense.

The long dress, backless, was of pink chiffon, on the lines of a Spanish dancer's, the bodice and the long-sleeved jacket in devoré velvet. To complete the ensemble there was a wide-brimmed green picture hat. Jess could hardly blame Peggy for laughing – 'dressed up like a dish of fish', as Peggy had put it – but she thought the reflection in the mirror of this strange young

21

woman had a certain elegance.

She went in fear and trembling in a taxi – her first ever – which dropped her at the foot of the steps of the Wellington Church, another example of Greek architecture she noticed, although it didn't help her on her long climb up the flight of steps to the entrance.

She was greeted at the top by a young man in a tailcoat who said he was Muriel's brother and had been told to look after her. She thankfully sank into a seat he led her to.

Muriel, she thought, looked dwarfed in her panoply when she came down the aisle on the arm of her father. The white dress and veil seemed to reduce her in some way to something like the sugar brides on the top of wedding cakes on permanent display in the City Bakeries window – actually made of cardboard, she had been told – and the bridegroom was disproportionately tall with thick-rimmed glasses.

He didn't fit in with her conception of the man who had made Muriel twitter excitedly over her Royal for the past few years, and for whom Jess, in her wanderings about the city, had chosen a Sleepeezee mattress in a panoplied bed. She had once had a dream of Muriel in a pink chiffon nightie lying in bed and Richard bending over her and saying tenderly, 'Sleepeezee.'

Muriel's brother, true to his promise,

whisked her off at the end of the ceremony to the Grosvenor Hotel, where the bride and groom and parents were waiting in a row to receive the guests. She didn't know what to say to Muriel. It wasn't the Muriel she knew saying, 'Nip into the toilet and fill the kettle, Jess. I'm dying for a cup of tea,' nor the Muriel who crashed and banged and rang bells at her Royal with cheerful abandon.

She had never been in company like this in her life. They all spoke differently, they all laughed a lot and made strange jokes with each other, like 'Do you remember that Casanova at the Hydro last year?' and burst into fits of laughter.

She experienced a profound shock when Muriel, hitching her long train over her arm, opened the dancing with her new husband. It seemed to her like a blasphemous act, that this bridal sacrifice in white should dance a vulgar fast quickstep with her new husband to shouts of 'Nifty footwork, Richard!' and 'Good old Muriel!'

Jess couldn't believe that all those people got on so well, used as she was to her mother's acerbic tongue. She thought of the Forsyte Saga, and that helped. This was a whole world she didn't know, a clan. She could feel the rules, like a structure, an underpinning. That was why they got on so well. They knew the rules.

She was a success at the Plaza when she took off the devoré jacket, or perhaps because she was like a strange bird that had strayed into the wrong forest. The men were intrigued, and she was never off the floor.

She zigzagged and swung to the Plaza band in the arms of various McEwan-taught young men who all said the same thing, more or less – 'Where have you been all my life?' She couldn't think of an adequate answer except once when she replied, 'I didn't know you'd been looking,' which had brought her partner near to apoplexy.

She couldn't think of much to tell her mother when she got home except the size of the wedding cake and a description of Muriel's outfit, and that everybody had been very kind, and no, nobody had mentioned her dress. Peggy listened with a supercilious air and said she would rather have a good night's jigging in the Scout hut, and Mrs Crichton lost interest in the whole thing. Jess was at a loss to know what her mother had expected – a signed certificate to prove that her dress was the best there? 'Hang it up in the wardrobe after you've covered it with that old tablecloth.' It was dismissed.

Jess didn't have the courage to tell her that she had left her hat in the Plaza.

Three

Jess missed Muriel's chirpiness, and although she was now designated as a shorthand typist, the salary was low.

Possibly as low as Mr MacIntyre's spirits, she thought. She guessed his business wasn't going well. He dictated numerous letters to her along the same lines, 'I shall be in your district this week and would like to take the opportunity of calling on you to discuss future business...' Initially, he varied them slightly with each recipient, but then appeared to lose heart and told Jess to compose them herself.

The chauffeur of his grey Daimler disappeared and he took to driving it himself, his navy-blue suit became shiny at the elbows and his little rosy mouth drooped miserably.

She spent long hours in the office alone when he was out on his calls, often polishing and repolishing the glass cabinets in his room containing models of early Clyde-built steamers. They belonged to another world, she thought, like Mr MacIntyre.

She looked out of the large windows on to busy St Vincent Place. Her mind, she thought, was no more occupied here than it had been at school. She was restless, there had to be more in life than this. She should have been studying. An image of the grey spires above the Kelvin swam before her.

Nessie Riddell, a distant cousin whom she met occasionally in town, couldn't understand her. 'You're only marking time till you meet some bloke and get hitched, Jess. Look at me and Bob. He's joined the Territorials, and we're going to save up for getting married when he gets allotted to Army quarters. We're both contented.' She admired Nessie's contentment.

She had a letter from the College Principal.

> Since you were the first of three in the course you have recently completed, we have decided to offer you free tuition at the College for a Commercial Teachers' Diploma. You are also eligible for entry to an Admiralty posting as shorthand typist, if that should be your preference.

She accepted the free tuition. She had tested her mother about her going to

London, but her response was as she had expected. 'Leave home! Over ma dead body! None o' ye leave this house until you get married!'

She had now plenty to do with her time. Three hours' attendance three times each week, the last year to be spent in a college in the South Side as a pupil teacher.

Her mother accepted this decision with unexpected pleasure. 'See, Peggy, there's someone who wants to get on! Pity you couldn't put your mind to something like that instead of chasing policemen!'

This was a sore point. Their mother had a deep-rooted objection to anyone in the police force. They were 'trash', 'rubbish'. Jess took no part in this, but she noticed that Peggy was coming in later and later.

'She's furious with you,' she commented one night, watching Peggy's flushed face and shining eyes as she undressed, her covert bursts of laughter as if there were some secret joke.

'Don't you start. You're her pet just now but it won't last.'

She took no further part in Peggy's affairs. She was now fully occupied with the exacting syllabus of the teaching course. Any homework she didn't get done at home she could at least do in the long idle hours she spent alone in the office at St Vincent Place.

She felt acutely sorry for Mr MacIntyre,

and tried to put on a semblance of busyness when he was there, which was seldom. His navy-blue suit grew shinier, she thought his shoes looked scuffed. She hoped he had an understanding wife at home or even a jolly family to cheer him up. He never mentioned them.

She saw a notice under 'Jobs Vacant' on the College noticeboard which appealed to her – *'Shorthand typist wanted for large busy office'* – and on impulse applied for it. The salary was much higher than she was currently getting. She told herself she would be doing Mr MacIntyre a good turn, but she still felt like a traitor, a rat deserting a sinking ship.

She was offered the job – she was always surprised that her demeanour seemed to suit her prospective employer – but she didn't relish telling Mr MacIntyre.

'Mr MacIntyre?' she said when he passed her the following morning on his way to his room. Even the seat of his navy-blue trousers was shiny, she noticed before he turned. His bowler was on at a jaunty angle, which made her feel worse than ever.

'I've been offered another job. I thought I would tell you in case you intended to ... get rid of me.' His blue eyes – seafaring eyes, she'd always thought – were bloodshot. For a moment they seemed unfocused, then she saw him straighten his back and look directly at her.

'Well, you've forestalled me in a way, Miss Crichton. I'm making arrangements to close down the business, and I should have had to dispense with your services, eventually.'

'Oh, I'm sorry,' she said. 'I could stay on to help you...'

'No, there's no need. One of my daughters ... she's given up the idea of going to the University. Come into my room, please.' Jess followed him.

'I should like to dictate a testimonial for you in case it's needed. I may say you have always given me excellent service.'

It was a splendid testimonial. Jess could have wept. He got up and took his bowler hat and rolled umbrella from the coat-stand. 'I shall be back before five o'clock to sign it.'

Something made Jess look out of the window before she sat down at her desk. She saw the portly figure of Mr MacIntyre, bowler hat at the usual jaunty angle, emerge from the doorway, stand leaning on his rolled umbrella watching the traffic, then cross the busy street. There was no grey Daimler at the kerbside.

Four

'I've fixed up for you to have some extra tuition for your classes,' Mrs Crichton said. She had a self-righteous look on her face.

'But I don't need extra tuition! It's time I need.' Jess had come in from the office, soaked by walking home along St Vincent Street in the rain, down the hill towards Anderston and west towards their flat. At least she hadn't to go out again to the College.

'Ten bob a week it's costing.' She wasn't listening. 'Mrs Thompson knows a teacher who gives extra tuition' – she seemed to like that phrase – 'and don't say I'm not willing to help you. It's tonight. That's the address.' She put a scrap of paper on the table. 'Aye, I've always said you're like your father, ambitious. Not like that Peggy, out gallivantin' as usual. I bet it's that policeman...'

Is she playing me off against Peggy? Jess wondered. 'You might have consulted me first.'

'Consulted you! The nerve! That's hard-earned money, that is.' She laid a ten-shilling note on the table. 'I worked ma fingers to the bone in the premises for you all, and that's all the thanks I get.'

Jess lifted the note and the scrap of paper. 'Thanks, Mother.' What's the point of arguing, she thought.

Bath Street at night was quiet. There were a few private hotels, not many houses now, only the BBC offices were lit up. The crowds for the King's Theatre would all be in and there were very few people about.

Here it was. An inconspicuous notice about private tuition and an arrow pointing downwards. She went downstairs to the basement, holding on to the iron railing, and rang the bell. She was expecting a receptionist, but instead a middle-aged man with smoothed greying hair opened the door. He had an air of shabby smartness.

'Hello!' he said. 'You must be Miss Crichton. I'm Mr Anderson.' He held out his hand. 'You found me all right. Come in.' He stood aside to let Jess enter into a narrow, badly lit hall.

At the same time as Jess was with Mr Anderson, above her in Sauchiehall Street Peggy was sitting at a café table in La Scala Picture House. This café had the unique advantage of giving its customers a view of the screen, a rather slant view, but a novelty nevertheless. She was with Donald Buchan, a policeman she had known for several months.

'Look at Marlene's face!' Peggy giggled. 'It's all squinty. Did you know she arrived off an airyplane wearing a man's suit!'

'A don't care what she was wearin'. A telt you we'd have been better off in the back seats than this.' He looked at her above his coffee cup. Melting eyes, she called them. They certainly melted her.

'So it wasn't the picture you wanted to see?' What was it about this man that made her go weak at the knees? Good thing they were sitting with a table between them.

'Well, a've got to get a chance somewhere.' Those melting eyes... 'Hey, since we're here, have a cake.' He held out a plate laden with fancies.

'D'you think I should? It'll make me fat.'

'A don't mind a few curves.' He eyed her lasciviously.

Peggy selected a cream pastry horn and dug her teeth into it. 'Ma God,' she said. 'A like the good things o' life.'

'A can give you the good things of life. But we'll no' get them here sitting looking at a squinty screen like two dummies.'

'Well, you can look at me instead.' She had demolished her cake in a few swift bites. She had enjoyed sinking her teeth into its

32

creamy softness. 'That was great. My good-ness, Donald, is that the time? A should be home, she'll be out o' her head.'

'All right. It's no' ma idea of fun, this any-how. A neither get to put ma arm round you or see the picture. Here,' – he glanced at the screen – 'I read somewhere that she's half a man! I bet she could do with a few cakes to fatten her up.'

'No' her! She's seductive like that. Hear me, seductive!' She was wriggling herself into her jacket, which was over her chair back. 'Hey, are you grudgin' me ma cream cake now?'

'A wouldn't grudge you anything, Peggy.'

'Provided I gave you something back?' She was on her feet. 'Come on, Donald, a'll have to go.'

He got up too. 'Will your sister not be in to keep her quiet?'

'Maybe by this time. She's arranged what she calls "extra tuition" for Jess. Ten bob a week. She, not Jess, is always shovin' it down ma throat. A just work in a grocer's!'

'Well, if you didny a wouldny have met ye.' He had been the policeman on the beat, and when he called in at the grocer's shop she had fallen for him, hook, line and sinker. She wasn't going to tell him that.

He paid at the cash desk and they left the cinema and went into Sauchiehall Street. It was a wet night and it wasn't as busy as

33

usual. The cinemas hadn't emptied yet. He put an arm round her as they walked. She liked the feel of him – tall, broad, a Highlander's build. She felt his hand come round under her armpit. She wriggled as it touched her breast.

'You're bad, Donald Buchan, did you know that?' When she looked up at him he turned her towards him.

'Here, you've got a bit of cream on your lip. I'll lick it off.'

'In the middle of the street! No' likely! That's why she doesny like policemen.'

'What's her objection to them as a matter of interest?'

'See, she's got fixed opinions on a lot of things. She thinks they're trash.'

'You watch it, Peggy Crichton!' His handsome face looked ugly for a moment. She glanced at him and saw she had gone too far.

'Poor wee soul! And all those lassies dyin' to go out with you.'

'Oh, there's plenty that would like to take your place, that's for sure.'

'You tell me that?' They walked on in silence. She liked making him angry, liked teasing him to danger point and then being nice again until they were both excited ... Wee quarrels were fine, as long as you didn't go too far. He fired her body. She knew he felt the same.

Jenny in the shop had warned her against him. 'He's a bad one that, Peggy. He thinks all the lassies should fall down and worship him.' It was exactly this dashing, cocky quality in him that had won her over, that and his 'little boy' appeal.

He had told her about his background on subsequent meetings. He was the adopted son of a miner and his wife in Airdrie outside Glasgow. Jack and Mary had waited ten years without her conceiving, and when a neighbour's young daughter became pregnant and didn't want the baby, they had been accepted as foster parents and had been allowed to adopt him. His real mother had later married a man who didn't want to have anything to do with her by-blow, and she had not objected to her son taking the Buchan's name.

Jack Buchan had the usual miner's build, scrawny, undersized, and his wife was much the same. As Donald grew up his large frame and ruddy fairness contrasted with the thinness of his adoptive parents. They worshipped him, probably realising that if Mary Buchan had been fertile they couldn't have produced anyone as handsome and as well built as Donald.

When he paraded in front of them in his new police cadet's uniform, they became his willing slaves. 'A clean job, son,' Jack had said, bursting with pride. 'I'm right glad you'll never get pit dirt on that!'

Peggy and Donald were walking past a dimly lit side street when Donald suddenly guided her round the corner and into an unlit doorway. 'Here!' Peggy said. 'A've told you, haven't I? A'm in a hurry!'

'So am I.' He pressed her against a darkened shop window with his body, his hands on her shoulders.

'You're bad.' She struggled, but not too much.

'A'm no' bad.' It was the little boy voice. 'A'm an honest bobby.' His mouth was against her ear. 'We never get enough time, Peggy. Will you come out to Airdrie with me? The folks like me to bring a lassie home. "Nae hangin' aboot street corners, son," they say. It would please them if you came. It would please me.' She felt his tongue in her ear. She was melting. She always did, although she could see through him. He was a rascal and he had her eating out of his hand because ... she had stopped thinking.

'Oh, God, Donald. You'll kill me!' She gave in for a minute or two to him kissing her, pressing her with his body ... he would drive her mad. 'You'll break the window!' She struggled free, straightening her skirt. 'You'll have to arrest yourself for molesting me!' She giggled. 'Aw right, I'll go out to Airdrie with you. It would be a nice run in the tram. And a'm goin' for mine!'

She half-ran from him back into Sauchie-hall Street, got to the stop just as a tram came rattling along the tramway lines towards her, and jumped on to its platform. Her last sight of Donald was of him reaching the tram stop, and she waved gaily. He waved back, his face dark with anger.

'Wavin' to your fella?' said a friendly man beside her.

'Aye,' she said. 'Ma fella...'

When she came into the bedroom Jess was sitting on her bed. She wasn't undressed.

'Have you been cryin'?' She noticed her sister's eyes were red.

Jess looked at her. 'Me? What a hope!'

'A wouldny blame you. Did you hear her? A wish to God I was oot o' this hoose. We only went to the pictures and she can't keep her tongue off me.'

'Because you go out with a policeman.'

'Here, don't you start! A get enough from her. We were at the La Scala café. Have you ever been there? You can see the pictures and drink your coffee at the same time. Real swanky.'

'No, I never get the time.'

'You shouldn't let her push you around. And bribe you with ten bob.'

'One ten bob.'

'What do you mean?'

'I'm not going back. He wanted to strap me.'

Peggy stopped in her undressing, mouth open. 'Strap you! Am I hearin' right?'

'Yes, strap me. He had it in a drawer.'

'And pull doon your knickers as well! The dirty scum! A bet she didn't believe you! A could get him run in. A could tell—'

'Don't bother. And don't let on I told you. I'm just not going back. I told her.'

'Well, you've saved her ten bob, that's something.'

'She didn't grudge me it.'

'No, she doesny grudge you anything.' Peggy sat down to peel off her stockings. She thought of Donald, his hand on the top of one of them half an hour ago. They were all the same, men. Though what Jess was telling her was different ... dirty. She heard her sister's voice.

'Are you ready for the light to go out?'

'Aye. A'm dead tired.' And yet she didn't sleep. She knew Jess wasn't sleeping either by her restless movements. No wonder, the dirty bugger! Donald, with all his faults, would never be like that, she hoped ... She would go to Airdrie with him. Maybe it was time to meet his folks...

Five

Jess's mind, as she also lay sleepless, was like a record playing over and over...

'Oh yes, I know Bath Street. And I've seen your notice.' She was chattering through nervousness. The narrow hall, linoleum-floored with dark brown walls, was poorly lit. 'I thought there would have been a receptionist.' She spoke with the knowledge of the many offices she had seen when she had delivered letters for Mr MacIntyre, which she now suspected had been to save postage.

'Betty, our receptionist, has just gone home. It's quite small here, but exclusive, a crammer, really. Highers, that kind of thing. I help them out. Will you follow me, please?'

It was a long corridor, very quiet, and she thought of them walking from the door in a tunnel. And yet there was an impression of people having been here – there was a stale, used smell.

He opened the door of a small room with a few desks and a table, and stood aside to let her in. 'Would you like to take your coat off?' He hung it beside his.

She smoothed her collar nervously. She was wearing a Quaker-like dress of grey marocain with a white collar and a black grosgrain ribbon simulating a tie. It was one her mother had made because she had got a bargain of the material, 'the very best', its only fault being that there wasn't quite enough of it. She looked at Mr Anderson and thought he was looking at the dress. It was shorter and tighter than usual.

'Sit down, please, Miss Crichton.' He took his place at the table in front of her. She brought out her notebook and pencil from the attaché case she carried, now acutely embarrassed. She couldn't relieve herself of the feeling that she was buried in the bowels of Glasgow with a strange man. She might be underneath one of the big shops, or cinemas, even La Scala...

'I thought I would give you a small test tonight,' Mr Anderson said. 'And when I correct it, it will give me an idea of where to start. Does that meet with your approval?' She nodded, opening her book. 'I'll give you the title, and you should write for about ten minutes. Now, the title is... "How I got here".' He smiled. 'Quite simple. Don't be nervous. Are you ready to start?'

40

'Yes.' She was well versed in examination techniques, and this was much the same, she told herself. *Write 200 words on the subject of* ... At least it was nothing to do with the usual stuff. She bent her head.

It was a funny subject, 'How I got here'. He knew how she got here. He'd know Glasgow as well as she did, and know there were several ways from her house – walk past the Mitchell and turn into Bath Street, or cut through to Elmbank Street and then along Bath Street ... And then the strange eerie feeling returned, of being in a deserted underground city, an empty beehive, all the activity and the buzzing hushed, with only two occupants, Mr Anderson and herself.

She began to write. Out of the corner of her eye she saw he had got up and was walking slowly about the room. He was humming quietly, like a bee. After a few minutes, it seemed, he sat down.

'Finished?' His voice was kindly. 'Time's up, I'm afraid.' She put down her pencil.

'Yes, Mr Anderson.' He was holding out his hand and she got up and handed him her notebook. He took up his pen, held it poised, and began to read.

The quietness hit her again. She could hear a clock ticking, and located it above the door. Ten to nine. She looked at the door. There was no key in the lock. Had he locked it? Don't be silly, Jess.

She looked at him. He was using his pen in an erratic fashion and she could see red marks appearing on the pages. He kept jabbing with the pen, brows furrowed. His face was a dull red. He hadn't liked it. She had been quite carried away by the subject, the way she always was when she was writing an essay. He looked up at her as if trying to match her with what he was reading. She tried to smile.

'Well, Miss Crichton,' he said. 'I expect you're anxious to know the result.'

She laughed nervously, and rushed into speech. 'I thought, well, you know the way I could come as well as I do. You'll know I live opposite the school where you teach, and I just had to walk up Elmbank Street and into Bath Street ... or I could have walked up St Vincent Street first and cut up ... and I thought, well you wouldn't want me to write just that...'

'That's not the point,' he said. His mouth had become stern, his eyes were pale and cold. Even his voice had changed, too level, as if he was restraining himself. 'When you walked in here, I expected that on your way you would have noticed what you were passing, used your eyes. For instance, if you'd come up St Vincent Street...'

'But I didn't—' He held up his hand.

'Let me speak, please. If you'd come up St Vincent Street, for instance, you'd have seen the church with its Doric columns. Do you know who built it?' His eyes were odd, pale, unblinking, as if it were a matter of life and death.

'No ... but I have noticed it often. But I came by—'

'Do not interrupt!' His voice was like a whiplash, and her astonishment made her draw back as if she had been struck.

'I'm sorry,' she said. 'I suppose maybe he was copying Greek architecture?' She could feel the blush creeping over her cheeks. It seemed even to fill her eyes. She saw his mouth clench in scarcely controlled exasperation.

'Leave it! That seems to be your chief fault, not using your eyes or your brain, a lack of attention to detail. Instead of describing what you saw you have written this airy-fairy rubbish!'

'I'm ... I'm sorry.' She was stammering. 'I'm sorry. Is the spelling all right?'

'There are a few mistakes. I'll overlook these. As I said before, that's not the point.' He rapped his pen on the desk. His head swivelled on his neck like someone who has had more than he could stand. 'A punishable offence, don't you agree?' She looked at him, confused, miserable, then smiled tentatively, thinking it must be some kind of a joke. Her heart was racing.

There was silence. She felt the edge of

nausea and swallowed. He said, slowly, 'What do you think I've got in this drawer?' He pointed.

'Got?' It was becoming a nightmare.

'Got! That's what I said. Got in this drawer!' He pointed again, his eyes looking at her were steady, that odd drained colour, lighter than his face. She watched a flicker at the side of his mouth. 'You're not deaf as well, are you?'

'No, Mr Anderson.' She felt her brows draw together. She was on the verge of crying with fear and vexation. A kind of sanity returned to her. Her heart slowed down. 'What have you got in the drawer?' It was some horrible kind of game.

'That's better. I'll tell you.' He paused. 'It's a strap.' He was smiling now, seemingly relaxed, even leaning back in his chair, but her fear returned with a rush. It wasn't a game. Her fear was dark, unfamiliar, something barely recognisable, even worse than the fear she could still remember about Danny and the horse, long ago in the premises. But that had been understandable, natural, straightforward. This was a question of not believing what she was hearing, or seeing.

She lifted her attaché case from the floor and got up, trembling so much that she could scarcely stand. 'I'm going home, Mr Anderson,' she said. 'I don't like it here. I

44

shouldn't have come.' She walked to where he had hung her coat, took it off the hook and put it on. She hunted in the pocket and found the note her mother had given her. 'Mrs Thompson said ten shillings.' She went back and put it on his table. She didn't meet his eyes.

'Oh, come, Miss Crichton – Jess, isn't it?' He was laughing at her. His face was relaxed, set in its normal lines. The flicker at the side of his mouth had gone. 'It was only a joke, a test. When you start teaching you'll be afraid of standing in front of your pupils, you have to know the fear and learn to ignore it.' She looked at him, uncertain, saw the drawer in front of him where he had pointed. *Do you know what's in here?* She hadn't imagined that, surely, nor the odd pale eyes.

'I'm going home,' she said. 'I don't feel well.'

'If you wish.' He was dignified. 'I'll escort you. I live in Partick. We can walk round to Sauchiehall Street and get the same tram home.'

She stood uncertain, still fearful, while he got up and put on his coat. She hadn't imagined it, she told herself. The ten-shilling note was still lying on the table. She pointed to it. 'That's yours,' she said. She daren't look at him.

He was beside her. 'If it makes you

happier.' He lifted it and stowed it carefully away in a wallet he took from his inside pocket. His movements were slow and methodical. She stood, petrified, her arms pressing against her ribs.

'Come along, Miss Crichton,' he said kindly. She turned and saw him take a key from his pocket and unlock the door. She had consciously to set her body in motion to walk the few steps to the door. 'You have to be careful at night,' he said. 'Intruders.' He stood aside to let her pass.

Her mind was working furiously. Her mother wouldn't believe her. She would say, 'You're imagining it. He's a teacher! Away wi' ye!' They were walking along the long narrow corridor and he was talking to her cheerfully about his methods of teaching and the successes he'd had.

She wasn't out, yet. She had an attaché case – she could hit him on the head with it. This corridor hadn't seemed as long as this before ... She tried to set the pace, walking quickly at his side but not wanting to get ahead of him. He could attack her, jump on her...

At last they were at the outer door. He unlocked it with the key that was in the lock, and stood aside to let her out, carefully locking it behind him. They climbed the basement stairs together and when they got to the top he stood, swivelling his neck, head upraised. 'Fresh...' He stood for another moment, head still swivelling. She was now trembling with the reaction. She'll never believe me, Jess thought.

They went upstairs in the tram because he suggested it. He wanted to smoke. Seated, he offered her a cigarette. She refused.

He blew smoke as he spoke. 'I like trams at night, lit galleons, streets like rivers ... Your style, eh, Miss Crichton?' She was dizzy with relief at being amongst other people. *Yes, airy-fairy,* she wanted to say. Instead words tumbled out of her, how much she liked Glasgow at night, the lights reflected in the streets especially if it had been raining but it always rained in Glasgow ... He laughed with her. She chattered on, 'I come from haunts of coot and fern,' she quoted to herself, still dizzy.

'Charing Cross already.' He nodded, glancing. 'Charing Cross Mansions. Built like a French chateau. Burnett, did you know that? And here's the Grand Hotel. Have you ever been there? Very popular for weddings.'

'No, I haven't, but I was at a wedding once, Wellington Church and the Grosvenor.'

'Nice place. Toney.'

'The food ... and afterwards we danced at the Plaza...' She couldn't stop talking about the wedding. On and on, pretending nothing had happened, trying to convince herself.

'What a pity life is not all enjoyment. But we have to work to be able to afford it. Next week we'll do Examination Techniques. I know quite a lot about that. But when you become a teacher you'll be glad I was able to give you a few extra tips. You're good teacher material.'

Jess nodded, putting on a pleased look. Newton Terrace, she saw, looking out. They were coming near her stop.

'Excuse me...' He was still talking. 'This is my stop. Thank you for paying my fare.'

He got up to let her pass. 'It was a pleasure.' He smiled, a friendly smile. 'Next week, then, same time and place?' She nodded, smiling too.

She jumped off when the tram stopped and kept running round the corner and along the street towards their flat. Once she had a flash of such pure joy that she jumped in the air like a child.

Six

1936
Maggie Crichton looked forward to their occasional Sunday visits to the Gray brothers. Sunday, in any case, was the usual day for Glaswegians, armed with flowers and gifts, to visit relatives scattered about the city. It was nice to be part of the custom. She was inspecting her family before they set off.

'That hankie in your breast pocket, James, doesn't look clean. Get a fresh one from the drawer!' This mythical 'drawer' was the bane of the family's existence, she well knew. James was the only one who could instinctively find out first time which one she meant. Jess got confused and guilty, and Peggy angry – but James was back in no time with the fresh handkerchief, full of confidence. 'And remember, it's for show,' she said, tucking it into his breast pocket with a point showing. 'Don't blow your nose on it.'

'Don't forget a said a had to leave right

away after tea,' Peggy said.

'Is it that policeman?' Maggie glared at her elder daughter, at the same time thinking how much Peggy resembled her when she was the same age.

Robert, a few years her senior, had been a catch; the youngest son of the Crichtons, who were farming gentry. She wouldn't have been seen dead with a policeman. It was always the dullest lad in the class who went into the Force. Wooden-headed. She'd break up that affair if it was the last thing she did.

She had been a flirt in the small community where she lived, but she had set her heart on Robert Crichton from the start. His mother hadn't liked her, had hated parting with 'my Robert' – probably thought she wasn't good enough.

'It's a concert in St Andrew's Hall,' Peggy said. Is she lying? thought Maggie. Nothing so genteel as a concert in St Andrew's Hall would please that one. You only had to look at her, the excitement in her eyes, like a damped down fire.

'Take a lesson from Jess, there,' she said. 'Neat and tidy and ladylike, no low necks and tight blouses for her!'

'Oh, aye, there's never anything wrong with her!'

They're as different as chalk and cheese, Maggie Crichton thought. She had often the same feeling with Jess as she'd had with Robert, a failure to understand him, a feeling of being shut out. He had been like Jess, distant. But bright, aye, bright.

'Who's got the flowers?' she asked. James waved a bunch of bronze chrysanthemums wrapped in florist's paper.

'Here!' he said, laughing. You knew where you were with James.

'Quick march!' Peggy said. Maggie Crichton knew when they were teasing her, but you had to laugh all the same. They could be worse.

She particularly relished the address of the Gray brothers, a red sandstone block of flats across the road from a bowling green and with a fine view of Kelvingrove Park and the distant bulk of the University. And the flat, – there was only one on each landing – was spacious, with an additional two or three attic bedrooms since it was on the top floor.

And, she had to admit, she quite enjoyed her encounters with Mrs Bell, the brothers' housekeeper – a stuck-up bitch. She rang the doorbell.

'Mrs Crichton and her family!' the woman said when she saw them. 'Come away in!'

Maggie stepped into the hall. The three of them were at her back. She took the flowers from James. 'Perhaps you would put these in water when you get a moment, Mrs Bell.' She was glad they had a Matthew Campbell wrapper. That should impress her.

'Oh, aren't they lovely!' You would have thought she was giving them to *her*! 'My, you've got two lovely girls there, Mrs Crichton. But this one' – she put her arm round James' shoulder – 'is my favourite.' Probably never had any, Maggie thought – probably wasn't a 'missus' at all.

She always liked this room – 'the drawing room', they called it – spacious, great windows giving on to Sauchiehall Street and the bowling green. And they were gentlemen, if old-fashioned – Peter with his bald head that ran into his bald face with its cheery smile, and Thomas, the elder, the boss, lips bunched under his fine Asquith moustache.

'Away to the window and watch the bowlers,' he said to James. He always did the ordering. 'And you, Maggie, and the girls, sit round the fire. I got Mrs Bell to light a wee one. When you get to September the days begin to draw in. My,' – lowering his voice – 'he gets more and more like Robert every time we see him.'

Maggie sighed and rolled her eyes to please him, seated in the comfortable armchair Peter had led her to. 'Aye, a often have a quiet cry. If only Robert had been spared to help me with the rearin' o' these three.' Out of the corner of her eye she saw Peggy look at Jess and glance ceilingwards, cheeky

52

besom. And Jess was just as bad, smiling at her.

'My, he was a handsome man.' This was Mr Peter. 'Personally I think Jess has more of a look of him. James has your dark colouring, Maggie.'

She nodded, pleased. They were all settled now round the small bright fire set in a tall white-painted mantelpiece which was many-shelved to house Thomas's collection of Glasgow pottery. They'd probably get a lecture on them later. She knew it off by heart.

'A handsome man,' Peter repeated. 'I first saw him when he wasn't a lot older than James, there, fifteen or sixteen, working far beyond his strength when his father died. We were grain merchants then and called regularly at the Crichton farm. A fine place, that.'

'That would be our grandfather's farm?' Jess asked. 'I never knew what it was called.' For a shy girl she was an awful one for asking questions. Cheeky.

'Yes, Jess, Woodburn was its name. It was sold up before you were on the scene. Your father had two brothers who had been at the Agricultural College in Hamilton and he was going on to the University to become a vet. The brothers had taken themselves off to manage a sheep farm in Australia, just for experience, but when your grandfather died, most of the running of the farm fell on Robert. The brothers stayed on in Australia. But you'll have told them all this, Maggie?'

'Aye, most likely. She'll have forgot.' She gave Jess a look, shook her head at her. Peggy at least was far away, a silly smile on her face.

'He had to sell up when his mother died and make his own way. There wasn't much left for him when it was divided. But he was ambitious, always was...'

'I was too young to know my father well, you see,' Jess said. She could feel her mother glaring at her.

'Wi' James just a baby and the premises to run, you can see a didn't have much time to sit down with any o' them!'

'Jess has an enquiring mind.' Peter had a soft side for her. 'And maybe she's a story-teller as well. Is that it, Jess?'

'It *is* a story, Mr Peter.'

'Aye, the story of a life. After the farm was sold up your father became manager of a wholesale milk distributors in Glasgow. You'll remember your first flat after you were married, Maggie?'

'Aye, that I do, but he always wanted his own place.' That had been a fine wee flat, right nice views out of the window – busy days with the two babies; busy nights, he was a fine lover...

'That's where we were able to help him.

54

Although he never had much need of helping hands. He had repaid the loan for that business in the East End in a couple of years. A grand head on him, and got the best out of his workers because he worked with them.'

'A was workin' as hard as he was!' Maggie Crichton felt her face flush. They never gave her credit for anything, the two brothers. 'We both worked our fingers to the bone.'

'We know you did.' Thomas taking over as usual. 'And a fine place you had there. Your fortune would have been made if ... Well, we shouldn't dwell on the might-have-beens.'

'Tea's ready.' Mrs Bell was at the door. And about time too, Maggie thought. And delving into the past never did any good. Nobody here knew how she had missed him, especially in bed. If he could only have been like that in the daytime. But he was a typical Crichton, single-minded. 'James!' she called, and he came obediently from the window. They all got up.

It was the usual spread, ham and pickles, scones, pancakes, Dundee cake, finishing with ice cream. She bakes a good Dundee cake, Maggie had to admit.

'Aye, nobody can make ice cream like the Italians, eh, Maggie?' Thomas was wiping his moustache. 'You'd agree?'

'Maybe so, but they took away jobs from our lads when they came back from the

War.' She was still peeved. A cheeky daughter turning up the past and now the Tallies. What did foreigners come to Scotland for anyhow?

'There's that, there's that.' Mr Peter was the peacemaker.

'Now, off you go to the Park and walk it off, James.' Mr Thomas said.

'And a'll have to leave, Mr Thomas,' Peggy said, rising. 'I've got an appointment.' Her chin was up, she was smiling confidently. Nothing would change that one when she had made her mind up, Maggie thought.

'They young ones...' She would give her a telling-off later. She watched Peggy open the door, shut it with a decided bang after her.

'Believe it or not, Maggie,' Mr Peter said with his quirky smile, 'we were young ourselves once.'

'We have a proposition to make to you, Maggie.' Mr Thomas was holding up his hand. 'You can tell Peggy afterwards.' She was mystified. 'What's the school like, the one James attends?'

'The school? Fair to middlin'. Jess went there. And the one he'll be moving up to isn't much better. Overcrowded places.'

The two brothers looked at each other. 'If he passes their Entrance Examination, in due course,' – she saw Thomas draw himself up – 'we would like to send him to the

Glasgow Academy, at our expense, of course.'

She could hardly believe her ears. The Glasgow Academy! Her hand flew to her mouth, and she turned to Jess.

'Did you hear that, Jess? Send James to the Glasgow Academy! Well, you left that school across the road because it was hopeless, didn't you?'

She didn't like to be reminded of her schooldays, Jess. It had always puzzled her. But now she was smiling. What a wonderful chance for James!

'Well, there's no doubt he'll pass the Entrance Exam, that's for sure,' Maggie said. 'My goodness, I'm fair knocked back.' She turned to the brothers. 'It's real generous of both o' ye. Isn't it, Jess?'

'Yes, it is. Most generous.'

'I don't know what to say, and you'll know it takes a lot to do that!' She knew she was giggling like a lassie, but the brothers looked pleased.

On the way home, James, who was just as flabbergasted, said to Jess, 'They'll all be toffs there.'

'Then you'll be one too. You make the most of it, James. You deserve it.' What wouldn't she have given for a chance like that, maybe to go to the University ... She had been a fool. What had possessed her to

57

be cheeky to Miss Pollock?

'Peggy will be really pleased for you,' she said. She wondered if Peggy would care. It was easy to see that her mind wasn't on anything as mundane as schools.

Seven

Peggy and Donald were in the tramcar going out to Airdrie to have tea with his parents.

'Do you realise I'm giving your Ma and Pa ideas, turning up with you?' Peggy said. 'You'll have to marry me after this!'

He burst into laughter, a full-throated laughter which made passengers in the seats upstairs turn their heads. Peggy saw a middle-aged woman nudge the man she was with. They both smiled indulgently. He was handsome without a doubt, vaguely familiar...

Once, long ago, when she was six or seven, there had been a fair-haired boy, with an extra something about him, even at an early age, an appeal ... He had taken her under his wing. She had worshipped him, though he never knew that.

Although it was the last thing she would do – agree with her mother about policemen – he wasn't quick, Donald, he was ... ponderous. He gave her the impression that

59

ideas took a long time to sink in. Ma would say, 'Lazy … they're aw the same.'

But, oh, he was a right smasher. Look at that girl across the aisle fair gawping at him, trying to hear every word they said and stealing looks at Donald. She pressed against his side, putting her head on his shoulder. A'll give you your penny's worth, she thought.

Donald looked down at her, like a king on his subject. 'Canny wait, eh? Never mind, you'll get your chance later.' She made eyes at him, to give the lassie a real treat. 'Cambuslang,' he said. 'Do you know here?'

'No, a never come out this far. A like oor end better, Sauchiehall Street and that, shops, and the pictures – three places to go to.'

'Don't mention that one we went tae! A waste o' good money.'

'The La Scala? What was wrong with it?'

'I've had a squinty neck ever since. If I pay all that I like to get a chance of a cuddle at least.'

'You're keen on cuddles, ur ye?' She saw the girl wasn't missing a thing, poor soul. What if I said to her, Would you like a loan o' him for a while? That would make her ears flap!

'Did you know I'm a musician?' Donald said.

'A musician? You mean, the piana?'

'No, but a can play it as well – anything. A've got a natural gift.' He waggled his head proudly. 'A'm in the polis pipe band.'

'You're pullin' ma leg.'

'No a'm no'. A've got a set at home. I'll give you a tune on them when we get in.'

'For God's sake, no!' she said. 'A only like them in a park, me at one end, them at the other. Have you no' got anything softer, like a penny whistle?'

'I've got a fiddle. Ma mother bought it fur me to see if a could play it. A can play anything.' She still didn't know if he were teasing her.

'You're wasting your time in the Police Force. You should be at St Andrew's Hall.'

'No a'm not. The polis suits me. And I've got masel' noticed already playing in the pipe band.' He was serious. She leant back in her seat.

'Well, that's a promise, then. A tune on the fiddle.' She glanced out of the window. 'Look at these bings! A don't think much of this place. Some scenery!'

'Here! That's how ma faither earns his wages. Doon the pit.'

'Oh, yes. A'm sorry, Donald.' She had seen his little-boy expression. 'Did a offend you, eh?'

'You'll pay for it later,' he said, with a slow smile. He turned round to her. He had bad eyes. For the first time she felt afraid of him,

61

glad that they were going to his house where his parents were.

'We're nearly there,' he said. 'We've passed Blantyre. Have you got your gloves and your scarf? Come on, we'll get down now.'

Peggy gave the girl a saucy look as they passed, making her lower her eyes in confusion. She immediately felt sorry for her. He was a smasher, all right. They stood on the platform, the tram hurtling along the lines. 'In a hurry to get to Airdrie,' Donald said. 'We're in a row of houses before we come into it. A cut above the rest. Here we are!' They jumped off, and as he strode along she had to half-run to keep up with him. She was just a wee smout in comparison. She liked the feeling.

They had finished their tea – as it was her second that day she'd found it difficult. His mother was a terrible fusser, constantly pressing her to 'try this, then'.

'I'll help you with the dishes, Mrs Buchan,' she said, thankful they had finished.

She shook her head. 'You're no' to touch a thing. We'll go ben the hoose. Did you know our Donald can play the fiddle?'

'Yes, he was telling me in the tram. A didn't believe him.' She laughed.

'Oh, it's no' a joke. If he hadn't gone into the Force he could have made his living in the halls. He has a perfect ear, his teacher said.'

'A pair o' them.' Donald grabbed his ears and waggled them. His parents laughed, looking at Peggy with pride.

'And he's a comic as well.' She saw they didn't like that. He needs bringing down a peg or two, that one, she thought. Spoiled.

She looked around the room. Almost every chair and sofa was occupied by dolls of all shapes and sizes, carefully dressed – even to hats and shoes. Their staring eyes made her feel uncomfortable. 'Are those yours, Donald?' she asked. She lifted a fat-faced one with a closed-mouth smirk dressed in a sailor suit.

'No, they're Ma's.' He spoke shortly. 'She's fond o' dollies.'

'Every holiday we went on a used to buy her one.' Mr Buchan spoke, almost for the first time. At the table he had eaten steadily, listening, his head going from one side to the other, but he had not contributed to the conversation.

'That was before Donald came.' She looked embarrassed, turning away as if to hide her face. A poor soul, Peggy thought. She had seen her blush. It would take a lot to make their mother blush. She had plenty of spirit. This one had none, not a fight in her.

Donald went over to the sofa where a violin case lay, lifted it and took out a fiddle.

'What would you like, Peggy?' he asked, settling it under his chin confidently. She looked at his parents, who were gazing at him with awe. What a crowd, she thought. A queer lot.

'*Comin' through the Rye?*' She still thought it was a joke, an embarrassing joke.

He played like a man at a concert, assured, expertly. She was astounded. His timing was perfect, the slow beginning, then the rush at the end. You could tell it was good – more than good ... professional. Anyone could recognise that.

She looked again at Mary and Jack Buchan. They were bursting with pride. They looked at her as if they had produced a miracle and wanted her to say so. And they hadn't even *had* him. That was a piece of luck for them. Adopting him, and finding they had been given a handsome lad, and then finding out that he had a natural gift as well. What a bonus for the poor souls! Donald was waiting for her opinion, smug, his bow poised.

'Well, how did you like that, Peggy?' Spoiled rotten, she thought. She wasn't going to gush.

'It was all right, but I bet you couldn't play a jig, an Irish jig.' That would test him.

'Could a no'?' She saw the smirks on his parents' faces. They nodded. This'll show her. He tucked the fiddle under his chin and he was away, the bow twinkling, the notes liquid, like a running burn. His father's foot was keeping time, his mother was clapping her hands. At the end Donald bowed elaborately. 'That's enough o' that.' He crossed to the sofa and picked up the violin case. 'Is there a fire in ma room, Ma?'

'Aye, son, a nice fire. You and Peggy can go in any time you like. We'll get the dishes done.'

Some devilment made Peggy say, 'Oh, no, it's very nice here.' There was something odd in this set-up. Unhealthy. Never in a hundred years would her mother offer them the chance to go into a bedroom.

'Don't be shy,' Donald said. 'They don't like me to do ma courtin' in public.' She got up reluctantly and followed him, wishing she could just open the outside door and run. It looked as if they were keeping a brothel. She caught the mother's glance. It was candid. 'Let me know if you would like a cup of tea after...' She could only murmur something. After what? This visit, she thought, has changed my mind about him. The glamour's gone, seeing him in his own background. There was something pathetic about the set-up – she couldn't put into words what she felt about it, just that she wanted no part of it, nor anything to do with him.

'My!' she said as she and Donald went

into a room off the lobby. 'You're spoiled. This is nice.' She still felt uncomfortable. It was the connivance of the parents – or were they completely under his thumb? For the first time in her life she thought she would welcome some of her mother's bossiness.

'When a started getting a good pay a said to them a'd go into digs or rent a house o' ma own, and they were that upset. They said a could have ma own place. They wouldn't expect me to sit wi' them – a could entertain ma friends here. So a said, aw right. They dote on me. The way you do.' He smiled at her, going to a cupboard beside the fire-place. 'Will ye take a dram?'

'No, thanks. And get rid o' the idea that a dote on you like them.'

He smiled as if to humour her. 'Well, you soon will. A'm havin' yin. A'll pour a wee glass oot for ye and ye can take it or leave it. Sit at the fire, Peggy. On the divan. A said a wanted the bed taken out and this put in. Looks quite nice, doesn't it?'

She sat down, mystified. And yet it made sense. Because her mother would never have countenanced such an arrangement, maybe other folks did. She knew her friends would be surprised, but then she didn't know a lot of people to sound out. Maybe you could call Donald advanced. Bachelor's quarters. She had heard of that. And, she thought, if a telt Jess, she'd say it was about time men, or even girls, had a room of their own. You couldny shock Jess though she was quiet.

Aye, maybe there was something in this. She looked around at the cosy room, the armchairs, his wee table with a pot plant on it and an ashtray. 'A'll take that dram after all,' she said. He brought her the glass, and sat down beside her with his own.

'D'you like it?' He looked round the room proudly. 'A did it all masel' – the wallpaper, the pictures and that. She's an eyeful, isn't she?' He pointed with his glass at a print of a Spanish-looking woman with a shawl round her bare shoulders. 'Cut it oot o' a mag. It makes sense this, ye know. A keep odd hours in the Force, and it's better havin' this place. A don't always like to go to bed right away, or a might bring back somebody wi' me. It saves me disturbin' them. Pa has to get up at four in the mornin'. An' she's got weak insides or somethin'.'

'This is pretty strong,' she said, taking a sip.

'Ach, away wi' ye. Knock it back.' She took another sip, and felt the fire running down her throat. She took another and then another in a spirit of bravado. She looked at the empty glass. 'I've tasted worse.' It was her first whisky.

'You fair knocked that back.' He was admiring. 'Lie back and relax noo.' She had been mad, drinking so quickly. 'Well, did you think a could play the fiddle?' he asked.

'A must say you were good.' The warmth flooding her made her feel more kindly disposed towards him. And it was more sensible, really, to act natural in his room, have a friendly drink, instead of making small talk with that pathetic pair outside.

'It's just a hobby,' he said. 'The teacher wanted me to have more lessons, but a always wanted to go into the Force. Power.' He leant over her. 'Power. That's the name of the game. The auld ones say they feel safe wi' me in the hoose.' He looked at her with his bad eyes, a long slow look. Do *you* feel safe, Peggy?'

'Whit way would a not? The polis are just all pose. It's the uniform. Think they're the bees knees wi' lassies.'

'No, we're the carers of the community. That's what the Chief said to us. Now a'm goin' to take care o' you.' He lifted her legs up on to the divan. Her head swivelled round and rested on some cushions. It was very comfortable, and the whisky was filling up her veins with a warm excitement. What would he do next?

'It's nice here,' she said. 'With the fire and everything...'

'Aye, nice.' He was half-lying on top of her.

'You look far too hot,' he said. 'A'll help

you off wi' yer blouse.' He began unbutton-
ing it.

'Leave ma blouse alone!' She smacked
feebly at him. Her hand didn't have much
strength in it.

'Leave it to Donald. A'm takin' care o'
you, remember?' He had her blouse off her
shoulders and now he was fumbling with his
crotch. 'A bet you get up to mair than this
wi' blokes.' She met his eyes and he was
smiling, slowly, keeping his eyes on her. He
heaved himself on top of her and she felt his
warm hard flesh between her thighs. The
whisky warmth drained away like an un-
blocked drain, leaving her cold and shaking
with rage.

'You've got a hell of a nerve!' Her voice
choked in her throat. She pushed at him
with all her might but it didn't move him an
inch. He laughed, pinioning her with his
body.

'Bit late when you've been leadin' me on
aw night.' She spat in his face, rage – partly
at herself – consuming her. She saw the spit
running down to his mouth, and as it
reached it he swore obscenely, drawing his
hand over his face. While he was distracted
she let out a loud sharp scream.

'Whit in hell do ye think ye're doin'?' he
said. 'Shut your gob!'

'A'll scream again if you don't let me up!'
She heaved with all her might, and he rolled

69

off her on to the floor. Before he could right
himself she ran for the door, pulling at her
blouse.

She heard Mr Buchan's voice outside.
'Anything wrong?'

She laughed, pretending to choke with
laughter, but it sounded as if she were
clearing her throat. She tried again. Better,
she thought. 'Your Donald's making me
helpless!' she spluttered. 'Tellin' me some
o' his jokes!' She laughed again, and this
time it was genuine. She had her blouse in
position, she felt Donald panting behind
her, and she opened the door before he
could draw her back. She saw his father at
the kitchen door peering along the lobby at
her. 'This light's awfy bad.'

'Oh, sorry, Mr Buchan!' she said. Her
mind was working like mad. 'Did you hear
me laughin'?'

'Aye, a heard ye. A was dozin' at the fire.
D'you want a cup o' tea? Mary's gone to her
bed. She's done too much the day. Said a
was to be ready to make you a cup.' Donald
was pushing behind her to be allowed out.
She stepped aside, safe now.

'She's easily amused this yin, Pa,' he said.

'Some of yer jokes, eh, son?' He grinned
feebly, and Peggy thought his eyes were
nearly dropping out of his head with tiredness. 'He's got a fund o' jokes, oor Donald.'

'A would like to stay an' hear more o'

70

them, but a'll have to be going,' she said, lifting her coat from a hook on the wall at the same time. 'Will you say goodnight and thanks to your wife? The tea was lovely.'

'Aye, aw right.' He walked with her to the door. Donald joined him. He's too thick, she thought. He can't think of a way to get rid of his father. She kept talking nonsense to the older man, turning to say to his son, 'A have to go, Donald. Ma mother worries. An' don't come with me. It's too far. You'd never get a tram back.'

'No, we're a bit far oot here.' He was still thinking, his brow furrowed. Don't scratch your head, she would like to have said. You might get a skelf in your finger. A head like wood, she thought. Ma's quite right – only the Police would give him a job. Thick.

'Goodnight!' she said, gaily, and went running down the stairs. What happened to that whisky? she wondered. It must have run out of the soles of her feet. Anyhow she was a lot quicker on them than he was, big clumsy lout with his divan and his nice fire and his pictures.

She wept quietly, her hand to her mouth, as she sat downstairs in the tram. A woman sitting beside her asked if she was all right. 'Aye,' she said. 'Got a cold starting,' and, smiling, 'That's what happens when a come to Airdrie!' The woman looked affronted and folded her arms on her chest.

'A've been visiting here for twenty years an' nothin' ever happened to me!' You're lucky, Peggy thought, her eyes dry now.

Her mother was sitting reading in the kitchen. Jess was an early bedder, her mother always reluctant to take to hers. Maybe she misses our father, she thought, realising that the thought had never occurred to her before.

Maggie looked up when Peggy came in. She didn't look angry, strangely enough. 'You'll be comin' home jist in time to go to work,' she said. 'D'you see the time?'

'Aye, but a telt ye a'm twenty-one and a still haven't got a key to the door.' She sat down. What a difference between her mother and that poor browbeaten soul at Airdrie.

'I've got news for you!' Her mother's eyes were bright. 'The brothers are going to pay for James' education at the Glasgow Academy! They brought it up when you'd gone for your "appointment".' She was sarcastic, and yet full of excitement.

'Is James pleased?'

'Of course he's pleased! It's a great chance for him.'

'So it is. He's lucky.'

'I've just been sitting thinking here. Remember that advert the Grays sent me about a dairy in Dennistoun ... in case I was interested?'

'Yes, but you said you weren't. That you'd done enough of working your fingers to the bone.' Her mother let that go.

'I've changed ma mind. Things are going to be different with James away all day – they get their lunch there – and maybe Jess will be the same. If you could come in with me, it would be easier ... give me time to keep an eye on the house as well.'

'A telt ye before...' Peggy stopped herself. The penny dropped. She could have jumped with joy. She wouldn't now want to be in the grocers with Donald coming in. That was a thing of the past. Put it down to experience, the whole set-up, his room with the divan, his poor parents under his thumb, the dollies with their glassy stares – pathetic, it was all pathetic. 'I'm ready for a change too,' she said. 'I'll come in with you.'

Her mother's eyes shone. She looked handsome, flushed, a good-looking woman ... Why had she never thought so before? 'You won't regret it. You'll be the manager, a step-up. You'll be level with Jess and James...'

'Maybe. Anyhow, that's it fixed. I'll get off to bed.'

'Aye, all right. I'm real pleased, Peggy. I'll just finish this story first. It'll settle ma mind.' Peggy glanced at the magazine her mother was bent over. *Peg's Paper*. A could tell you a story that would beat any in that! she thought.

Jess was sitting up in bed writing.

'A thought you'd be asleep,' Peggy said, beginning to undress.

'No, a've got exams tomorrow, and I couldn't get any work done beside her. James ... did she tell you?'

'Yes, that's great for him.'

'He'll do well. And then it was your policeman, on and on, what she thinks of them...'

'Pity. She was wasting her breath.'

'What do you mean?'

'She thinks she's worked a fast one on me. She's offered me the job as manager in this dairy in Dennistoun ... and I've taken it.'

Jess looked at her. 'You know why she's done that. She wants you away from your policeman. Even willing to take on a shop on the other side of the town ... She's a warrior.' She smiled, and Peggy thought, she's all right, Jess – different from me, but all right.

'The thing is, a got rid of Donald tonight. It's finished!'

'The policeman!'

'Aye, he's not ma style.'

'Gosh, if she knew that! Did you go off him?'

'Yes,' she said. 'Right off.' She let out a gale of laughter. 'And him the best fiddle player in Glasgow!'

Jess waited for an explanation, then bent her head to her books. That was all she was going to get. She was all right, Peggy. Smart.

Eight

More than three years in the large city office where she now worked had given Jess at least a surface sophistication.

She had learned to accept the fact that the counter clerks, who at first had lined up to take her out to the Golden Divans in Green's Playhouse, soon lost interest when she wasn't prepared to give them their half-crown's worth of canoodling in return. She thought Mr Anderson was to blame for that.

She had also learned, in the crowded and varied inhabitants of a city, how to recognise any deviation from the norm – something which was never discussed at home, although her mother became incensed at a certain lady with an Eton crop and a tie who haunted the Central Station.

There was one of similar gender in the office, a dark-haired woman with red lipstick and teeth that crossed at the front, who attempted to woo Jess with presents of Fuller's fudge. Jess learned quickly how to accept the fudge, which she loved, and turn down the woman's suggestions to come up and see her wee flat. Unlike her mother, Peggy, or even her cousin Nessie, it was difficult to shock her. She had an early total acceptance of the vagaries of life. This surprised even her, knowing how shy she was in social situations.

She knew she surprised the girls in the typing pool when, curious to know why she turned down invitations from the counter clerks, she told them she had run the gamut from A to B, quoting Dorothy Parker. Jess Crichton had a certain something, they decided, but she was odd.

Miss MacDuff, the head typist, didn't think so. Miss MacDuff had golden hair parted in the middle with a neat bun at the back. There was no sign of hairpins and it was commonly thought that it was a wig. She didn't look young in spite of her small pink face – indeed her complexion reminded Jess of that of an elderly dwarf whom she had once seen in Hengler's Circus.

Miss MacDuff's opinion of Jess was one of obvious approval. She was easily the best and most accurate typist in the pool. 'I'm older than you may think, Jess, and I'm beginning to look out for a successor. Since the first day you came here I was impressed. You seemed to have the qualities I was looking for ... But, well, I'll say no more for the time being.'

She had a brother in Australia, and she had confessed to Jess that 'the great outdoors' had a strong appeal for her. She came back to the subject from time to time. 'I'd feel happy in Australia with my brother if I knew you were at the helm. You're not boy-daft like the rest of them here. Only wanting to get married. But there's more to life than that...'

Jess wasn't quite sure, but she was too busy to bother much. She was now a pupil teacher in the South Side College three evenings a week, and any spare time she had she played tennis or went walking – the company was advanced in its thinking and provided clubs for their staff.

She was convivial, but didn't make close friends. There was always Nessie, faithful, devoted to her Bob, a ready listener, never speaking ill of anyone. She knew where she was with Nessie.

Although it seemed to Jess that she had no skills with young men, strangely enough she had an easy rapport with Mr Craven, the owner of the College, who also taught Business French and German. Miss Evans in Bookkeeping told her he was divorced and had a son of thirteen or thereabouts. Mr Craven was mature, Jess thought – unlike the counter clerks – and ran the College with a sense of humour. He had a crease on one side of his mouth where it quirked, and was liked by all his staff – particularly Miss Evans, who confessed to Jess that she longed to iron his shirts for him. She too had noticed their rough-dried state.

Jess puzzled over the fact that she got on so well with a young middle-aged man like Mr Craven, whereas the young men gave her difficulty.

She said to Peggy, 'It's not that I'm worried about it or anything, but how do you know, I mean, learn, how to talk to boys of your own age?'

'Talk to them!' Peggy said. 'You don't talk to them! They're not worth it. They're all dead from the neck up. You just ... string them along, and then when you get tired of them ... or they turn out...' She had stopped, then said, 'You just chuck them!'

Jess had meant to go on to the next problem, being touched and fondled, then wondered why she was asking at all, since she had never met anyone who really appealed to her in that way. But at the same time she didn't want to be groomed as Miss MacDuff's successor, a celibate head typist. Yet.

James gave her no worries. She often made his tea, as her mother and Peggy were later than her in getting home from the dairy in Dennistoun. She and James had some interesting talks. They were the right age for each other.

But this night she made a quick meal for him of bacon and egg stuffed into a roll, as he was in a tearing hurry to get back to rugby practice at the Academy. She watched him eating, or wolfing, and thought what a handsome fourteen-year-old he was, full of confidence. Maybe the school had something to do with it. She remembered her lacklustre performance at hers, and her ignominious departure.

'Thanks, Jess,' he said. 'You're a brick. Jock was telling me' – Jock seemed to occur a lot in his conversation – 'that he has to make his own tea if he's going back to the school. Well, chin-chin!' He lifted his rugby gear and was off. She heard the outside door bang behind him.

A success story, she thought, as she began clearing the table. He was a good investment for the Grays, and their mother was still lost in admiration for him in his school uniform.

'Pull the peak down further, James. That's the way they Academy boys wear it.'

A protest from him to the effect that he was regularly punched on his way home by boys from another school fell on deaf ears. 'They don't matter. They're just jealous.' Even when he came home with blood-encrusted nostrils and a swollen lip it didn't make much impression. 'Stand up for yerself, James! They'll soon get tired of it. It's

80

only jealousy.' He had told Jess that he had to take a different way home every day and hide his cap under his blazer.

There was no doubt about it, they all basked in his glow, especially the Gray brothers, who liked a good investment. This was confirmed when they were shown his term reports by a jubilant mother. A credit to the whole family, they said. Even Peggy nodded and smiled, a quieter Peggy these days.

When Jess had asked her if she would like to come hiking with her she'd said, 'Not likely. It's all right for you, sitting on your backside all day.' You had to leave Peggy alone.

And now it was ice-skating, she thought, drawing the curtains against the early dusk. It was a pity Peggy wouldn't try that.

To Jess, Crossmyloof Ice Rink was like a miniature Switzerland. She had attacked the art of skating with her usual enthusiasm, and become obsessed by it. If only she could dance on skates ... If only she could join the speed skaters, that select band who flew round the rink when it had been cleared for them. If only...

Nine

1937

Jess had often seen Ronnie Wilcox when she had occasion to go into the Finance Department on some errand for Mr Brough, from whom she took dictation – the leonine head too big for his body, skin stretched tightly over his high cheekbones. Even his smile seemed stretched, and he jumped to her request as if he was on an elastic band. This particular day he said, tightly, as he handed over the file she wanted, 'Haven't I seen you at the ice rink?'

'Possibly,' she said. 'I'm at the learning stage.' She didn't like the intensity of his gaze. His eyes were very blue, Nordic eyes, his hair was fair. He should have been handsome but there was something wrong. She said stupidly, because he made her nervous, 'The girls I generally go with have given it up, but I love it.'

'Are you going tonight?'

'Yes, it's my only free night. Sometimes I go on Saturday afternoons as well.'

'I'll look out for you,' he said as if it were a matter of indifference, and turned away.

To safeguard herself she didn't go that evening but instead went out with Nessie Liddell. They didn't see each other as much now, as Bob was stationed in the nearby barracks at Maryhill. They were saving up to get married.

'How about you and me having a last fling next summer?' Nessie said. 'Bob says that man Hitler is up to his tricks. There's trouble brewing.'

'Yes, I've read something about him.'

There were no political discussions at home, but Mr Brough had told her his son had gone to Spain to fight for the Republicans. 'That's bad enough,' he had said, 'but most people think the big one will follow quite soon.' 'You mean total war?' He had nodded. 'That's it. Spain's just a rehearsal.'

'I know a great place in Skye, bed and board for two guineas a week,' Nessie said. 'Maybe Peggy would come too?'

'No, Peggy's in the doldrums. She's running a dairy with my mother and she doesn't like it.'

'She should get spliced. She's the right type for it. A'm not so sure about you.'

'I'm in no hurry.'

On Saturday afternoon the house was quiet. Jess's mother and Peggy were working and James had gone to visit the Grays. On impulse she decided to go to the ice rink. She had forgotten her conversation with Ronnie Wilcox, or chose to forget it. She liked skating, would like to dance on skates ... Why shouldn't she go?

She was making her way carefully round the rink when Ronnie Wilcox braked suddenly beside her.

'You didn't come last night,' he said with his tight smile.

'I was busy.' She went on skating, sorry he had seen her. He made her uneasy.

'I'll help you.' He held out his hand, and she had to take it.

They did a sober round or two and then slowly he increased his speed until they seemed to be flying round the rink. It was a wonderful feeling, exhilarating, and she forgot her objection to this odd young man. Skating was the thing, especially skating like this, feeling like a bird, the other skaters a blur. She was intoxicated by the speed.

'You're a natural,' he said when they slowed down. 'Come and have a coffee.' She accepted, and walked beside him on skates, her legs trembling with reaction. She needed that coffee.

The exhilaration left her. He ordered the coffee, thanked the girl effusively who brought it, then relapsed into silence. Each time she looked at him she caught him looking at her. He was nervous, and she felt sorry for him, but her effort to make conversation was a failure. He said suddenly, 'Ready to go back, then?' The tight smile.

'No, thanks, Ronnie.' She had made up her mind during the silences. She put her cup down. 'I've had enough. I'm tired.'

His eyes, very blue, stayed on her face. If she had been Peggy she would have said, What are ye starin' at?

'I frightened you.'

'What an idea!' She laughed nervously. 'You didn't. I liked the speed.' She got up clumsily on her skates. 'Thanks for the tuition.' She made herself smile.

'I'll come every Friday and Saturday. And any time you say. I'd like to help you.'

'Thanks,' she said again.

On the way home she puzzled about him. And about her own feeling of unease. He was nervous, she told herself, unsure. He couldn't help his mannerisms. She'd see...

When she got into their bedroom Peggy was already there, sitting up in bed reading.

'You should try skating, Peggy,' she said. 'It's great.'

'No, thanks. Haven't time. A wasn't born lucky, like you.'

She changed the subject. 'Is the shop going well?'

'It's no' like Woolworths, and on top of that, she's never pleased ... Talk about jumping from the frying pan into the fire!'

'Are you sorry you left the grocer's?'

'A'm sorry about a lot o' things. The only satisfaction a've got from this is that she bought the shop to get me away from Donald and she didn't know a'd broken it up myself. Sometimes a wonder, though...'

'Nessie's talking about booking next summer for Skye. Would you like to come?'

'Go with two other lassies? That'll be the day!' She returned to her book.

Jess stayed away from the ice rink and missed it. The next weekend was dreary. James was spending the weekend with a schoolfriend – a source of great satisfaction to their mother – and on Sunday Peggy was with her old friends from the grocer's.

She and her mother took a tram to the Botanical Gardens. At first it went well. Her mother talked incessantly about the big house where James was staying and the letter she had received from his schoolfriend's mother. *Would you be kind enough to lend James to us ...* She had it off verbatim, and repeated it once or twice, but soon grew tired of that and the hydrangeas and said she would have to have a cup of tea.

She grumbled about Peggy. She wasn't doing the ordering well enough. 'You have to have full shelves all the time to attract customers.'

'Maybe you should do it, then?'

'But a made her the manager! A can't be

there all the time. A only bought the place out o' the kindness of ma heart...'

The outing was a failure. Her mother had finished up by saying she couldn't understand why her two daughters were already old maids.

There was a letter for Jess on Monday morning in unknown handwriting. Her heart sank.

Dear Jess,
   Did I offend you last week? I went on both Friday and Saturday and you didn't turn up. You shouldn't stop coming just when you're getting your confidence. With my help you could become an expert in no time. Please don't let me down. I'll be waiting...

'Who's your letter from?' her mother asked.

'Nessie.' Lying saved a lot of time. 'She's saving up to get married.' She took care to lift the letter from her plate.

She made a conscious decision to ignore it. If she went to the ice rink he was bound to be there. She didn't want to skate with Ronnie Wilcox. It was a pity, because she had enjoyed it.

That evening he was waiting at the foot of the office steps. 'Hello, Jess,' he said, stepping forward.

'Oh, hello, Ronnie.' She was confused. 'I'm in a hurry. I teach tonight. I have to grab a sandwich before I go.'

'Could I join you?'

'No, thanks. I meet a friend there. Usually.'

'You're trying to put me off.' There was that agonised smile, and again she felt sorry for him. 'Why did you not answer my letter?'

'There was nothing to say. I've been too busy. I was waiting to see if I had any time.' She felt miserable. 'I'll come when I can, Ronnie.'

'Friday evening? That's your night off, isn't it?'

'I'm afraid I can't.'

'Saturday afternoon, then?'

'I'll do my best, but you know how it is ... Things to do...'

'Don't think I don't understand.' His eyes were full of understanding. 'I was in the same position when I was studying accountancy. Hardly a moment to myself. But you need a break. Try, will you?' It was a long speech for him. His eyes were beseeching, his smile almost sweet.

'I'll see,' she said. 'That's all I can say. Now, I must push on...'

She didn't go on Saturday, but she was so miserable about it that she gave in and asked Peggy's advice. 'How do you get rid of someone who's pestering you, Peggy?'

'Is there somebody pestering you?' She looked amused.

'Letters, and waiting for me at the office.'

'Tell him to bugger off. Unless you don't mean it?' She sat down to pull off her stockings. 'Look at ma ankles! Standin' aw day! Sometimes you do mean it at the time, and then you wonder if you've done the right thing?'

'Why should that be?'

'You're the clever one. If there's nobody else on the scene you kind o' miss ... Ach, work it out for yersel'.'

'But do you not feel sorry for the man?'

'Sorry! Sorry for myself more likely. You need, y'know, a bit of excitement ... an' that.' She hadn't got over the policeman, Jess thought.

'I can do without the excitement.'

'Aye, but you're different from me, just a child yet in spite o' all your typin' and teachin' and fancy talk.' She shrugged. 'Any roads, when it comes to the bit they're none o' them worth it. Not yet anyhow...' She got up. 'A'm away for ma bath.'

Another letter came on Friday morning. *Dear Jess, Don't let me down. I'll be waiting.* It was printed in black ink, big bold characters. She felt a stab of fear, followed by anger. There was no address at the top and she tore the letter up in small pieces and threw it on the kitchen fire.

That day one of the typists asked her if she would buy a ticket for the tennis hop on Saturday, and she decided to go. Her anger was growing. She was being kept away from something she had liked doing! She went to the dance with two girls in her department, her face more made up than usual, wearing a black dress with a garish necklace from Woolworths and high-heeled black slippers.

In the dance hall the two girls went off quickly with two young men, and she was left sitting alone on a bench. The hall with its wooden floor and tall dusty windows was a far cry from the Plaza. She looked around carefully. At least there was no sign of Ronnie Wilcox.

Bill Johnson, one of the counter clerks, asked her to dance, and she got up, relieved. He was safe enough, and he had never asked her out. He was tall, rangy, his good looks spoiled by acne and greasy black hair – but he was a good dancer. His mother ran a dancing school and he frequently partnered her.

'What brings you here, Jess?' he asked.

'I intended to skate and changed my mind. You would make a good skater, Bill.' She was feeling the ease of being with a born dancer, light-footed with a rolling gait which expertly steered her through the crowd.

'Just the same thing. I've done a bit of

figure skating. And dancin'. Stopped going for some reason.'

'So did I.' She gave herself up to the pleasure of dancing with him, in spite of the nearness of the acne.

He danced with her exclusively, speaking little, but there was no unease. At the last dance he said, 'I could teach you dancin' on skates. It's just like this, if you think of it. Balance. Confidence. Having the right body. You've got that.' It wasn't a flirtatious remark, she knew.

'Waltzes, and tangos?'

'Waltzes first, maybe. A'll take you next Saturday, if you like. We pay our own. That's how I like it. And I never take lassies home.'

'That's how I like it too.'

When she turned into her own street she saw Ronnie Wilcox leaning against the wall of the janitor's house, across the road from her flat. Or had she? She didn't look again, but hurried into their close and ran up the stairs as if she were being followed. She got into the house, breathless, her heart beating rapidly with fear.

Ten

She chose her dress with care for her Saturday's dancing at the ice rink – a short black skirt which she rolled up at the waistband to make it even shorter, and a white jumper with a polo neck.

'Don't let her see you in that outfit,' Peggy said. 'She'll skin the hide off you.'

'I'm wearing my coat. It's long enough. Besides she's out with James, remember?' They were at an Academy concert, 'Arias from Well-known Operas', which had amused the girls. Any woman singing on the wireless made their mother shout, 'Put that squeakin' teenie off!' 'Where did you get those!' Peggy said. Jess was fastening a pair of swinging false diamond earrings – not her usual style, she knew.

'Woolworths. I'm going dancing with a boyfriend.'

'They'll no' let you in like that!'

'It's at the ice rink.'

'My God! If Jenny hadn't booked seats at the Empire it would have been worth coming to see that!'

Jess rummaged in a drawer, selected a woollen cap and put it on. 'There!'

'A hat with a toorie on the top!'

'They all wear them.' She patted the round woollen ball. 'I'm off. You'll be late for the Empire if you don't stop painting your face like a...'

'Hoor!' Peggy laughed. 'It might be better than working in that shop.'

She met Bill Johnson practising figures at the barrier. 'Grab that!' he said when he saw her. 'And watch me.' He didn't comment on her outfit. She doubted if he had noticed.

She was quick, following his example with little difficulty. At the end of half an hour she could skate backwards and make a simple three-point turn with confidence. When he took her in his arms and said 'Try them now!' she executed the steps easily. 'No bother, eh?' he said. 'Again.' He coaxed her with his body to follow his movements, a slight swaying to one side and then the other ... It was easy. She could do no wrong. 'You're ready,' he said.

She looked up at him and smiled gratefully. He was wearing a red 'toorie-top' – Peggy's word – which matched his acne, and a violently-striped pullover and black, tight trousers.

The recording system blared the *Blue Danube*. The floor cleared. Bill Johnson held out his hand. 'Come on,' he said, and skated with her to the centre of the rink.

It was easy, a doddle, she thought delightedly. She was dancing on ice. Bill Johnson, acne, toorie-top and all, was an angel. He had been made in heaven for the express purpose of showing her how to waltz to the *Blue Danube* – the same swaying motion as he used on the ordinary dance floor, the same slight pressure with body, hands, or knees when necessary – and there they were, waltzing with ease amongst the other skaters.

'Da-da, de-dum, tum-tum, te-tum,' he sang, swinging her round. 'Da-da, de-dum, tum-tum, tum-tum,' and bending slightly towards her. 'It will be the tango next.' He whirled her round again, and as her head turned she caught a glimpse in the crowd at the barrier, of a face, skeletal, fair hair ... He whirled her again, a triple whirl. She lost the rhythm, her blades tangled with his, and they were both down on the ice.

'Whit in hell did ye do that for?' He was furious as he struggled to his feet, then helped her to hers. Dancers whirled past them.

'I'm sorry, Bill. Oh, I'm sorry! I was doing fine and then I thought I saw...'

'You shouldn't be lookin' about you. You're not that good.' He winced.

'Are you hurt?' He hadn't asked if she was. She didn't feel anything, only shame.

94

'We're gettin' in the way.' He held out his arms and they joined the dancers, but it wasn't the same. The communication between them had gone, she was shaking with shock, and after a few turns he said, 'Ach, it's no' any good. An' ma leg's hurtin' like mad. Did you hurt yourself?'

'No.' She shook her head.

'Only your pride.' He gave her a wry smile as they skated slowly off the rink. There was a ripple of clapping from a few people in the crowd.

'You shouldn't look at folks,' he said when they sat down. 'You lose your concentration ... Ach!' His face screwed up with pain. An official was at their side.

'Anybody hurt?' And to Jess. 'You could do with a cup of tea. Are you okay?'

'I don't know.' She could hardly speak.

'Ma leg's hurtin' like mad,' Bill said. 'Look!' He touched the front of his trousers and held up his hand. It was wet with blood.

'You'd better come along to the first-aid room. You too,' he said to Jess as he helped Bill to his feet.

They went with him, where another uniformed man gave her a cup of tea. 'That'll put some colour into your cheeks again,' he said.

'Bill's leg has an ugly gash in it, caused by blades when you fell,' the official said. 'Most likely hers, but that's the luck o' the game.

95

A've seen broken legs before now.'

They told Bill he could have a taxi to take them home, and he said all right – as long as he didn't have to pay for it. 'A only brought money for the tram,' he said.

'Well, we'll pay for it,' the man smiled. 'This lass doesn't look as if she could walk far.'

'I'm all right,' Jess said.

They sat for a long time waiting. She felt so guilty that she couldn't bring herself to speak.

'You were doin' quite well,' Bill said. Perhaps the idea of a taxi pleased him. 'It's just bad luck wi' ma leg. It'll take a time to heal.'

'I can't tell you how sorry I am.' She was fighting back the tears.

'It's done. But don't look to me for a partner for a time. A'm goin' to stick to ordinary dancing till I get over this.'

'I don't blame you,' she said, looking at the floor.

They sat in the taxi without speaking. The only consolation was that the accident had prevented her going back to the rink and perhaps meeting Ronnie Wilcox again. He would have seen her fall. Would he think it served her right, or would he be sympathetic?

The taxi dropped her first and when she said 'Goodnight,' he only replied with a grunt. He had let out a few groans on the journey. His leg was obviously hurting, but she guessed he had a mother who would cosset him.

In a spirit of bravado she went into the kitchen when she got home. She had heard voices. James and her mother were sitting at the table having a late-night supper. She took off her coat and flung it over a chair. The room was hot from a glowing fire.

James looked up. 'Have you been dancing the Highland Fling, Jess?'

She looked down at her short skirt. 'Oh! It's got caught up!'

'What sort o' outfit's that?' her mother enquired, but she was evidently in good humour.

'I was skating. They're all the same. How did you enjoy the concert?'

'Madame Thingamajig was in fine voice.' Maggie laughed at James as she spoke. 'We had refreshments at the interval, and the woman beside me was quite friendly. Talked about how she loved opera. A said a was quite keen on it myself.' She laughed again like a young girl. 'We had to mingle, that's what the headmaster said, "Please mingle."' She looked at James, her face creased with laughter. 'So we mingled.' Well, she's in a good mood at least, Jess thought, amused at them.

'I prefer the *Barber of Seville* myself.' James

waved his hand.

'Where's *his* shop?' her mother said. James looked at Jess, shaking his head in mock despair.

'You two are out of your minds,' Jess said. 'I'm going for a bath.'

'Leave some water in the tank for the dishes,' her mother's face sobered. 'That other one's not in yet. She'll get a good piece of ma mind!'

'Why don't you sing it?' Jess said, lifting her coat and making for the door.

She discovered a bruise on her shoulder, and one on her ribs, and her body ached. But she didn't feel so badly now about the tumble. The clowning of James and her mother must have cheered her up.

She tried not to think of Ronnie Wilcox's face in the crowd, which had caused all the trouble to begin with. She was now deathly tired, and crawled into bed. She didn't hear Peggy coming in.

On Monday morning she spoke to one of the counter clerks, and after the usual ribbing found out that Bill Johnson wasn't coming in.

'The gigolo's got hurt in a fight or something. Don't waste your time on him. He's only interested in the dancin'.'

She managed to get his address at last and went upstairs to the typing pool.

98

Ronnie Wilcox was waiting for her that evening when she went down the main steps leading to the street.

'I thought I'd just see if you were all right ... after your fall.' His chin was lifted, his face expressionless.

She was suddenly furious, the depth of her anger surprised even herself. Those piercing blue eyes fixed on her, and had he been trying not to smile? She was so angry that for a moment or two she was speechless.

'I'll walk you home, Jess. Maybe you need a bit of support...'

'You will not walk me home!' she shouted, not worrying who heard her. 'First, because I'm going to the College, and second, even if I weren't, you're the very last person I want to walk me home ... or see, ever again!' Nothing would wipe off that smile, she thought wildly. 'Stop following me!' Her voice was still raised. 'Do you hear?'

It was as if he were deaf. Or stupid. 'I know you don't really mean it. I could take you speed skating ... You won't want to dance ... now...'

'Keep away from me!' She felt she would explode. 'Do you hear!' She was on the point of running away from him when she saw Mr Brough coming down the steps. He was as untidy as ever, an old raincoat, a bashed soft hat which he was raising to her.

'Good evening, Miss Crichton,' he said,

and passed on. She thought of catching up on him, then dismissed the idea. No one must know about this.

She turned to Ronnie Wilcox again. 'Mr Brough lives at Kirkhill. He's going for his train. I'm walking to the station too. My College is on the Circle Line, so I can go on the same train. If you dare to follow me I'll shout my head off and he'll hear. You'll be in trouble!' He looked taken aback. 'I mean it,' she said. She left him, walking a few yards behind Mr Brough. He was in a hurry, shambling along, not looking back.

She turned her head. Ronnie Wilcox was standing where she had left him, his eyes following her. He looked pathetic, although his head was still up in that peculiar gesture. His hands were in his pockets. One foot moved on the pavement, like a blind man's cane. She whipped up her anger. He's got to realise that I don't want anything to do with him.

The picture of him was still in her mind as she sat in the station tea room drinking tea. She couldn't face anything to eat. She saw his dejected figure, the foot moving in that peculiar way on the pavement...

She wrote a short letter to Bill Johnson late that night in the empty kitchen.

Dear Bill,

I can't apologise enough for tripping you up at the ice rink. I found out that you were off work, and wanted to say that I hope your leg will soon get better. I know you would never have fallen with anyone else.

Best wishes for a speedy recovery,
Jess

That's the end of dancing on ice, she thought, sealing it. And the end of speed skating too. Short but sweet. She felt tired, a bone tiredness. She hoped she would sleep.

Eleven

1938
By a stroke of luck Jess overheard in the office that there was a back entrance which led on to a side street, and she had been using this for a few weeks. It seemed as if she had shaken Ronnie Wilcox off, and she breathed more easily.

She would put it out of her mind. They were into 1938 now, and the possibility of a war was occupying many people's thoughts. She began reading the papers more thoroughly. Hitler had invaded Austria, and Mr Brough thought it was only a matter of time.

Nessie had begun to talk about their trip to Skye. Bob was saying he might be called up for active service, and the holiday would be their last chance before anything happened. 'You get off with Jess while you can,' he had said.

The firm rented a swimming baths in Dennistoun, and Jess started going there. She had never gone back to the ice rink. But she soon realised she had been congratulating herself too soon. A letter arrived one morning from Ronnie Wilcox, and she read it sitting alone in the kitchen.

Dear Jess,

I waited and waited for you. It worried me so much that I've been off ill.

What I wanted to say to you is that you aren't ready for figure skating, and I don't think you ever will. Don't believe what Bill Johnson says. Everybody knows what he is.

If you'll only tell me where to meet you I'll stop bothering you. We'll have a good talk and you'll see how suited we are to each other. I'll not even bother you about skating.

The thing is, I have to see you, to talk to you. I can think of nothing else. I'm torturing myself thinking about you. Please take pity on me. I'm not eating, or sleeping, and I'm even making mistakes with figures in the department. The boss has told me to watch my step.

You wouldn't like me to lose my job, would you? I mean what I'm saying. I've never been out with another girl in my life. If you don't see me I don't know what I'll do.

Ronnie.

She put her head in her hands. She didn't weep. Who could she talk to? He would lose his job if she complained. She thought of telling the Gray brothers, but no, they were too old. 'All passion spent.'

'What's wrong, Jess?' She looked up at James' voice. He had his school trousers on, his vest, but no shirt.

She tried to smile. 'Me? Nothing. Just tired.'

'Do you not like your job?'

'Oh, yes, I like it.'

'What is it?' She looked at him and thought for a second he had their father's eyes, the eyes she still remembered when he had told her they had a wee brother. He seemed mature, and she wondered if it was the influence of the Grays with whom he frequently stayed, or the school, or that he was simply blessed with an equable disposition in this family of moods. The one that got away, she thought...

'It's nothing, really. Feeling sorry for myself.'

'You're never that. Hey, Jess, I can't find a clean shirt.'

'Sorry. I was ironing them last night. Take one from that pile over there, white-collar worker!' No, he was only a boy yet. She'd have to solve her own problems.

But she thought of the letter constantly, with a mounting feeling of dread. If she told

Ronnie's boss it would get him into trouble – he might report him to Mr Brough. He had his own worries. His son had been sent home from Spain injured. 'He'll get better just in time for the big one,' he said gloomily.

Besides, she had no proof. She had torn up the first letter, burned the second one. Meantime the only thing she could do was keep out of his way, but it wouldn't take him long to discover that she was slipping out the back way. And yet the image of his dejected figure stayed with her, how when she had looked back that evening he had been standing there, shoulders hunched, that wandering foot...

Nothing happened for a few days and then she began to see him again leaning against the wall of the school, in front of the janitor's house. When she looked out of the window he was looking up at their flat.

Peggy came in after work one night and was making a cup of tea in the kitchen. Jess had her pupils' books spread across the table for correction.

'Whit are ye lookin' out o' the window for?' She had caught Jess in the act.

'It's that man in the office again. I'm beginning to think I'm imagining things.'

'You're looking scared stiff. Let's have a dekko.' She walked over to the window and lifted the curtain.

'Aye, it's the same wee bachle. Do you want me to go down and tell him to bugger off? A could lift him up on ma hand!'

Jess laughed at her. 'No, he'll get tired of it. Sometimes I get ... kind of sorry for him.' She felt better with Peggy there.

'Sorry! He's got a hell of a nerve! If a was still seeing Donald a could tell him to bash him up.'

'Oh, for goodness sake! I'll deal with it myself. Are you still not seeing Donald?'

'I told you that was over. A didny like him enough to ... well never mind. You take a leaf out o' ma book and don't waste your time or energy on anybody you know isn't right for you. And that wee bachle across the road! Well a wouldny waste the time o' day on him! Here, Jess, would you like me to throw a pail o' water over him, the way we do with cats?'

Peggy had cheered her up. 'Don't go mad.' She changed the subject. 'There's a note from Mrs Thompson asking you and me to tea tonight. The Grays are taking mother and James for a meal to celebrate him doing so well last term.'

'The boy wonder! No, a can't go. A lassie in Dennistoun has asked me to go to their picture house tonight. It's one a want to see. You go.'

'One of us should. But I've got all these to correct...' She indicated the pile of paper.

'Take your tea from her and come back. You make heavy weather out o' everything.'

Maybe she did. But she felt better. She bent to her work.

'Well, it's just you and me, Jess.' She had given Peggy's apologies to Mrs Thompson. 'Joe's had to be on duty tonight at the school.

She bustled about the kitchen where the meal was already set, a dumpy wispy-haired woman with a button of a nose which was made redder by frequent rubbing. She suffered from catarrh, the common Glasgow complaint. 'Draw in your chair, Jess.'

She sat down before a heaped plate of mince and suet dumplings thickly embedded with currant-like blobs of mince, all swimming in a glutinous Bisto gravy which had overflowed on to a mountain of mashed potatoes. Dinner and tea in one, Jess thought, lifting her knife and fork.

'You keep oot o' ma road, Tommy.' Mrs Thompson's remark was directed at her huge, spoiled black cat. It came and sat at Jess's feet, looking enviously upwards at her plate.

Mrs Thompson sat down opposite her and poured them both a large cup of orange tea. 'That'll help to wash it down.'

'It's far too much, Mrs Thompson.'

'Eat it up. It'll do you good. Would you like

some HP sauce?'

Jess declined.

'You like where you're teachin', Jess?'

'Yes. Mr Craven, the principal, is really nice to work to, fair-minded, and with a sense of humour. And I get on well with the girls.'

'Well, you're just a lassie yourself.' She looked at Jess over her teacup. 'Remember that Mr Anderson?'

'Difficult to forget.'

'I always felt to blame for that. And you were quite right. Other girls here complained about him, called him "Slimy Joe". Well, eventually it got to the headmaster's ears and he was sacked.'

'I'm not sorry. My mother didn't really believe me, you know.'

'I did. But she's a strong-minded woman, and I was a bit doubtful at first. He didn't accept any money, she said.'

'He did. But it's over and done with, Mrs Thompson. I'm just sadder and wiser. Sometimes I wonder if I'm wise enough.'

'Nobody ever is, at the time. Eat up, Jess.'

'It's really good, but I've let it grow cold with talking.'

'I'll heat it up for you.' She half-rose.

'No, don't bother. I've really eaten a lot. Besides Tommy here's just waiting for my leftovers.'

'Well, if you're sure.' She lifted the plate and put it down in front of the tom. It squirmed with pleasure and then crouched over the plate, a picture of lust.

'I could take another cup of tea, though.'

'Here you are, then. And a wee chocolate biscuit to finish off with?' It was easier to agree. And at that minute she had made up her mind.

'Mrs Thompson, when we were talking about Mr Anderson, I thought I'd ask you about something else. Supposing that Mr Thompson saw someone loitering about the school, at night, what would he do?'

'Is it someone you know?' She was astute.

'Yes, there's a man in the office. He wants me to go out with him. I haven't time for him, I don't like him ... and I'm busy, as you know.'

'Aye?' Mrs Thompson's eyes were on her.

'I've seen him some nights, looking up at our flat, leaning on the wall of the school, sometimes in front of your house. I'm a bit worried. I don't like it. I've told him I want nothing to do with him.'

'A follower? It's no' unusual. If Joe sees him he'll give him a piece o' his mind. A'll tell him. Most likely he'll threaten him wi' the polis. He wouldny mention your name. He's the janitor of the school. Responsible.' It didn't sound much like the peaceable Joe that Jess knew, but she accepted it.

She imagined the scene, Ronnie with his head up, facing the enemy, then retreating, shoulders bent. Mrs Thompson was looking at her kindly.

'A think a know you, Jess. You don't like to hurt folks' feelings, when sometimes a piece of direct talking is what they need.'

'I did that. Really lost my temper.'

'But you're still worried. Well, so would I be.' She polished her snub nose vigorously. 'It's not right – not as bad as Mr Anderson was bad, but upsetting all the same. You've got to look at those things clearly, trust your own feelings. You're no' daft. You just leave it to Joe.'

'All right.' She still felt miserable. 'I've got nothing against him, except that I don't want to have anything to do with him.' Remembering Peggy, she added, 'He's not for me.'

'Right. Joe'll put the fear of death in him. The poor soul's maist likely daft about ye. You're a bonny lass. And with takin' ways. There will be somebody for you when the time's right.'

'I'm in no hurry. Thanks, Mrs Thompson.' She tried to speak brightly. 'That was a lovely tea but I've got to get back and get on with correcting books. Mother and James will soon be back.'

'My, that was a good thing those friends did for him! She's always talkin' about it.

And the Grays! A think she's taken by their flat up there among the toffs.'

'Yes, she's in her element.' They laughed together.

Twelve

Although Jess had been a pupil teacher at the South Side College for a year, she had a day off that week to sit her Finals. In spite of her worries about Ronnie Wilcox she had the enviable attribute of concentrating on work when it was demanded. In fact, it was a welcome respite.

She ran into Bill Johnson when she was back in the office, still limping a little, but he bore her no grudge. 'It was just bad luck, Jess. But no more for me for the time being. I'm busy helping out my mother at the Dancing School.' It was finished for her too.

On her way home that evening she saw Mr Thompson sweeping the pavement outside the school gate. All her worries about Ronnie Wilcox returned. She stopped to speak to the janitor.

'I hope you didn't think it was cheeky of me to ask you to speak to that man, Mr Thompson?'

'No, you did right.' He leant on the handle of the brush. 'Even if he had nothing to do with you I don't like people loitering near the school. It's my job to keep an eye on them.'

'How did he take it?'

'Frightened. He said he was sorry, and I said to see that it didn't happen again. No bother. No fight in him. Not like some.'

Jess saw him in her mind, his head back, the smile. Mr Thompson said he had been frightened...

'You couldn't shout at him. A said, "Look, lad, you'll get into trouble with the polis if they see you hanging around," and he was backin' away as a spoke, and saying, "Sorry ... sorry ..." He's an odd one that, Jess, kind o' pitiful. Something wrong there. You're well rid o' him.'

All the satisfaction she had been feeling about her exams drained away. She should-n't have asked Mr Thompson. 'I wish I hadn't mentioned it...'

'Don't feel that. A've instructions to tell loiterers to clear off. That's my job.' He drew himself up, a scrawny figure in his navy jacket and peaked cap. He took an evident pride in his job.

'Well, thanks anyhow. You'll be thinking it's me who's the odd one – first Mr Ander-son, then this...' She didn't want to use Ronnie Wilcox's name.

She told Peggy that night when they were both in their room. 'Mr Thompson spoke to that man who was loitering. Told him to clear off.'

'What?' She looked distracted. She's been having a row with mother, Jess thought.

'Remember? The man I told you about. Across the street. You saw him.'

'Oh, that wee smout!' She was busy rummaging in a drawer and didn't look at Jess. 'Good riddance to him, I say. You'd be better with nobody, like me.'

Jess gave up. 'Well, thank goodness my Finals are over, if I've passed...' she said to change the subject.

'Your Finals!' She mimicked Jess's voice. 'You don't have to worry. You were born lucky!'

A week later Jess went into the typists' room, aware that the girls were talking amongst themselves, their faces grave.

'Come away, Miss Crichton,' Miss Mac-Duff said. 'Is that everyone here?' She looked around, and stood up, bracing her shoulders as if to give herself courage. There was something ominous here, Jess thought, something I have to face. She waited, tense, quelling the feeling of terror. 'Some of you may have heard already.' Miss MacDuff's voice was firm. 'But I regret to have to tell you that there's been a tragedy in the office.' Silence. No one moved. 'Ronnie Wilcox of the Finance Department has been found drowned in the Clyde at Anderston.'

There was silence for a further moment or two, then everyone was talking, a confused murmur. Someone said, 'We'd heard, Miss MacDuff. It's awful.'

Another voice separated itself from the muttered talking. 'I heard his parents had reported it and the Police have been making enquiries. I hope they don't come in here.'

'I'll deal with things if they do. Don't worry.' Miss MacDuff still stood erect. 'It was the river police who found the body. He's an only son. He didn't make friends easily. They'd been worried about his behaviour recently, both at home and in the office. He'd been off ill. Mr Mackieson told me he had been making mistakes in his work.'

'Maybe Mr Mackieson gave him a ticking off,' someone said.

Miss MacDuff held up her hand. 'We mustn't speculate. Anyhow, these are the sad facts. There is no point in further conjecture. As far as could be ascertained, the young man took his own life. We will never know why.' She looked around. 'Now, can I ask you all to get on with your work? We're going to have a busy day. Thank you, girls.' She sat down.

One of the bells on the wall went. 'That's you, Miss Crichton.' She was businesslike now.

'Yes, Miss MacDuff.' Jess managed to

walk out of the room, not looking to right or left. Could she slip into the Ladies? No, Mr Brough would ring again and that would get her into trouble. Her throat ached with tears, her head throbbed.

Had it been Mr Thompson's threat that had made Ronnie Wilcox drown himself? The last straw? Had he walked to the Clyde that night and deliberately walked in? It would be dark. He would walk slowly in and be submerged with scarcely any noise, the water would close over his head...

Her mind whirled. It was her fault. But Mr Thompson had said that he would have spoken to him in any case. And she had burned the letters! Had she subconsciously thought that they would be incriminating if they were found? No, no. She hadn't thought, it had been an instinctive reaction.

She had reached Mr Brough's room. She knocked and went in. 'Good morning, Mr Brough.'

He looked up as she sat down. 'Good morning. I'm in a hurry. Would you take a letter to...' She took one and then another and another, her mind on this terrible thing, her hand moving automatically over the page.

'That's the lot, Miss Crichton.' She was gathering her papers when he said, 'I suppose you've heard the sad news about Mr Wilcox in the Finance Department?'

'Yes. Miss MacDuff told us.' She had begun to rise but had to sit down again because her legs seemed to give way.

'You knew him, didn't you?' Was this a trick? He had seen her talking to him that time outside the office. He might even have heard her.

'Yes, I knew Ronnie. I had been to Crossmyloof with him once or twice.' She listened to her calm voice.

'A loner, they say. Elderly parents. Well, there's no accounting for some things. My lot fought like cats and dogs when they were growing up. Then the eldest goes off to fight in Spain...'

'How is your son? Is he getting better?'

'Much better. We're getting him home this week.' His face softened.

'I'm glad. Well, I'll get on with these, Mr Brough.'

She got through the day somehow, her mind a welter of thoughts. Should she tell someone about the letters? Mr Mackieson? The Police? But if she went to either of them it would only be her word. She had burned the letters. They might think she was making it up. People, mad people, did that – went to the Police for notoriety.

Her mother and Peggy were out of the question. She didn't stop to analyse why. Of course they might read something in the papers. Or Mr and Mrs Thompson? He would get all the newspapers in the school. She finished her letters before closing time and took them to Miss MacDuff.

'Thank you, Jess. I hardly need to look at these. By the way, how did your Finals go?'

'My Finals? Oh, all right, thank you.'

'I hope you're not thinking of leaving us?'

'I don't think so. I'm not sure about full-time teaching.' I'm not sure about anything.

'Well, I wouldn't attempt to influence you, but remember, my job will be open in a year or so. My brother is building a new bunga-low at the moment. "Ready for you when you are, Polly," he writes.'

I can't think about teaching or jobs, Miss MacDuff, or your bungalow in Australia. I can only think of Ronnie Wilcox's body being pulled out of the Clyde ... Would his mouth be stretched in a smile even when he was cold and stiff?

She wept the whole way home, regardless of passers-by. When she got in she put her head round the kitchen door. 'I ate something today that didn't agree with me, Mother. I'll not take any tea.'

'I'll wait till Peggy comes in. You might face it. It's tripe.'

Then she was sick. She was glad of the excuse to creep into bed. She pretended to be asleep when Peggy came into the room.

She expected that the Thompsons would

say something about Ronnie's death, but she heard nothing. Maybe they were being tactful.

She still agonised about going to the Police and telling them about the letters, but as the weeks passed and discussion died down in the office, she decided against it. She had burned the letters. She thought of consulting Mr Brough, but he was a busy man with his work and family. He had enough to worry about. She dismissed each idea in its turn. What she was looking for was someone who would reassure her, help her to assuage the awful guilt that she was responsible for Ronnie's death.

Reason told her she should not have guilt. She couldn't be responsible for his behaviour, and as for the warning from Mr Thompson, well, the man had only been doing his duty. But at her instigation?

They said he was a loner, and unfortunately, he had become obsessed by her. But she hadn't encouraged him, had she? In her anxiety to excel in skating, she had accepted his company, but that was all.

There would be other factors. Elderly parents, out of touch with the young; Mr Mackieson reprimanding him, warning him that he might lose his job. Oh, yes, there were plenty of reasons, but she knew the real one. He had appealed to her in a letter and she had ignored it.

One night she was so disturbed that she gave in and said to Peggy when they were alone, 'Remember the man from the office who hung about outside?'

'Are you on about that again? Has he given it up?'

'Yes. He drowned himself.'

She looked at Jess, a peculiar look. 'Drowned himself, did he? In the Clyde?" She seemed to be au fait with drownings, perhaps because of her policeman.

'Yes, at Anderston. That would have been on Donald's beat, wouldn't it?' She had remembered his name.

'Oh, aye. He was always pullin' stiffs out o' the water. Dead drunk, then they fall in. Did you ever go out with this one, I mean, *out* with him?' The emphasis was meant to be significant.

'No, only skating. That was all.' Liar. She couldn't bring herself to tell Peggy about the letters.

'There are folks like that. I don't mean drunks. Just odd. Better out the road, put themselves out o' misery. A can tell you a'm sometimes tempted to do the same thing myself. She comes into the shop and complains, alters the way the shelves are arranged, says I've got to tempt the customers! What does she want me to do? The *Dance of the Seven Veils*?'

Jess spluttered. It was no good. If she

120

wanted to tell the whole truth it would have to be to the right people, the Police. But, why? The verdict, one of the typists had said, was that the victim had taken his own life while of unsound mind. It was a closed book. All the telling in the world wouldn't alter that fact. Ronnie Wilcox didn't exist any more.

The keenness of her regret faded as time passed, leaving only a deep dislike of herself. She wasn't like Peggy, who believed in herself and her opinions. Nor like James, well balanced, happy in his school and with the background of the Gray brothers – where he had become almost one of the family. Everything was going well for James. She suspected it always would.

When the letter came announcing that she had passed her Finals with Honours she was unmoved.

Mr Craven was delighted and said they must celebrate. She smiled wanly and said there was no need. True to his word he took Jess and Miss Evans – possibly for decorum – to have dinner at Danny Brown's.

He was a splendid host, she thought, amusing and yet kind, listening patiently to Miss Evans' lengthy tale about her next-door neighbour and her dustbin – probably lengthier because she confessed to enjoying a 'little tipple' now and again.

'Drink up, the night's a pup,' he adjured

her, refilling her glass and throwing a laughing sidelong glance at Jess.

'Do you know, Miss Evans,' he said, 'my son, Jock, wanted to come along tonight too, but I told him he'd have to get on with his homework. I think he's enamoured of you.' She blushed into her glass.

'My brother has a schoolfriend called Jock,' Jess said.

'Is it James?'

'Yes.'

'One and the same. Young Turks both of them. James Crichton knows his way round our kitchen better than I do myself.'

Well, well, she thought.

He dropped off Miss Evans and then Jess. 'She lives with an elderly mother,' he said. 'A bit of a penance, I believe.'

'Well, she enjoyed herself tonight.'

'I'm glad.' He had reached her close and when he stopped the car he turned towards her. 'You know we'd all be pleased, indeed highly honoured, if you would become a member of our full-time staff.'

She thanked him, and said she would think about it.

He nodded and said, 'Okay, just remember the offer's there.' It was too definite, too soon, she thought, like tying up her life in a neat parcel. Like becoming Miss Evans Number Two. First, she had to come to terms with Ronnie Wilcox's death.

Every week after work, she went to Dennistoun to the office Swimming Club. Sometimes for company she would call at the shop and go home with Peggy.

She chose an evening when she knew her mother wouldn't be at the shop as well. She cherished the wish that she and Peggy might become real confidantes. Their mother, these days, was in a springtime frenzy of house-cleaning, shaking the life out of carpets, beating them to death with a cane beater in the back green, washing the net curtains of their accumulated winter soot ... Everyone had their own method of coping with their problems. Perhaps she took her liking for exercise from her mother.

Thirteen

Peggy looked up when the shop doorbell tinkled. It was Jess, in a loose camel coat over a smart skirt, and that peculiar hair of hers – brown with streaks of silver in it. It was damp at the ends. She would have been swimming at the Baths. Always up to something.

'What bring you here?' She resented that look of smartness Jess always had. No amount of fancy dressing could make her look like that.

'I've been swimming. I thought I'd come in and go home with you.'

'Good for you.'

'You don't seem to be very busy.' Jess sat down opposite her at the scrubbed wooden table.

'It never is. Nothing like "the premises". That was different...' She looked around disparagingly.

'Somehow I don't remember it as well as you do. But you're right. I remember the tiled wall pictures, and the counter and shelves of a streaky kind of marble...'

'D'you not remember the biscuit boxes with glass lids? You asked once if you could have one to make a doll's house. You didny get it. But look at this place. No comparison ... stone floors, whitewashed walls. And a've to scrub all those shelves and table every day ... It's like a byre. But then a've never been given a choice, servin' behind a counter aw the time...' She saw Jess's eyes fall. She didn't like those remarks, but you couldn't make Jess fight. She'd tried it often.

'Do you think Mother's beginning to regret buying this place?' Jess ruffled her damp hair. She had nice hands. And those clothes ... better than a white apron.

'It's not exactly makin' a loss, but it's no' makin' a fortune. No, it's James being at the Academy that's taken her fancy now, and aw the social affairs that go with it. She's always across at Mrs Thompson's boasting about it. About you too. Passing to be a teacher.'

'Not to me.' She saw Jess's eyes fall again.

'Oh, yes. You're the success story this week.' She had a pang of shame, and got up. 'Well, it's about six. I'd better get ready to lock up.'

'Would you like me to count the till?'

'No, it's done. It's in the bag.' Jess knew it, and the little leather pouches which had been used in 'the premises'. Details like that came back. She remembered the kitchen table there being covered with coins and how she had thought it was all the money in the world.

'Do you remember the kist behind the curtains in their bedroom, Peggy?'

'Aye. It's still in her bedroom. She decks it up with a fancy shawl and cushions...'

'Have you anything I can do for you, then?'

'Yes, take that bag of doughnuts there. They didn't go well today. Thursdays the wives have no money left for fancies. Scones are better. They can always fry them with a bit of bacon.'

'It must be awful when you're not busy.'

'You don't know the half o' it.' She stood up and put on her coat, lifted the Gladstone bag with the money in it and felt in her pocket for the keys. 'There'll be no more folks in tonight. They'll all be getting their teas ready.'

'I'll carry the money bag.'

'No, you might get knocked down.' She smiled at her sister, feeling a rush of affection for her. She wasn't bad, Jess, she shouldn't grumble to her. It wasn't bad here either, and there was always the fun with the girls up the town. 'Come on, wee yin,' she said.

They were in the front shop when the bell on the door pinged and a tall young man in working clothes, fair-haired, pushed in.

126

'Hey!' he smiled at Peggy. 'Am I too late? A just want a half pint o' milk and some boiled ham. And a loaf, if you have it.'

'You don't want much.' This was more like it. She knew when she was at home with a situation. And handsome, too, a cut above the rest – even above Donald. 'Ach, no, you're all right. You've just caught me in time. Is it for a sandwich?'

'Aye, a'm workin' on a building site in Duke Street. A'm in digs in Dennistoun.'

'Oh, aye.' She threw off her coat, glad she had on her tight blouse. She uncovered the slicing machine and expertly inserted a side of ham. 'Would four slices do?'

'Fine. And a bit o' butter if you don't mind.' She threw a glance at Jess, eyebrows raised. 'He doesn't want much, does he?' She returned to the young man. 'If you speak to me nicely I might do even more for you.'

'Aye? Whit's that?' His eyes were dancing.

'Like make them up for you.'

'Is it a knife you want, Peggy?' Jess handed over one she took from the drawer under the counter. She felt invisible to them. She looked at the young man and saw his mouth had fallen open.

'Did you say Peggy!' he asked.

'Yes.'

'A thought you did. You two didn't used to live in a wee dead end across the road from

127

Renfrew Ferry?'

'A long time ago...' He wasn't looking at her.

'Peggy Crichton!' he was saying. 'Is it Peggy Crichton? D'you not know me?'

'No.' She was puzzled. 'What's your name?'

'Noble Murdoch. We lived there too.'

Her eyes widened, her face flushed. 'Noble Murder! By all that's ... My God! The wee fair-haired lad wi' your father's cap on, aye showing off...'

'That's me! As large as life!'

She turned to Jess, her eyes flashing. 'You remember him, Jess? Always up to something. Followed me around like a shadow...' She threw a flirtatious glance at the young man.

'I was only four, but, yes, I remember, all being crowded into a small space, and—'

'The Co-op door!' Noble Murdoch said. 'Good for you. Peggy and Jess Crichton, from the past. It's past believing!' And then the three of them were laughing, remembering, exclaiming, exchanging their memories. When they calmed down at last Noble asked Peggy, 'Where are you stayin' now?'

'Off Sauchiehall Street, but our mother bought this shop ... to keep me out of mischief.'

'I'm not surprised.' His glance was admiring. 'Ma mother died and ma father married again. I've been a bit of a drifter since I grew up. A have an aunt outside Perth and a go there sometimes to help them on the farm. I like that best. I like the hills, and the space.'

'So do I,' Jess said.

'You haven't changed much.' It was Peggy he was speaking to. Their eyes were eating each other up.

'I'll make the sandwiches,' Jess said. She took up the slices of ham on a sheet of greaseproof paper, lifted a loaf from the shelf where they were covered with a cloth and retired into the back shop.

She could hear their voices, their laughter, and as she cut and spread the slices of bread with butter and then ham, she remembered how Peggy and Noble Murdoch had gone everywhere together when they were children. So long ago. In their first house, before 'the premises'. When she took the finished sandwiches back to the shop they looked at her as if they didn't know her.

'It's after six,' she said to Peggy. 'I don't want to hurry you but isn't there a rule that you have to be out of here by six thirty? A police rule?' She wondered if the word 'police' penetrated her sister's consciousness, but doubted it.

'You're right.' Peggy said it regretfully. 'They're strict round here.'

'Do you still want your sandwiches?' Jess

said to Noble Murdoch, feeling like an arm of the law.

'Oh, aye, thanks.'

Peggy reached down under the counter and got a paper bag, which she gave to Jess. 'Here you are. For Noble Murder!' She suddenly let out a peal of laughter. 'That takes me back. Noble Murder! We aw called you that.'

'Because nobody could spell. Happy days. Well, a'm keeping you girls from your tea. I'd better get on. How much do I owe you?'

'Oh, have them for auld time's sake,' Peggy said. 'Give them to him, Jess. A've counted the money now.'

'Well, that just means a'll have to come back tomorrow and pay you.' He took the sandwiches. 'Thanks, you've saved ma life.'

'A'll hold you to that. Tomorrow. You're a witness to that, Jess.'

'A don't need any witnesses. Nothing will keep me back!' He waved the paper bag like a flag and turned for the door. Before he went out he called, still looking at Peggy, 'How to get sandwiches for nothing!' The bell jangled behind him.

Peggy turned to Jess, her face full of excitement, a little embarrassed. 'A can hardly believe it. Noble Murder! Do you really remember him?'

'How could I ever forget him?' she teased. 'Yes, I remember him. Always laughing. And you followed him about like a wee dog.'

'Yes, we were soulmates. A wonder if...'
She looked shy – for Peggy – then, as if to
change the subject, said, 'Do you remember
Mrs Buckup?'

'Mother's friend? Yes. How did she come
by that name?'

They told their mother about Noble
Murdoch when they were all sitting round
the kitchen table later. 'Aye,' she said. 'A
taking lad. And May Buckup. I've never had
such a good pal as her. Mrs Thompson isn't
in the same street. May and I had the same
interests – those classes we went to after the
War finished. We painted these cushions a
have on the kist in ma room. Hand-painted.
Her man wasn't called up either, so that
made a bond. Then your father bought the
premises and we moved away. Aye, that
wee street and May ... It was the best time
... But your father ... well, ambition ate into
him.'

'What were we like, Ma?' Jess said, wishing
they could meet someone like Noble
Murdoch every day. Their mother was rarely
as mellow as this.

'Well, you were a peely-wally wee thing.
Got awful sore throats. And there was that
time when you followed Peggy...' She shook
her head. 'And I thought you were dead!'

'But she wasn't,' Peggy said. 'And you gave
me a good skelping.'

'That was a relief. But you! Those bold black eyes of yours! You were always up to some mischief.'

'Once you did run away,' Jess said. 'I remember Mother and I going to the police station. We were both crying...' She had cried because it was expected of her, although she was sure that her sister would be all right. She always was.

'A had found a ha'penny in the gutter and gone over in the ferry to Renfrew masel'!' Peggy looked proud. 'Then begged another one from somebody to get back. A polis nabbed me when I got off the ferry.' She looked at her mother. 'A was always keen on the polis after that!' She laughed.

'Jess never gave me any worries. Playin' in those nice fields you could see from the window wi' another wee lass called Bessie Brechin.' Where are you now, Bessie Brechin? Jess thought. We were happy...

'Jess followed me to school one day,' Peggy said.

'Mary had a little lamb,' James said, who was the only one eating, but managing to look bemused between mouthfuls.

'I wanted a schoolbag.' Jess laughed at him. 'This was all before your time. Miss Clewes. That was the teacher's name...'

'Aye, it was a happy wee corner, that,' their mother said. 'Just a short street and the fields in front of us, a fine view, and the

Co-op below us, that fine and handy.' She gazed at her lost vision of paradise and shook her head. 'You say that lad's mother is dead?' She turned to Peggy.

'Aye. He has an aunt in Perth he goes to'

'That was Morag. I remember her comin' for her holidays to visit Jean Murdoch. Aye, it was a fine wee corner that ... So he doesn't have a home now?'

'No, the father married again.'

'Oh, men don't wait long before they jump into somebody else's bed...' She looked at James, who had his head down. 'But it's different for widows.'

'Aye, it's different for widows,' he said.

'Will you listen to him at his age!' Her face changed, became wistful. 'A had you when we were in the premises...' She looked round at her family, 'Well here a am, and another war comin' if you believe aw they say. But a was happy then...'

'I'll do the dishes,' Jess said.

In their bedroom later she said to Peggy, 'I wish she was always like that. Gentler.'

'Aye. As it should be. Well, she took to the mention of Noble Murdoch any roads.' Her smile was rich, secret.

'So did you.'

'Maybe I did.' She was too casual. 'It was funny, though, him walkin' in like that. He could have gone into any shop.' She was brushing her hair. She said to the mirror, 'A wonder if he'll come back tomorrow?'

'If he doesn't you'll be short of one and six.'

'One and nine. He'll be back.'

She got into bed, tucked herself in and asked Jess to put off the light.

Fourteen

'Let me tell her,' Noble said. He had Peggy pinioned with his body against the table in the back shop. She didn't seem to mind. Her arms were round his neck. 'She likes me.'

'Just see how much she likes you if you tell her you're taking me away to Perth wi' you!'

'Ach, a've a way wi' wummen! You can vouch for that, can't you?' He bent down and kissed her. 'Can't you?' He kissed her again, this time more passionately. She sighed, loving the weight of him against her.

'Don't start that, Noble Murdoch. There isny time for it. The last time when a had to dash to attend to a customer, she asked me if a'd got a fright or something, ma cheeks were aw red and ma eyes were funny!'

'You should have told her it was love.'

'Aye, it's love aw right.' She stroked his cheek. 'It's no use, ma dear. She wouldny hear o' it. Just tell her, and then see since you're so sure.'

'Maybe Jess could put in a word for us. A

like your sister. She's sad, though. A think it was that suicide...'

'She's like me. She'll no' talk aboot it. Oh, she may be ma mother's favourite, along wi' James, but she wouldny have a bit o' influence wi' her! She's convinced she has to be faither an' mither to us an' so she's twice as strict. And snobbish! Nothin' but the best is good enough for us.' She came out of his arms. 'Come on, we'll go and get it over with...'

'Aw right.' She saw his handsome face was unhappy. If I had any sense, she thought, I'd run away wi' him tomorrow and tae hell wi' her.

'Well, how is Mr Noble Murdoch the night?'

Maggie Crichton was inclined to be flirtatious with young men if she favoured them, and while this one wasn't so well-connected as she liked, she knew his background – and by God, he was handsome, with those come-hither eyes that she'd often wished Robert had had.

'A nice piece o' rump steak, Mrs Crichton,' he said later when they were seated round the table, and, looking at Peggy with mischief in his eyes, 'Maybe the last decent meal a'll get.'

'Whit d'ye mean?' Peggy saw the instant suspicion in her mother's eyes.

136

'A've got the sack. Came quicker than I expected. Got ma marching orders.'

'That's bad.' The flirtatious smiles had gone. 'Have you got anything else lined up?'

'Aye. Fortunately. Ma Aunt Morag has offered me a job on the farm. A bothy goes wi' it. A thought...' He looked at Peggy. 'A thought a'd just take Peggy wi' me.'

'But you're no' married!' She reared back in her chair. 'Nae daughter o' mine leaves this house unless she's married!'

'We could get it done there.' Peggy faced her. It would be a help if Jess said a word or two but she was sitting there, dumb.

'Am a hearin' right?' Her mother's face looked ready to burst. And then, lighting-like, as if she was gathering ammunition, she said, 'Whit kind o' job?'

'Muckin' oot the byre.' Peggy could have killed him. 'Cleanin' oot the pigsty. Anything that crops up.'

Maggie Crichton turned to Peggy, grim-faced. 'So, you would go up there, live in poverty an' sin, after runnin' a shop an' being your own mistress!'

'A widny be happy runnin' a shop and being ma own mistress if Noble was at the other end of the country!' She looked at her sister for support.

'Peggy's old enough to know her own mind, Mother,' Jess said.

She was cut short. 'You keep oot o' this. A

137

haven't worked ma fingers to the bone to give you two everything you needed for one o' ye to go off and live in a hovel wi' a man!'

'We'd get married! A told you that!'

'Whit's aw the rush, eh? Tell me that!' She clamped her lips together, waiting. Peggy said nothing. 'Tie yersel' up to someone livin' on someone else's bounty, never a penny to rub against another, you who's had the best o' everything!'

'The best o' everything!' Peggy's anger equalled her mother's. 'A like that! Dragged away from school and put to work in a shop, no advantages, no nothin'!'

'Because you weren't prepared to work for anything, like your sister here...'

'Work!' Peggy's face was scarlet, her black eyes were flashing. 'A've done nothin' else but work! Look at my hands!' She spread them out on the table. They were clean, scrubbed red, the nails short and ridged. There was the loud noise of Noble's chair being scraped back. He got to his feet and came round to stand beside Peggy, putting his arm round her shoulders. 'A've had enough o' this slangin' match! Peggy would be better to just come away wi' me. We'll get married up there.'

Maggie Crichton was weeping now, wiping her eyes. 'That's it, then. So you're just goin' to walk away without a stitch after aw a've done for you, for the lot o' ye, nae pleasure in ma life, ma family ma only concern, and me withoot a man...'

Jess shot a glance at Noble. She wanted to say, don't fall for it ... Off you two go...

Noble Murdoch wasn't a fighter. He still had his hands on Peggy's shoulders. 'A don't want to come between you and your mother, lass. Supposin' a go up to Drumairn tomorrow. That'll give you time to sort it out.'

She'll find ways to keep me, Peggy thought. The shop, lack of money. She had none of her own. She thought of the bag of money she carried back every day, but, no, she couldn't ... She gave in and got up. 'Aw right,' she said. 'But no' for long. A mean it. Come on, Noble, a'll see you oot.' They walked out of the room together, Noble's arm still around her shoulders.

It's true love, Jess thought. Tonight she's given in for his sake, but she hasn't given up. She knew her sister.

She started to clear the table. She lifted the plate from her mother's place. She was sitting, silent, an elbow on the table, her hand supporting her chin. Her eyes were dry. She's planning, Jess thought, planning her campaign. Just like Peggy.

What's at the root of it? she thought, washing up the dishes at the sink. Is it genuine concern on my mother's part for the well-being of Peggy, of not being prepared to let

Noble take her away until they were married? Or is it deeper than that, a kind of jealousy – her mother liked Noble – fear of being eventually left alone, Peggy being the first one attempting to leave?

And then there was her snobbishness. Look how she preened herself at the Gray's house, that spacious flat, how she patronised Mrs Bell, the housekeeper, how she boasted to Mrs Thompson about 'the premises', about her son being at the Academy. And, of course, she's jaloused that Noble will never rise far. He's not ambitious, but he will be a good husband, possibly an exciting lover. He liked women ... It's Peggy who's been born lucky, she thought.

On an impulse she put down her drying cloth and went into their bedroom. She had heard the outside door bang and then the bedroom one.

Peggy was sitting on the edge of the bed and Jess sat down beside her.

'It'll turn out all right, Peggy,' she said. She saw her sister's eyes were tear-stained.

'You've never been in love the way we are.' She didn't lift her head. 'She tries to ruin everything, but she won't ruin this. A'll leave just as soon as a get the word from Noble.'

'Is he just seeing to the bothy?'

'The hovel? Aye.' She turned to Peggy, her eyes dry. 'A don't ask for much. A'm not like

140

you, readin' and teachin' and all the other things you do. A just want to be with Noble. When you're in love you'll know what that means.' The doorbell rang. 'That'll be James,' she said. 'You'd better go and let him in.'

James looked happy when Jess opened the door. He was carrying his schoolbag and the laces of his rugby boots were tied together and slung around his neck. 'I was asked to play in a practice match, Jess!' he said as he came in.

'Great! Did you do well in the scrum?'

'You should have seen me! Away with the ball! Gosh, I'm starving!'

Their mother was on her feet to greet him when they went into the kitchen, her face wreathed in smiles.

'A was just wonderin' when you'd be in, James. Somethin' to eat now, eh?'

'I'll do his meal, Mother,' Jess said.

'A'm quite capable.' She scarcely looked at Jess. 'Egg and chips, eh, James?'

'Double portion of chips, please.'

'Well, whatever next? "Double portion," he says. A hope you didny use all the hot water.' She half-turned to where Jess stood. 'James will want a bath.'

Jess went to bed.

141

Fifteen

It seemed to be an armed truce between Peggy and their mother, with Jess and James in the middle.

'Why does she not push off to Noble?' he asked her. 'Noble's okay.'

'I think she's trying to please them both.'

'She'll never do that.'

She smiled at him. He wasn't a little boy any longer. 'Then Noble has to get the house ready for her. She'll leave when he sends for her.' And looking at him, Jess added, 'I forget you're growing up. I expect you talk amongst your friends about ... things.'

'Yes, some of them have sisters.' He shrugged. 'I'm more interested in rugby.'

The thought occurred to her. 'This Jock you speak about. Mr Craven, the Principal at my College, has a son with the same name.'

'It's the same Jock. I've met his father. Easygoing. They're good pals. And he doesn't mind us cooking up stuff in the kitchen ... We couldn't make it any untidier than it is!' He laughed.

'Why didn't you tell me who Jock was?'

'I didn't think it was important.'

'I don't suppose it is.' But she could understand the attraction the Craven household would have for him – three males, instead of two sisters and a mother who persisted in fussing over him as if he were a child.

In their bedroom she had given up asking Peggy any questions. All she would say was that she was waiting to hear from Noble. Jess had to follow James' example and get on with her own life.

She had met Mr Craven one evening in the staffroom. 'You're doing wonders with that problem class of sixteen-year-olds,' he said. 'If you ever want to come full time I'd be more than happy to have you. Have I said that before?'

She smiled at him, wondering if it was time to change, but hung back. There was Peggy ... She would like that problem settled. 'I'll think about it, Mr Craven,' she said. 'After the holidays.' And there was Ronnie Wilcox, still in her mind, especially at night. She would make Skye the watershed.

She looked at him, saw the tiredness in his face, but still the essential good humour. He made a good boss. 'And then there's the prospect of a war...' she said.

'Yes.' He nodded. 'It's rushing to meet us. I don't know how that would affect the College. Did you see that Hitler has ordered the Brownshirts to burn all books?'

'That would please your problem sixteen-year-olds.' They laughed together. He's an easy man to be with, she thought, middle-aged, though. But then, what had that to do with it?

As if to complicate matters Miss MacDuff told her she had decided to promote her to take Sir Bernard Carruthers' letters. He was one of the directors. 'You're reliable, Jess,' she said. 'Miss Campbell is leaving to be married and there's no one else I could trust.'

'Thank you, Miss MacDuff,' she said. 'I appreciate it.' She couldn't give in her notice after that.

She had never known anyone with such impeccable manners as her new boss, which at the same time kept her in her place. He rose when she came in each morning, drew out her chair, said, 'Please tell me if you have any difficulty.' then proceeded to dictate with brisk efficiency. Mr Brough had bumbled his way through his letters, had often asked Jess to compose them. She was bowed out of Sir Bernard's room with the same exquisite politeness.

In her first week with him, the news went

144

round the office that his only son had been killed in the Civil War in Spain. She was appalled. That was two young men who had felt the urgency of war, who hadn't been able to wait. Mr Brough's son had at least escaped with his life.

Sir Bernard's demeanour didn't change, but when she stole a glance at him she was moved at the signs of grief in his face – the sunken eyes, the lines round his mouth. She would have liked to say how sorry she was, but felt it was impossible.

On a summer Sunday afternoon, it was still so warm after tea that she suggested to James they go to the Park. Peggy was in her room, but shook her head when Jess asked her if she would like to come too. 'I'm busy,' she said. She didn't meet her eyes.

The two of them set off. 'Mother's gone to the Grays,' she said. 'It's with your school report.'

'I think she fancies Mr Thomas.' He laughed. He was licking an ice cream she had bought him, a double nougat wafer, his favourite.

'I asked Peggy to come,' she said.

'She's biding her time.'

'How do you know so much, little boy?' She laughed at him.

'A spectator sees most of the game. That's where you make a mistake, Jess. You worry for the whole world, get too involved.'

145

'Well, who wouldn't?' They had reached the Park and were sitting on the grass near the bandstand. 'Do you hear what they're playing? All the songs of the last war. Sad. Nessie's Bob has been called up for active service.'

'I wish I'd been older. If you're in the OTC, you're officer material. That's what I'd like.'

'I hope it's all over by the time you're eighteen. *Take me back to dear old...*' She hummed the tune. 'Do you hear it?' The brass band was playing *sotto voce*. 'So poignant ... that's the word...' She lay down on the grass, feeling a nostalgic kind of sadness sweep over her. The people sitting around them were quiet, as if they felt the same. The old order changeth ... The words came into her mind. The quietness around them had an ominous quality, as if everyone was waiting, dreading...

'That was a great wafer! Thanks, Jess.' She heard her brother's voice as if from afar off. 'I'll have a walk round and see if I can bump into any of my school pals.'

'Okay.' She lay where she was, thinking of that first war when she was born, of her father who had never fought in it, and now these young men, sons of Sir Bernard and Mr Brough who had been so impatient that one had rushed to his death. Had they felt the coming change, the looming dread? She must have lain longer than she meant to, for she suddenly realised that the brass band had stopped. She sat up quickly. James was nowhere to be seen. Well, he'd come home in his own time. She had a sense of urgency. She must get back. She shivered as she stood up.

Mrs Thompson opened the door to her. One look at her face confirmed her premonition.

'What's wrong, Mrs Thompson?'

'Oh, Jess! Am a glad you've come back! Your mother came over to me in a terrible state. Peggy's gone to Drumairn!'

'But she was here when I left!'

'Maybe. But your mother had gone to her friends, the Grays, and I think...'

'Come in and sit down, Mrs Thompson.' She led the woman into the kitchen. 'I'm sorry you've been so upset.' She felt an immediate resentment towards Peggy. Why hadn't she told her, been frank? But Peggy had always been like that, kept her own counsel... 'Where's my mother?'

A quavering voice came from the bedroom. 'Is that Jess, Mrs Thompson?' Jess got up.

'I'll go. Don't worry. I'll take care of things.'

Her mother was sitting up in bed. Mrs Thompson must have persuaded her to take off her skirt and lie down, as perhaps the only thing she could think of to calm her. She brandished a letter when she saw Jess. 'Read that!'

Jess took it. 'Dear Mother,' she read, 'I'm going to Drumairn. Noble has sent me money for a taxi and the train. I'll be staying with him until the banns are declared. Don't expect me to come back. Peggy.'

'Well?' Maggie Crichton was in a high state of agitation. 'Well?'

'You must have expected this.' Jess handed it back.

'But livin' wi' a man and her not married!'

'She doesn't really mean that. It'll be in his aunt's house.'

'You don't know Peggy as I do. And to think of the sleekitness of it, crawlin' away when my back was turned! What will the Grays think?'

'Never mind the Grays. You can tell them any tale you like. Say she's being married at Perth. That Noble's working there...' Mrs Thompson had appeared in the room, curiosity having overcome her shock. Maggie looked towards her.

'See, Mrs Thompson! She's sidin' with her! Thank God you never had a family. You work your fingers to the bone for them and this is the thanks you get.'

'You get away home, Mrs Thompson,' Jess said. 'Your husband will be wondering where you are.'

'All right, Jess.' She bent towards Jess's mother and patted her shoulder. 'You'll get over it, Mrs Crichton.' She was rewarded with a look of disdain.

'I could bring you a nice bowl o' soup?' Mrs Thompson believed in turning the other cheek.

'There's never been a shortage of anything in *this* hoose, thank you all the same. There's no need for borrowing here...'

Mrs Thompson departed with a pained look at Jess, who followed her to the door to thank her. The woman was sympathetic, laying a hand on Jess's arm. 'You've got a job on your hands there,' she said. 'Good luck.' There was a glimmer of a smile as she turned away, one that said that Jess would need it.

Jess went back to the bedroom. 'I'll bring you a cup of tea.' Her mother was lying back on the pillow, her hand over her face.

'There's no need for that. I'll get up. I'm not an invalid.'

She was feeling calm as she stood by the stove waiting for the water to boil. Mrs Thompson had got the heavy end of it. Her mother was a fighter. She would be up and planning before long, just as Peggy had done.

She turned and saw her, fully dressed, except that she hadn't combed her hair. It gave her a pathetic look. She sat down carefully, like an old woman. 'A don't know what James will say, and him an Academy boy. Living in sin in a bothy with a farm labourer.' Her voice was weak.

'Just say Peggy's gone off to Perth. To Noble. James expected it anyhow.'

'What have you been saying to him?' Her voice suddenly strengthened.

'Nothing. But he's not daft.'

She gave her mother her tea and sat down opposite her, ready to listen, to take the brunt of it. As long as it didn't prevent her going to Skye ... What had been a watershed now seemed like a lifeline.

Sixteen

Crossing the Kyle of Lochalsh to Kyleakin with Nessie Liddell, Jess felt as if she had escaped from prison. James had behaved normally; that is, he spent most of his spare time with school friends, relying on the fact that his mother would approve.

Jess hadn't been so successful. All the attempts to console her mother failed, and in the end it was Mrs Thompson who urged her to go off to Skye.

'She'll be like that till she gets word, and there's no point in you missing your holiday waiting with her. She'll not thank you.' The woman was right.

When Jess said with false cheerfulness that she was off tomorrow, she was met by the same glum face and the remark. 'Aye, you all please yourselves.'

It was a fine day for crossing. She looked around her. The space and the blueness, the expanse of the sea – a sea field – brought the same joy to her as those summer fields of her early childhood.

'Great, isn't it?' Nessie said. 'Forget your worries.' Nessie came from a large happy family, and all of them were a reflection of that happiness.

'That's what I'm going to do.' Their two mothers didn't get on. Maggie Crichton thought Nessie's mother was 'always in a muddle'.

'A can't imagine your place. But then we're a daft lot. Leave it to James, Jess. Just wait till you taste Mrs MacDonald's baking.' Maybe that was the answer, to enjoy the simple things.

She was drinking in the scenery, sea and mountains – the same blue as the sky – the swift movement of the ferry with its trail of frothing whiteness, the happy chatter amongst the other passengers, some of it in Gaelic ... The whole scene seemed to wash away her guilt about 'clearing out'.

'You lassies will be lookin' for a roll in the heather?' the skipper said. There was a roar of laughter from the other passengers.

'Here's hopin',' Nessie said. 'Can you introduce us to some nice lads?'

'We're all nice on the Island.' There were nods of approval.

It was a short walk to Mrs MacDonald's croft set on a heather-clad brae overlooking the Kyle. The table she sat them at was laden with scones of every variety, pancakes, a comb of honey, slabs of butter, and dishes of strawberry jam. 'This'll tide you over till you get your real tea,' Mrs MacDonald said.

'See, what did I tell you?' Nessie smiled at Jess.

They couldn't wait to get out once they had paid a visit to their bedroom – white-curtained, bedspread white, a bare wooden floor and a view from the window of an infinity of sea and sky. They walked back to the jetty to see the next boat coming in, feeling already like old inhabitants, then strolled along the road for a mile or two, and, on impulse, when they saw a bus trundling towards them, hailed it to stop and climbed on. 'Two to Ardvasar,' Nessie said, armed with foreknowledge. 'It's the seat of the MacDonalds of Sleat,' she told Jess.

'We'll call in and see them, then.' She felt light-hearted. Skye was having its effect already.

'I've never met a titled person,' Nessie said. 'I wonder if they're different from us?'

'My boss is titled. Yes, there's a difference. Subtle, but it's there. For instance, his son was killed fighting in Spain and yet I felt it would be out of place to say to him how sorry I was.'

'Oh, well, he wouldn't need your sympathy. He'd likely have a wife to give him a good cuddle. Our Pa gives ma Ma a good cuddle if she's upset. It works wonders.'

They were lucky. Day followed day with perfect weather – a rare thing. 'Usually I get tired saying to ma visitors, if only they'd come last week,' Mrs MacDonald said. 'This is a pleasant change. You'll see, it'll keep up while you're here. I feel it in my bones. My Lachlan's home for the weekend. He says it's always good weather when he comes, just to make him homesick when he goes away.'

They didn't see any of the lads the skipper had told them about, except an occasional one working in the fields, but Mrs MacDonald assured them that they would all come out of their holes this Saturday. It was the village dance.

'That's when all the datin' goes on,' she said. 'I met ma Robert there, God rest his soul.' She wasn't bitter about being left a widow, Jess thought.

Nessie was the right companion for her. Happy-natured, not introspective, they walked on the heather-clad hills, got bitten by midges, stood under a waterfall bare naked to cool them down, took the bus to Portree, and bought a record of Gaelic songs to play on Mrs MacDonald's gramophone. At night she would 'learn them', as she called it.

Jess felt happier than she had been for a long time. My life's too circumscribed, she thought. Here I can enjoy the simple things, new places and people. 'A change is as good as a holiday,' Nessie had said, and she was right. The present was unclouded, worries about Peggy and their mother seemed far away, as well as the ever-present regret about Ronnie Wilcox's death. 'You're a different lass here,' Nessie said.

The weekend came, and with it Mrs MacDonald's son, Lachlan. He was an engineer on the Clyde, curly-haired, laughing-faced like his mother, and dressed in what he called his Highland costume – a hairy pair of plus fours and tartan socks with green tabs above stout brogues. He kept the girls in a constant state of laughter at the table.

'I've told these lassies you'll escort them to the village dance tonight,' his mother said.

'And that's a fine thing to be doing,' he agreed. 'But you have put me in a fearful predicament, Mother. I don't know which one to fall for first.'

'He's a terrible tease, you know, and he's not tellin' you he has a lovely young lady in Glasgow, a teacher. They're going to be married at Christmas.'

'Will she not mind?' Jess asked.

'Not a bit of it,' Lachlan said. 'She's generous-hearted, my Maureen. She believes in sharing a good thing.'

It was a dance such as Jess had never experienced, having been used to the more formal staff dances she went to at the Grosvenor or the Plaza. It was held in a wooden hut at the side of the water, with a fiddler playing, relieved at times by a piper and another fiddler for the occasional waltz to cool them after their exertions dancing eightsome reels and *Strip the Willow*. Even those were interrupted by the ear-splitting 'hooches' from the men.

Nessie and Jess were whirled until their heads spun. 'Let's see what the ferry has brought us this time,' one of Lachlan's friends said, and, eyeing both girls appreciatively, 'This is the best yet.'

'Now this one's spoken for,' Lachlan said, putting his arm round Jess. 'But here's the other beauty just waiting to bestow her charms on someone like you, Hamish, my boy.'

'He'll do,' Nessie said, and was whirled away.

'Now you're mine for the night,' Lachlan said to Jess. 'Have you ever tried scooching?' and putting one arm round her waist, took her hand with the other one, and with outstretched arms, their hands clasped, they charged through the crowd – he nearly shattering the windows with his loud 'hooches'. As every other couple in the hall was doing the same, there were frequent collisions.

'Worse than driving a motor car in

156

Glasgow,' Lachlan said. He was very handsome, thought Jess, with his laughing face,
his open-necked white shirt tucked into the
waist of his kilt – the picture of a brawny
Islander.

'All I need is a kilt like yours,' she said,
breathless.

'You're fine as you are. A real bonny dress,
that.'

'Thanks.' His happiness was catching.
They dashed about the floor until they were
exhausted. Finally they sat down.

'What we need is a drink to wet our
throats now,' Lachlan said, mopping his
brow. 'We'll go into the back.'

The small room he led her into was
packed with dancers. 'Make way for a young
lady from the city,' Lachlan shouted,
pushing her forward. Nessie was already at
the counter with her partner.

'Oh, my,' she said to Jess. 'That was tre-
mendous. What are you havin' to drink?'

'Lemonade?'

There was a roar of laughter from Lachlan, and he said to his friend, 'Did we hear
right, Hamish? What's lemonade, eh?'

'Don't bring your city ways here, Jess. You
might corrupt us. Even the taps run wi'
Highland whisky instead of water.'

'Well, whisky and lemonade?' she said.

'You wee devil!'

'I'm havin' it neat,' Nessie said. 'You only

live once.'

'Well, here's to it!' Jess raised her glass to Hamish.

'Highland whisky?' Lachlan said, raising his.

'No, life. Here's to us!' She took a generous sip, then another one. 'And the whisky as well!'

The four of them strolled outside with their glasses and leant against the wooden walls of the hut to cool down. The Kyle was indigo, silver-edged where the waves reached the shore – such small waves that they made a soothing, lapping noise as they touched the sand.

'They're lucky, aren't they, Jess?' Nessie said. 'Livin' in a place like this. Clean, quiet...' She leant against Hamish who had his arm round her waist. 'I like a good cuddle,' she said. 'It makes you forget your worries.'

The whisky was also running through Jess's veins, and she felt relaxed. If Lachlan had cuddled her, even kissed her, she wouldn't have minded. But there was his young lady in Glasgow...

'Lachlan's got a young lady in Glasgow,' she announced, to remind herself.

'Yes, but it doesn't cramp my style.' He turned Jess round against him and planted a hearty whisky-flavoured kiss on her mouth. She staggered slightly.

'Drunk again?' He smiled down at her.

'No, I'm just pleasantly—'

There was a great skirl of pipes and a man appeared in the doorway. 'Take partners for the quadrilles. Full set, ladies and gentlemen!'

'Throw back your whiskies, girls!' Lachlan shouted. 'This is going to be the experience of your lives. Come along!'

Jess had never danced a set of quadrilles in her life. 'How do you do it?' she asked Lachlan as he hurried her along.

'Don't worry. Hamish and I are the great exponents in these parts. Isn't that so, Hamish?'

'Aye, they pay to see us. That's Geordie McCallum, the caller!' There was a man going about the hall arranging sets. The four of them took their places.

The caller went to the end of the room and climbed up on the platform. 'Five figures!' he shouted out. 'Be sure there's somebody who can push you around if you get lost.' There were boos of derision. The bagpipes were skirling, the noise filling the hall. Hamish bowed to Nessie, Lachlan to Jess.

'Set to your partner!' Geordie was shouting, and they were away. The whisky seemed to run into the girls' toes – they were light-footed and sure, only needing a few helpful pushes from time to time.

'Did you ever know anything like this?' Lachlan shouted as he whirled her before parting company and dancing away. At the last moment another two dancers had joined them who were adepts, and in no time Jess felt she had been dancing quadrilles all her life. The Highlanders were nimble dancers. The three men were big and brawny, but they had surprisingly neat feet that seemed to twinkle as they pointed and whirled, their kilts swinging higher than the girls' dresses.

Jess learned how to hold her arms in the air, elbows bent, finger and thumb of each hand pressed together as she set to her partner. She quickly picked up the steps pointed out by their feet, whirled, bowed, and moved on to the next partner. The pipes swirled, the men hooched, there were bursts of laughter, the shouts of the caller's voice grew louder – all inhibition went out the window. The whirling grew more frantic, longer, the toes more pointed, the speed quickened, the heavy kilts swung. Sometimes when she caught Nessie's eye they both exploded with amazed laughter as they were whirled away again.

The final set came to an end in a frantic burst of prolonged whirling of the girls so that their feet left the floor completely. Jess felt as if she were flying through the air, her body thrilled with excitement, and she was breathless when Lachlan finally set her down. It had been pure joy, she thought, laughing up at his flushed face.

She curtseyed to his bow, and said to him, 'I'm sorry it's over. Great!' The caller was applauded, then the piper, then the fiddler. People streamed to the back room for drinks, talking excitedly, congratulating each other.

'That was a bit different from the dances I go to in Glasgow,' she said to Lachlan, accepting her whisky without a murmur this time. 'Mostly waltzes and foxtrots.'

'Yes, but you can't get rid of your inhibitions that way,' he replied. 'Maureen has to go to some dances like that and I have to get into my dinner jacket and black tie. She says I could wear the kilt, but I don't like to in Glasgow. It's not right, somehow. The men who wear it have never been past Balloch. It belongs to places like this – the Kyle at the door, all my friends, the liquid nourishment.' He laughed, holding up his glass.

'I'm ashamed of myself,' she said. 'I've never had a glass of whisky in my life, far less two. It's terrible.'

'You're a great girl for apologising, I've noticed. Who are you apologising to?'

'I don't know...'

'Are you always letting yourself down?'

'Often. I shouldn't really be here. My

sister left a note and went off with her boyfriend. My mother took it badly. I've left her ... to put up with it.'

'Guilty again? I'll have to teach you how to get rid of that. My Maureen would be the one for you.'

'Your mother says she teaches psychology?'

'She does. At the University.'

Jess was surprised, impressed even. But why should she be?

'I met her at the Union. I sometimes go in for a drink. I took my degree at Gilmorehill.'

'Did you?'

'Oh, yes, we're the great ones for learning in the Islands. Set off with our bag of oatmeal on our backs for the big city. Anyway, we were chatting at the bar, and I thought, this is the woman for me. Right away. She must have had similar thoughts. "What you see is what you get," she said.'

'Did she say that?'

'No, I read it in her face. Trusty.'

'I expect she's beautiful?'

'She is to me, but not as beautiful as you ... You're blushing. Has nobody ever told you that before?'

'You're pulling my leg.'

'See, you don't believe in yourself. No, Maureen hasn't your slenderness, nor your suppleness – I watched you dancing. She says she's got short legs, and she's got black no-nonsense hair – yours kind of falls about in interesting shapes. And it's an interesting colour. But what a sense of humour she has! Yes, I said to myself, she's a stayer. And her eyes are beautiful.' He put his head on one side. 'Hey, listen to that. The fiddler's playing a waltz. I'm partial to a waltz.'

'How are you getting on, Lachlan?' Hamish had joined them with Nessie. 'I saw you giving Jess the old spiel.'

'He was telling me about Maureen,' she said.

'You want to keep your mouth shut, my lad.'

'I wouldn't be surprised if they're both married,' Nessie said. She was flushed with dancing and whisky. 'But who's caring, eh, Jess?'

'We just came for the whisky,' she said. 'And the dancing. Come on, Lachlan!'

They danced a slow waltz and then a polka, which replaced the romance in the men's eyes with devilment. Lachlan never left her side. She was glad. He was a fine dancer, and when she forgot Maureen she could enjoy being in his arms as the lights were lowered, enjoy the laughing comments as they passed his friends – 'Are you not for sharing that beauty, Lachlan?' – enjoy how he bent over her when they were waltzing and how he put his cheek against hers. What

163

the eye doesn't see, the heart doesn't grieve over, she said silently to Maureen. She would understand that two people could enjoy an evening together, could like each other. She was probably doing the same, and she had the added advantage of understanding her motives. If *she* had gone to the University she could have studied psychology too, instead of working in an office and teaching shorthand and type-writing in the evenings.

They were making a ring round the dance floor. The fiddler struck up the national anthem, and it was sung lustily by everyone there. Jess joined in, thinking this was the best dance she'd ever been at in her life. She looked round the circle and didn't see Nessie or Hamish anywhere.

'I don't see Nessie,' she said to Lachlan.

'Hamish'll be showing her the other joys of the Island. He's an adept at that.'

'Maybe we'd better wait for them.' They had said goodnight to almost everyone, shaken hands with others – she had been warned to 'watch her step' with Lachlan.

He guided her down to the shore and said, 'Sit down and relax. We'll wait here for Nessie.'

'All right,' she said. Why bother about Nessie? It was a beautiful night; the water was calm. She lay back and listened to its soft lapping at the pebbles.

'I always put my feet in the water,' Lachlan said. 'It's part of the ritual. It brings me close to the Island, reminds me of what I miss...' He was taking off his shoes and socks, sliding down the turf until his feet were covered. 'Aye, that's it,' he said. 'Slide down, Jess. You have to experience this.' She did, sliding down the turf on her back, taking off her slippers, undoing her suspenders, rolling down her stockings, taking them off and balling them. The water was cool, and as soft as velvet.

'It's good,' she said.

'I knew you would like it. It's a remedy for all complaints.' He slipped his arm round her as they lay.

'It would be perfect if there was a moon,' she said.

'Ah, you don't want perfection.'

'No, I shouldn't be greedy.' He sat up to look down at her. She met his eyes. 'What would your mother say if she could see you now?'

'Ach, the old one doesn't care what I get up to. She trusts me. You're a rare wee lass for worrying about what people would say if this and that.'

She didn't mind his criticisms, thanks to the whisky. 'If I stayed here longer I wouldn't care either.'

He kept looking at her. 'What's your mother like?' he asked.

'As different as night and day from your mother. She's not like anybody's mother. But then, my father died when she was young.'

'So did mine. Drowned when he was out fishing. But me and Ma got through it, and now she's happy and I can leave her. She says he's still in the house. It didn't ruin her life. In a way it enhanced it. And she likes her guests coming. Likes to show off her baking.'

'It ruined our lives.' She didn't like herself for saying that. She should take a leaf out of Lachlan's book. 'Oh, that's a bit of an exaggeration.' She steadied her voice. 'I mean, we ... no, it's only me. I don't seem to take a balanced view of problems. I tend to bottle them up, worry too much. It's just when I see you ... everyone here ... there's no strain. Nessie's in her element. But me, there's this feeling of dread – what will it be like when I get back? And now Peggy's gone, and James, my brother, comes in and out regardless ... Oh!' – she swirled her feet in the water – 'I don't know why I'm talking like this. It must be the whisky...'

He turned to her and took her in his arms. 'What you need is someone to talk to, and to be loved. You don't know how good it could be.' He held her closely against him. It was wonderful, she thought – the tweedy, heathery smell of his jacket and the strength of his arms.

She pressed herself against him and he lifted her chin with his hand. In the half-light she saw his face – sweet, strong – before it came down on hers and he kissed her mouth, long and warm and hard. She was breathless when he released her.

'What about Maureen?' she said.

'Maureen?' He repeated the kiss, and this time it was fiercer, urgent. Jess thought that before it was too late she must remind him of that short, sturdy girl whom he knew was for him.

'That's enough, Lachlan.' She met his eyes, and then he sighed and released her. They both lay down close to each other.

'I'm a devil when roused,' he said and laughed. 'You did right to remind me. We'll lie quiet and think of Bonnie Scotland.'

'It's beautiful,' she said. 'The pale morning light.' She watched the lazy flap of two gulls over the water, listened to the soft twittering of waking birds, the lip-lap of the water.

'Tell me,' he said, 'what else you're bottling up and I'll tell you what Maureen would say to you.'

'How do you know there's anything else?'

'Highland intuition and the benefit of knowing a teacher of psychology. I go back tomorrow. It's your last chance.' He slipped an arm under her and drew her closer.

'Come on,' he said. 'Treat yourself instead of punishing yourself.'

'You're right. I'm always trying to prove myself. But it's never enough.'

'It's no good bashing yourself against a brick wall.'

'I know you're right. I've seen tonight how to really live in the present, how to let myself go ... almost.' She laughed and he gave her waist a quick squeeze.

'Aye, moderation in all things.'

'There's something else on my mind,' she said. 'Something I can't get over.'

'Go on,' he said. His voice was level.

'This young man I skated with in the winter. He became obsessed by me. It was ... frightening. He wrote letters. Sometimes he printed them. Black. Menacing. He waited for me when I came out of the office...'

'Poor soul,' he said. She knew he didn't mean her.

'Then when I looked out of the window of our flat at night, there he was. Or when I came round the corner. I told him and *told* him...' She stopped. Lachlan waited. She had to go on. 'This is the bad bit. There's a school opposite us, and I kind of complained to the janitor about him. And he said he would ... move him on. I know he did this, threatened him with the Police...' Again he waited without speaking. 'That night, I'm sure it was that night, he walked to the Clyde and drowned himself.' She breathed quickly, tried to calm herself.

'You think that ... being warned off was the final straw?'

'I'm sure it was. You see, inside he was terrified by people, but he pretended to be self-confident.' She remembered the wavering foot. 'But I kept quiet. Didn't tell a soul about anything. When it was announced in the office, I didn't go to the Police to tell them that it was because of me he'd drowned himself.' She breathed deeply several times in a kind of relief. She listened to the tiny stirring sounds of the morning.

Lachlan spoke slowly. 'How were they to know, you reasoned. You knew that if he had left some kind of note mentioning your name they would have come to you. At least you *thought* they would. But there was the suspense.'

'Yes,' she said. 'There was the suspense. And I couldn't talk to anyone – James, too young, my mother and Peggy always at each other, absorbed in their own affairs. I was Jess, successful, no worries – don't bother about Jess, she's all right.'

'Don't bring pity for yourself into it. It's simple. Go to the Police and tell them about this man. Unload. You've no idea of the relief you'll feel.'

'I haven't even the letters to show them. I

169

tore them up. They might not even believe me.'

'One look at your face, Jess, will convince them you're telling the truth.' He put his cheek against hers. 'You're a very loveable girl.'

'Loveable! But will they think so? Policemen?'

'Anyone would think so.'

She smiled at him. 'I feel different. Buoyant. Yes, that's the word – buoyant! I just needed to talk about it. Yes, I'll go.'

They were smiling at each other when Nessie appeared behind them with Hamish.

'We've been looking all over the Island for you two,' she said.

Jess got up. 'Tell that to the Marines.' She saw Nessie's dishevelled hair, and thought, well, well...

'We've been lying here talking, waiting for you,' Lachlan said. He had pulled some tufts of grass and was wiping Jess's feet and his own. 'And having a wee paddle.' He looked around for her shoes and put them on her bare feet. 'There now,' he said. 'Got your stockings?'

'In my pocket. That's us ready, then.' She felt light-hearted, secure, new.

Hamish had an old farm motor and she sat in the back with Lachlan. He steadied her with an arm round her waist, talking quietly.

'I didn't finish, Jess. Your friend who drowned himself took a bad way out. The best way is to try to understand yourself. He was beyond that. But you're not. Maureen's a great one for telling people to go back to their roots. Maybe if she'd seen your friend she could have helped him. But you can do it for yourself. You'll find it salutary. That's a great word of hers.'

'How do I do it? Go back to my roots?'

'Think. You've peace and quiet here. Meditate. Anyone can do it. You'll see a pattern. The child is father to the man...'

'Listen to the sweet nothings he's whispering back there,' Hamish said. 'He's got them printed. Has them off by heart.'

They sang *Over the Sea to Skye* and *The Skye Boat Song*, and after Hamish dropped them off Lachlan escorted them into the house and saw them upstairs to bed. 'The old one'll be fast asleep,' he whispered. His mother's voice came clearly to them from her bedroom.

'Have you brought those lassies home safely, Lachlan?'

'Yes, Ma, safe as houses.' They smothered their laughter.

At their door he kissed them both, and whispered into Jess's ear, 'Remember.'

'What a night!' Nessie said, sitting down to take off her stockings.

'You've brought back half that haystack

171

with you.'

'You're imagining things.' She ran a hand over her hair, saying casually, 'Hamish has a few days off. He'd like to show me some more of the Island...'

'I bet he would. What about Bob?'

'There's two kinds. One you have a good time wi', the other kind you marry. Bob's the marrying kind. A'll have to settle down with him.'

Jess looked at her admiringly. 'Well, I'll say one thing about you, Nessie. You know what makes you tick ... You go ahead with your plans. I'll be busy.'

'Lachlan'll be away tomorrow, though.'

'But the memory lingers on.' She laughed.

'You're a deep one, Jess.' Nessie gave a prodigious yawn. 'It was a great night. I'll never forget it. When a'm washin' Bob's shirts, and cookin', and runnin' messages, and scrubbin' ... a'll never forget it.'

She collapsed on her bed.

Seventeen

1938
Solitude was unknown to Jess. School, college, a busy office and clattering type-writers, a background of crowded city streets where you had to be quick-witted to avoid bumping into passers-by. And at home it was the same – not very large for four people, and where you only used a bedroom for sleeping or dressing. She could hear her mother's impatient voice: 'What are you doin' in there?'

Maybe going back to her roots would explain her mother as well.

Meditation. She had heard the word. Lying in a bracken-lined hollow halfway up the brae behind the cottage, Nessie away with Hamish, she didn't know how to *think*. She'd never had time to think. *Go back to your roots.* She heard Lachlan's voice. She closed her eyes, heard the high sweetness of the lark's song. It wasn't thinking, or even imagining; it was like watching a film being played backwards, flickering...

★ ★ ★

1917

She was intrepid, Peggy, right from the beginning.

'Wait for your wee sister!' our mother shouted, but she was off, long plaits tied with red ribbon dancing on her back. My hair was short with a butterfly bow on top – the pain of the short hairs being caught in that bow came back to me, made me even now screw up my face. I was following Peggy, my little legs in their white socks going like pistons.

'Peggy! Wait for me!' I cried as she jinked between fat women carrying thin shopping bags – it was wartime. She turned back to me and made a 'Go-home!' face. I plodded on.

I bumped into a man with a white stick and a dog and he said, 'Bloody mind, will ye?' and a woman nearby glared at me and said, 'Ur ye blind too?' I fell, picked myself up and ran on, my eyes fixed on the dancing red-bowed plaits.

She had reached the main road and was standing at the edge, her head turning right and left, and then she made a dash between the traffic and was on the other side where the road leads down to the ferry.

The ferry! I thought. Mrs Stewart who read magic cups and saw your fortune; Mrs Stewart who made marzipan sweets shaped and coloured like little carrots and turnips and strawberries and put them in pleated paper cups ... No, not without me! I thought, and plunged into the road after her...

Sudden darkness, like going into a tunnel, and clashes of metal – a large hand coming out of the darkness and pulling me into the air. A strange face hung above me. 'Mammy!' I shouted.

'You gave me the fright o' ma life!' The strange face had a green cap above it with a shiny black visor, there was the gleam of brass buttons, and then I saw more faces and one, nearer than the others, saying, 'In the name o' God, it's a wee lass!' And another one, looming, and saying, 'Is she deid?' I reassured her by bawling lustily, 'A want ma Mammy!'

The green cap was looking round. 'Does anybody know this wean's house? Ma car's being held up!'

'I know it!' said a woman with a scarf tied round her head like a turban. 'And that's her sister! That cheeky wee thing with red bows on her hair.' I turned my head just in time to see Peggy jink behind one of the ample women.

'Come oot o' there!' the driver commanded. He caught Peggy by a plait. 'Just you lead us to your Mammy's house.'

I was in his arms. Peggy was walking in

front with her head bowed like the chief mourner. There was a crowd of women following and I could see the driver's moustache going up and down while he muttered. 'They weans! The tram's goin' to be late and a'll get blamed...'

Up three flights of stairs. The driver was puffing. Peggy was still walking in front of us; there was a clatter of footsteps behind us like a posse of horses. She knocked on our door and turned to face us. She had her chin down and she was glaring up at me like a trapped tiger. The door opened.

'In the name of God!' my mother shrieked. 'Is she deid?' Everybody seemed to want me dead. I gave a loud wail for her benefit, and she grabbed me out of the man's arms.

'She could have been,' the driver said. 'Folks should keep an eye on their weans; folks shouldny let them roam about busy streets. Ma timetable's aw to buggery an' a'll get hauled over the coals...'

Peggy, half-hidden by all the women, piped up. 'A didny do nothin', Mammy.'

The driver interrupted. 'Aye, Missus, you can thank your lucky stars she's *no'* deid.'

'Better to be born lucky than rich,' said a woman with crossed arms. *Born lucky* ... The words echoed still.

'Caught her in ma cow catcher!' The driver was anxious to tell his side of the story. 'Followin' the other yin most likely. A busy road, that. If it hadn't been for me puttin' ma foot on the cow catcher she wouldn't be here the day...'

'Aw right, aw right!' My mother had found her voice. I could feel her bosom rising indignantly against my cheek. 'A'm sorry you've been held up and a'm much obliged to you for bringin' her home. You get inside, Miss!' This to Peggy, who slunk in. 'Good day to you all.' My mother shut the door on the driver and his posse. 'Into the room wi' ye.' Peggy disappeared. I knew she was in for it. So did she.

'An' you're just as bad,' my mother said, standing me on the wooden side of the sink and stripping me rapidly of my dress, socks and knickers. Her face was red and I noticed her eyes were watering. 'Who would have weans?' She addressed the overhead pulley. The canary in its cage above me sang a recitative.

She washed my legs, face and hands, put on me a clean dress, knickers and socks. Even then I noticed her remedy for most things was water and soap. I don't know who was supposed to feel the better for it. She put on top of my dress a hug-me-tight, a peculiar garment knitted from odd wool left over from Army socks. It crossed on my body at the front and the ends were pulled tight and tied at the back. It was as good as a cuddle – a rare occurrence in our house.

'You stay here,' she said, and went out of the kitchen. I knew where she was going. Peggy's loud yells confirmed my suspicions.

I liked sitting on the wooden sink. There was a fine view of the fields which stretched up to the railway bridge and beyond. It was my favourite place, and my favourite thing was to be there with Bessie Brechin, who shared my interest in setting up a shop composed of sorrel, clover, strawberries – actually red seeds stripped from a weed – and the *pièce de résistance*, mirrors made of loops of grass which contained our spittle. Bessie had shown me how to do it, and how to hold a buttercup under customers' chins to test if they liked butter. So far, we hadn't any butter, but Bessie was working on it.

In bed that night Peggy told me she hated me. I didn't blame her. But I envied her enterprise and wished I had thought of going over on the ferry too. When I asked her how she was going to get the halfpenny for the fare back, she said, 'Beg, stupid.'

I realised that Peggy would always have more courage and enterprise than I had. I saw the difference between us, even then.

1938
When the girls were having their tea that night Nessie asked Jess if she wasn't bored being alone. She said no, it was a rare treat.

'Hamish has a few more days off...' Nessie

178

shrugged as if it were a matter of no importance.

'I hope you're not forgetting Bob,' Jess said.

'Temp— ... temp— ... What's the word, Jess? You're the clever one.'

'Temporarily.'

'That. But I wouldny have missed this holiday and Hamish for the world.'

Mrs MacDonald came in at the end of her sentence. 'You know Hamish is engaged to a nurse in the Glasgow Royal?'

'Yes, he told me, Mrs MacDonald.' Nessie bent her head to her ham and eggs.

It struck Jess that douce Nessie with her Bob in the background was another one with enterprise.

Eighteen

1938

'Are you sorry to be going back?' It was Nessie's voice. Jess was looking out of the train window at the bone-white sands of Morar.

'Yes. Are you missing Hamish?' Jess teased her.

'No, that was a real tear but it's over.' She was pragmatic. 'Are you missing Lachlan?'

'No. But I'm glad I met him. He gave me some good advice.'

'Is that all?' They smiled at each other, and Jess looked out of the window again. The Morar sands had disappeared. The past took their place.

1918

Peggy beat me in everything.

Skipping ropes she could do the French way – double ropes, jump into where they crossed – whereas I was still doing single.

Then she was at school; she was six and I was four. Miss Clewes, who got tired of my wistful face day after day at the school gates, relented and took me in at four and a half.

And Peggy had a boyfriend, Noble Murder, the son of Mrs Murdoch who lived up our close. Once free from school, she scaled wash-house roofs with him, ran races, was his willing slave in everything he did. Especially the Pin Game...

'I'm just going to take Jess down to the street to see the stars, Mammy,' Peggy said.

'All right. But watch her!' Since the tramcar incident she had decided I looked 'peely-wally', which meant liberal doses of Virol and cod liver oil. She strapped me into my hug-me-tight, and cautioned Peggy again. 'Just down to the street, mind!' She looked cheerful. She was always glad to get us 'out of her road'.

The sky was frostily bright with thousands of stars, but there was no time to look at them. I was dragged past the night scene into the doorway of the Co-op, where already there were quite a few children. Noble Murder was there wearing his father's cap to give him authority.

The area we stood in was about twelve feet square, the distance between the stout inner door and the outer iron gate which ran on wheels. Ordinarily it was closed at night, but the lock had been broken, – the manager was convinced it was 'they weans' – and so far he had been unable to find a man to fix it, all able-bodied ones having been called up.

Children kept crowding in, like emptying two pints of milk into a pint pot. We were commanded by Noble to move closer. 'Move closer!' Peggy echoed, and pushed me against a girl who had a funny smell.

When the space was crowded to capacity, Noble Murder ran the gate along on its wheels to close it – we must have looked like animals in a cage – and announced grandly, 'House full!'

Peggy shouted, stepping slightly from the script, 'Anybody who comes in late canny get in!' I saw Noble nod approvingly at her.

'Now!' he said. He was taller than everyone else there, and he made an imposing figure with his broad shoulders and his father's cap pushed back on his fair hair – noble-looking, in fact. 'Now,' he said, 'you ones have to keep your traps shut while a tell you aboot this game. A made it up masel'.'

'A helped!' Peggy shouted.

'Aye Peggy Crichton's in it too.' He gave a reluctant nod.

'Are we ready, then?' He looked round the packed space, waited a minute or two. Tension was high. Peggy pushed me forward, the smelly girl became smellier, and a boy whom Noble had earlier referred to as Fatty nudged me forward again with his fat stomach.

'Now, watch ma hand! A'm putting it up with a pin in it for you all to see.' My vision was bounded by jerseys front and back, left and right, so I had to take his word for it.

'A'm goin' to count to ten. Don't think of anythin' else but listenin' for me to drop the pin. Are you ready?' There was a low murmur.

'Right! One, two, three ... pin back your ears ... four, five, six...'

I listened as I had never listened before. My little bosom tried to swell in its confined space as I thought of being the winner. That would show them!

'Seven, eight...' My ears were aching with listening. I could hear the distant hoot of a boat on the Clyde and cursed it. Shut up! But Noble had heard it too and had paused.

So had my heart. I was the only person on an uninhabited island; I had banished the pygmies to another one, with all the squawking parrots and chattering monkeys; told the sea not to wave ... And then I heard it, the tiniest scrape, totier than that ... there wasn't any word totier than totier. 'A heard it!' I shouted. 'A heard it drop!'

There was silence for a second, then I heard Peggy laugh, then Noble, followed by all the children, the space was filled with laughing faces turned towards me. I saw fingers pointing, the whole world was laughing.

'What is it?' I whispered, and then, summoning my courage, shouted, 'I did so hear it! Just a wee scrape as the pin landed...' Noble's face was red and bursting, and I heard Peggy behind me, choking with laughter...

I turned and looked at her. 'Peggy, a did so...' My voice faded away.

She stopped spluttering for a second, had to shake her head several times before she could speak. 'You couldny have. There never was a pin! It was a game!' The smelly girl exploded, sending out waves of smell. I looked round, defeated, and saw Noble's red face under the big cap, mouth open in a paroxysm of laughter.

'A'm goin' home!' I said.

'She wants her Mammy, poor wee soul,' Noble said, wiping his eyes. 'Take her, Peggy, the wee thing...' His minion obeyed, shoving me through the crowd in disgrace.

I ran up the stairs as fast as I could, Peggy at my heels, breathing noisily. 'Slow down!'

When our mother opened the door she smiled kindly at me. 'Well, did you see the stars?' She was in a good mood because we had been 'out o' her road', but I pushed past her and ran into the front room, where I flung myself on the horsehair sofa.

'What's wrong wi' her?' I could hear her asking Peggy.

I put my hands to my ears.

What I didn't realise at the time was that I was the typical younger sister, someone to be pushed around by the elder one. Probably it was what Maureen might have called a well-known syndrome.

Did it shape both our characters? Our mother could have helped here, but she tended to side with Peggy, possibly because they both had the same temperament. In any case she was an unmotherly mother, intent on her housekeeping and her classes with May Beauchamp, a neighbour. Both of their husbands were in reserved occupations, and I expect that was the bond.

I heard Mrs Buckup – as we called her then – say to our mother, 'If we'd worked in munitions, Maggie, we could have had fur coats.'

'Aye, and no knickers,' our mother commented. I wished I could have made her laugh like that.

But they sallied forth together to their various activities to help the troops, serving in canteens when we children were at school, and knitting Army socks interminably at night. How many skeins of khaki wool I must have held while she wound it into balls! They always had a good laugh together, shared secrets. She was not the stern disciplinarian we knew at home.

We saw little of our father. He was manager of a creamery, and because of shortage of staff, he left before we were up in the morning and arrived home after we were in bed at night.

But he was always gentle. I had nightmares after the tramcar episode, and once when I called out, he came into our room, and, cradling me in his arms, took me into their bed.

There I was wakened once more by the bed swinging up and down, and odd noises coming from our mother. I climbed out and ran back to Peggy. I told her our mother had been groaning. 'He's probably killing her,' she said.

But when I look back I realise I associated him mostly with our little milk churn, which fascinated me – a glass jar with paddles set in the wooden lid. Every weekend he would bring home an illicit supply of cream, which we churned, Peggy and I fighting to be the one to turn the handle. We were told to keep quiet about the resultant butter, and when I asked Peggy why, she said because the Germans would shoot us. That became my new nightmare.

I do remember our mother's sadness when we moved to 'the premises' in the East End. 'I'll miss May,' she said, snapping shut the wicked snout of her fox fur before we quitted the flat. 'We had some great laughs. But that's what it's like when you've got a man who's ambitious.'

'Will you miss Noble?' I asked Peggy, but she only shrugged and turned away so that I couldn't see her face.

There were a lot of things I would miss. Miss Clewes, who had told me if I worked hard, not like my sister, I could become a teacher – there was no higher ambition, it seemed.

But most of all I would miss the summer fields where I had spent so many happy times with Bessie Brechin. Our latest scheme had been to find a four-leaved clover and sell it for a princely sum.

Peggy carried the canary and I had the milk churn in a bag, although our mother had said that we wouldn't need it in the new place as we were going to the Land of Plenty.

Nineteen

1938

'So you're back?' Her mother's greeting was typical.

'Yes, Skye was lovely.'

'A dreary place when it's wet.'

'We were lucky. Have you heard from Peggy?'

'Not a word. Well, she can stew in her own juice. Why should I worry? I've the shop to run that she walked out and left without a thought.'

Actually, Jess thought, she looked quite spry the following morning setting off for the dairy, although she said before she left that she was going to see the Gray brothers and ask them to put it on the market. But the fire and ire which Peggy's departure had caused had died down. I should be used to her quick change of temper by this time, she thought.

When she went into Sir Bernard's room on Monday morning, he looked up with a smile. 'Ah, you're back, Miss Crichton?' He rose and seated her as usual, saying as he did, 'I understand you've been on holiday?'

'Yes, Sir Bernard.' She was able to look up and smile without shyness.

'Where have you been?'

'Skye. I never imagined it could be so beautiful.'

'It cast its spell on you too? That light...' They exchanged smiles. She had the feeling of basking again in that pearly glow, feeling the warmth of Lachlan's arms round her.

Sir Bernard was regarding her, rather than merely glancing. 'It seems to have done you good.' Then, after a slight pause, 'Shall we get on?'

They were nearing the end of his dictation when there was a knock on the door.

'Come in,' Sir Bernard said, his eyes on the letter he was holding. Jess looked up and saw a young man hesitating in the doorway.

'Oh, sorry, sir,' he said. 'I was told—'

'Giles!' Sir Bernard rose to his feet. 'What on earth are you doing in Glasgow?'

'It's a long story.' He grinned. 'Sorry.' He looked at Jess. 'I didn't realise you were busy. The porter said ... I'll come back.' He half-turned towards the door.

'No, no. I've nearly finished. This is my nephew, Miss Crichton. Giles Imrie.' The young man bowed and Sir Bernard waved him towards a chair. 'Sit down there for a minute or two, Giles.'

'Right.'

Jess was intrigued. He's aristocratic, she thought ... no, that's not quite the word. But his accent's different from his uncle's...

Sir Bernard finished, thanked her, and made to get up, but his nephew forestalled him, jumping to his feet and opening the door for Jess. She got the impression as she passed him of a dark lean face and a white smile.

He was still in her mind as she typed. He was like someone who had stepped out of the Forsyte Saga, she thought – Wilfrid, perhaps. She remembered Fleur had fainted when he first kissed her. Fanciful.

She went to the Anderston Police Station before going home.

When she was shown into the sergeant's room after waiting quite a time, she had lost any nervousness. This is what she had to do.

'It's about Ronnie Wilcox,' she said.

'The young man who committed suicide?'

'Yes.'

He got up and went to a filing cabinet, returning with a folder. 'Is there anything you wish to tell me?'

'I knew him, you see, and I thought I'd better come to you. I should have done it earlier.'

'Go on, Miss Crichton.' His head was down. He was turning over the pages of the file.

She found the relief so great that it lent her fluency. 'I've worried a lot about it. You see, he ... pressurised me to meet him – we had skated together. When I refused, he sent me disturbing letters – I tore them up.' She looked at him but he merely nodded for her to go on. 'Then he started hanging about outside our flat, at nights. I told the janitor in the school opposite, and he threatened to tell the Police. I've felt his death ... on my conscience.' She stopped. The relief was great. Lachlan had been right. 'And I thought he might have left a letter mentioning me ... I know I should have come to you long ago.'

'There was no letter. You say you tore up his letters?'

'Yes. Right away. It was an immediate reaction.'

'I understand. It's a pity you've worried ... If only you'd come to us earlier. It's always better to be frank with the Police. However, it's of no account now. The case is closed. Apparently he was an unhappy and disturbed young man. He had a history of mental illness, and had been on medication for some time. The doctor's verdict was suicide while of unsound mind. You were never under suspicion. Does that relieve you somewhat?'

'It does. Oh, it does. I'm so sorry. Poor Ronnie.'

'I'm afraid we see too many like your friend here in Glasgow. We only manage to save some. But thank you for coming.' He got up. He was a busy man.

She said when he was showing her out, 'I never knew his parents. How are they?'

'They're elderly. It was a bitter blow for them, but...' He shrugged. 'I'm afraid there's nothing we can do. Or you, for that matter. Good day to you, Miss Crichton.'

Her attitude to her mother changed. She was tolerant, listening patiently to her when she complained about Peggy's behaviour.

'The first thing you'll hear is that they've been married. I could take you and James for a weekend to Perth and we could visit them.' Her mother nodded, her eyes brightening.

James was a leavening presence, full of tales about his school, asking questions about Skye. And could she speak Gaelic now? And did the men all wear kilts? 'Only at dances,' she told him. In some ways Peggy's absence meant a quieter household.

And another good thing was that for the first time in her life she had a room to herself. It was the greatest luxury to lie in bed and let her mind wander – back to Skye, and Lachlan; back to those early days when her mother had been a young married woman in wartime, and when they had left their first flat and those summer fields for the 'the premises'. It was like lifting a dark veil...

1925
'It's ugly,' I remember saying and my mother, in a temper, had lifted her hand threateningly.

'What kind of word is that? It's a big step up in the world for us, owning a business like this. Get down on your knees and thank God instead of using words like "ugly"! The very idea!'

It was long after we had left the East End that I realised it was the lack of green which had so offended me, and the long mean streets with the tenements defaced by chalked words and drawings. They provided me early on with another kind of language. At eight I had acquired a rich, secret vocabulary.

Peggy settled in quicker than I did. She and Susan, the young maid who looked after us – our mother was far too busy running the shop – became friends. Peggy at thirteen was old for her age, and certainly brighter than Susan at fifteen. I, at eleven, was naive in comparison.

When our brother James arrived, it was a delightful shock, but Peggy, primed by Susan, was blasé about it. She quickly made herself useful downstairs, washing milk-cans in the huge sinks of hot water, helping the assistants to skim butter from the vats, ordering the milk-boys about, even holding the ladder when our father had to climb up the sides of the large coolers where the milk was pasteurised.

My role, which I loved, was to look after James – to wheel him about in his high grey perambulator, and, when he was walking, lead him by the hand into the bakery to watch the scones and pancakes being made on the large hot plates, or into the creamery to see Daddy. Sometimes, if Peggy was there, officious in a red rubber apron, she would say, 'Out o' ma road!' but our father always took time to speak to us. I worried in bed at night about him always looking so tired.

I was popular with the milk-boys because some were in my class at school and because I let them have a drink of milk when nobody was looking. I had a favourite, Danny, a poor little lad who looked, and probably was, half starved. There was a lot of unemployment, and as a result, drunkenness. Danny's parents, I'd heard, were both 'on the bottle'.

But the one employee I hated was Paddy, who looked after Dobbin, the horse that pulled the milk-truck. Paddy tickled me in the wrong places and squeezed me and attempted to 'give me beardie' – rubbing his bristly chin against mine. My reason for being in the stable was because I was trying to make friends with Dobbin, an unfortunate name for a bad-tempered splay-backed old Clydesdale.

'Hello, Dobbin,' I'd say. 'I'm Jess, come to see you.' Peggy said I was daft in the head, and that I should keep away from the stables and that dirty old man. I took her advice.

Once when we were lying quietly in our beds, watching the shadows sail round the walls – these were made by the tramcars across the road turning into the depot – I said to her, 'Do you miss our last place, Peggy? Those fields ... I had nearly found a four-leaved clover.'

'You're daft,' she said. 'You and that other one, Bessie Brechin.' I missed Bessie, and our make-believe shop, the long waving grasses, the insects which hid in them ... those summer fields.

'Is there nothing you miss, though?'

'Aye,' she said, and her voice became soft. 'A miss Noble.' She turned on her side. 'Go to sleep and don't bother me.'

When I was ten I was sent to music lessons 'up the brae' to Miss Bouverie's. It was our father's idea. 'That poor soul only gets half a pint a milk every second day, and sometimes a half-pound of margarine. Never butter.'

'Margarine!' That was a heinous crime in our mother's eyes. 'What do ye want me to do about it?'

'Send the girls for tuition. It'll help her out. There won't be many pupils for her these days.'

Peggy said she didn't want to go but I was willing. In two years' time it was evident to Miss Bouverie that I'd never be much of a pianist, but she had become my best friend.

'You're too romantic in your playing, Jess. You haven't enough *brio*. Beethoven and Bach are beyond you, but if you practice, Chopin could become your *forte*.' She liked musical terms. 'And,' she added, 'if you don't discover the two giants, you at least will discover yourself.' These words stayed with me.

'What will you be playing tonight, Jess?' my father asked me as I came into the kitchen. Mother and Peggy were washing up and he had the table covered with papers. Doing his accounts. He looked up with a smile, and I tried to be funny. *'Show me the way to go home!'*

Peggy guffawed. 'Better than all those daft scales and things.'

'They go through ma head,' our mother said.

'Don't mind them.' My father's head was bent over his accounts. I thought what a tired back he had. Did he ever regret taking on 'the premises'?

'Come away in,' Miss Bouverie said when

I arrived. 'We'll go into the drawing room.'
She always wore black with amber beads.
Her grey hair was fixed on top of her head
with a Spanish comb, and on cold nights
she wore a patterned shawl with black
fringes.

The fire crackling in the grate was
reflected on the elegant rosewood side of
the Bluthner. Only pupils who had reached
a certain stage were entitled to play on it,
and I had reached those dizzy heights.

I loved the room with its dried grasses in
huge vases on either side of the fireplace, the
ivory knick-knacks, the fans, and most of all
the appliquéd Egyptian figures who pro-
cessed round the room in profile on panels
of linen. Once I'd had a dream in which one
of those figures had been that of Miss
Bouverie's, her hands held horizontally
front and back.

I knew her language by this time. Strange
words had become familiar: 'Diplomatic
Corps', 'Shepherd's', 'our boys' (who were
servants), 'programme dances', her 'ayah'
(who had been a superior kind of Susan).

'Tea, Jess?' Miss Bouverie was officiating
behind her silver kettle perched on a small
burner. She enjoyed this ceremony as much
as I did. It gave her a chance to talk about
'the dear old days' in Cairo, the musical
soirées, Colonel Wainwright who had been
her escort but in the end had turned out to

be a cad. 'Not like your dear father whom I always call one of Nature's gentlemen. So beautifully mannered...' I could have listened to her all evening.

Later I played my piece on the Bluthner reverently, and, I thought, better. At least she praised my rendering of the Chopin waltz I had been practising. 'Nothing is gained without a struggle, Jess. Remember that.' When she bent over me to make a mark on my sheet of music, her amber beads swung in front of me, bringing me all the mystery of the East.

She saw me off saying I was to cross the Sahara quickly. This was our private joke about the stretch of empty ground I had to negotiate before I got down to the main street. It was very dark. The shopkeepers' houses were rarely lit; Miss Bouverie said they all lived in their kitchens. 'Not real gentry,' she had said, 'like your father.' I wondered if he was giving her an occasional round of fresh butter, a delicacy made in the creamery and stamped on the top with a Scottish thistle.

But I had reached the road safely and was hurrying along, thinking about Miss Bouverie saying she hoped I would catch the camel train, and how she thought my father was one of Nature's gentlemen. She could do with an occasional round of fresh butter to fatten her up. She had looked bony and

198

gaunt tonight, and her drawing room fire had been very small. She missed the Cairo sun, she often said.

I scurried along, my music case bumping against my legs. When I came near the premises I noticed there was the usual knot of men standing at the corner, the bane of my mother's life. She was always threatening to go down to them and give them a piece of her mind. 'You'd get more than you bargained for,' I remembered my father saying to her. 'They're in an ugly mood these days.' Beardmore's, the large engineering firm near us, was paying men off, Susan had told us. Both her father and brother were idle.

She was sitting at the table with Peggy when I went in. I thought how strange they looked, how solemn. Was she telling Peggy about Beardmore's?

'What's wrong?' I dropped my music case, overcome by a strange kind of fear. All my father's papers were spread over the table, almost as if he had been called away suddenly. 'Where's ... Daddy?' I saw his Ready Reckoner lying open beside the papers. 'Peggy?' She didn't move. 'Peggy!' She turned and I saw my fear reflected in her eyes. 'What's wrong?'

'He ... fell off the chair.' Her hand went to her mouth. Fear was choking me; I could hardly speak. 'Why ... did he do that?'

'How should I know?' She flared with sudden anger. 'He was sitting here ... working ... and he just ... fell off. On to the floor. Didn't he, Susan?'

'Aye, just fell off.' Her eyes were wide.

Our mother came into the kitchen. She looked strange, wild-looking. Her bun of hair was partly undone, there were wisps hanging over her face. She looked at me. 'So you're back. You and Peggy are goin' wi' Susan, her Ma has said it, so you can keep your coat on.'

'What's wrong with Daddy?'

'A don't *know*!' Her voice was shrill. 'The doctor's with him.'

'Could I peep in?'

'Do whit you like.' She collapsed into a chair and put her head in her hands.

I went into the bedroom and crept near the bed. The doctor sitting beside him turned when he saw me and waved me back. 'This is no place for you.'

I stood where I was. The man lying on the bed wasn't like my father. He was making a terrible noise in his throat and his tongue was jutting from his mouth, huge, white, underneath it was a dark purple ... His tongue frightened me.

'Go on,' the doctor said. He was taking something out of his bag. The terrible breathing sound filled the room. I turned and fled.

My mother looked up at me. 'Well?' she said.

'He's ... very bad,' I could only whisper.

'A don't know...' Her voice rose. 'What's goin' to happen. I don't know...' It tailed away. She put her head in her hands, shaking it from side to side. Susan looked at us, biting her lip. Our mother's voice came to us, dull, defeated. 'You two get off with Susan. I've got enough to worry me.'

'Wull we take James, missus?' Susan asked.

'No, leave him. He's sleeping.' She didn't raise her head.

The doctor appeared. 'You'll have to keep the house quiet, Mrs Crichton,' he said. She stared at him. 'It's touch and go. He needs very careful nursing. The crisis will be soon. I'll go back and arrange for a nurse.'

'Yes, doctor.' When he'd left the kitchen she turned to us, her face strangely flushed. 'I told you! Off ye go with Susan, you two. She's packed your night things.'

We went with Susan, and now I see we should have hugged her and said we'd rather stay ... anything rather than leave her alone. But ours was not a hugging family. No wonder I was so fond of my hug-me-tight – and remembered so vividly the time my father had put his arms round me when James was born.

Susan's mother gave us some milk and

thick slices of bread with jam on them – no butter – and bustled us off to bed with Susan and three younger sisters. My heart gave me no peace; it lay like a heavy, hurting ball in my chest. 'One of Nature's gentlemen' – the words came to me now. Nor could I forget the sight of that huge, swollen tongue...

Peggy kept nudging me to move over. And I kept saying to her, 'But he'll get better, won't he, Peggy?'

'He's only thirty-five, Susan says.'

'Is that young, for a Daddy?'

'How do I know? Mary!' She let out a strangled shout. 'This wee besom's kicking me to bits...' I moved to the edge of the bed and lay there for the rest of the night, sleepless.

I remember we were hustled out of the house the next morning after Susan's mother had given us a bowl of lumpy porridge, which I sat staring at, especially as she had poured over it a watery 'sour dook' – skimmed milk, very different from the rich cream we got at home. Peggy didn't touch hers either but she looked so stern that I didn't dare speak to her.

When we got home, Susan pushed us into the kitchen in front of her as if to shield herself. I saw our mother standing in front of the fire and the look on her face was terrible. She made a roaring kind of sobbing noise. 'Oh, my God, missus,' Susan said. 'Whit is it?'

'He's dead, that's what it is!' Her howling kind of sobbing frightened the life out of me.

James was playing on the rug and he laughed when he saw us. She bent down and picked him up and blundered towards us. Peggy and I made no move and she collapsed into a chair at the table as if she had lost her strength. James slipped off her lap and went back to his wooden blocks as if, even then, he wanted to keep out of it.

She was keening, her head down on her arm on the table. 'Left without a man, three bairns, these big premises, everybody stealin' from us ... It's his own fault! I kept telling him, *telling* him he was working too hard, but would he listen, oh, dear, no, you could never get anything out o' him. I used to say, "Why d'ye no' shout at me sometimes, anything's better than that quietness," but everybody liked him, didn't really know him, just liked him, I got all the blame for everything...' The dirge went on and on...

Peggy and I were rigid with fright and shock. Susan was the only sensible one. She went to our mother and put her arm round her.

'Now, now, missus, you hivny to go on like that. You'll do yourself an injury. Think o' the lassies. It's their father too. Come on,

James, get up on your mother's knee.' She lifted him from the rug and put him down on her lap, then she turned to us. 'Come and give your mother a cuddle. You're aw she's got.'

We obeyed, embarrassed, and James, thinking it was a new game, chuckled. Tears came to our aid, awkwardly at first, but then, kneeling beside her, they were real. I thought, this is what she wants. A tableau. A public manifestation of grief.

And then, suddenly, it came to me. I thought, he's not here, he'll never be here again, and my sobs were deep and hurtful.

'Whit did the doctor say, missus?' Susan said.

'Double pneumonia.' Our mother lifted her head. 'Double! He might have got over it being young but his heart was bad, over-strained. That heavy work. But a telt him! Leave it to your workers, I said...' Her sobs began again, but more subdued.

When we were in bed that night I said to Peggy, 'Are you crying?'

'No. Whit's the use? But things will be different. Susan says everybody respected our Dad, but not her.'

'Did they?' But I could only think of how I was going to miss him. In the middle of the night I heard my mother sobbing, and I'm sorry to this day that I didn't get in beside her and comfort her.

Twenty

1938

Jess had a new feeling of maturity since the Skye holiday, as if she had learned how to live. She remembered the thrill at her early school when Miss Clewes had said, 'Now, class, we are going to practise joined-up writing.' Perhaps Lachlan had shown her the way to see her life in the same way – as a whole, tying up the past with the present.

She understood her mother better, that possibly her bouts of bitterness were because of her husband's early death, the loss of companionship and even sexual love, which would account for her anger and perhaps envy of Peggy. They were very alike in temperament.

Jess also had a new sense of enjoyment in her daily life. She recognised that part of the attraction in working for Sir Bernard was that it gave her a glimpse into another style of living, to be at ease in the world, to have natural authority. And there had been his nephew, Giles Imrie. She was surprised how often her thoughts came back to him.

And she enjoyed her evenings at the College. The girls she taught were so near her own age that she had established a friendly bond with them. They often walked to her train with her, waved her off. It was pleasant to be liked.

And Mr Craven was complimentary. One evening he approached her in the staffroom. 'Great results for your class, Miss Crichton! The best ever. I'm still hoping we can coax you to come to us full time.'

She smiled at him, noticed again his clean but badly-groomed look ... Perhaps he was busy getting his son, Jock, off to school in the morning and hadn't time to spend on himself. 'One of these days,' she said. 'I like to keep my feet in both camps.'

'We lack attraction here,' he said to Miss Evans, who had been drinking coffee with Jess at the time. 'What can we do about it?'

'What about that circular you got in the other day? You were telling me about it.'

'Oh, yes! I had this great idea, Miss Crichton. I'm having a new prospectus printed. I thought if I could say we had special short-hand speed classes for journalists...'

She laughed at him. 'And I have to teach them?'

'Yes. But good as your speeds are, I'd like them higher. This circular came from the WEA. They have readers at the Christian

Institute, graded. With your skills you could attain dizzy heights there in no time.'

'He's a schemer, isn't he, Miss Evans?' But she was attracted by the challenge.

'Before you go any further, Jack,' she replied, 'you would have to make it worth Jess's time.' Jess saw that the use of first names was including her in the hierarchy.

'That goes without saying. "Advanced Speed Writing." That's what I want on our new prospectus ... How about it, Jess?' He smiled at her as he used her name. 'You'd get a certificate easily. Say a hundred and forty words per minute? I'll give you an advance in salary from this month. You're a witness, Beth.' He included Miss Evans.

'It's tempting,' Jess said, laughing. 'I think you've won me over.'

'It's your charm that does it, Jack,' Beth Evans said. Jess saw her look. Fifties, with an ailing mother ... Was she in love with him? She was curious about *his* age. Forties? Anyhow, much older than her.

She met Nessie for coffee one evening en route to Bothwell Street and the speed writing classes.

'You look different, Jess,' she said. 'That holiday must have done you good.'

'It did. A lot of good.' She thought Nessie looked sad. 'You'll be missing Bob, now that he's away.'

'Aye. But he's ma man. Skye did something to me too. The thing is, wi' the War coming nearer every day we're wonderin' if we shouldn't just...'

'Get married?'

'No, you know ... you're not daft. We haven't money to get married yet. It's makin' us think...'

'Oh! Well...' The thought of war must be changing a lot of people's morals.

'Peggy didny wait, did she?'

'Time will tell. She hasn't said anything to me. Anyhow she's with Noble now. Peggy has always known her own mind. What our mother says or thinks can't hurt her now.'

'She has courage, your Peggy.'

'Yes, she's always been like that.' Peggy climbing up on roofs with Noble although she risked a 'skelping' from their mother, planning the Pin Game with him; Peggy, in her rubber apron at 'the premises' ordering the milk-boys about; Peggy now in her love nest in Perth ... She had always been in charge of her life.

I wish I hadn't decided to come here tonight, Jess thought later as she went through the doorway of the great Victorian building which stretched along Bothwell Street. She wished she had eaten something with Nessie. She was starving. Well, I'm here, she thought as she knocked on the door of the dictation room, excused herself to the man at the desk, and sat down quietly. The reader had paused for a second or two until she got seated, saying, 'The book is *The Heart of Darkness* by Joseph Conrad. Speed one hundred and thirty words per minute,' and then gone on reading.

It was hard going at first, but she was soon in the swing and able to take in the meaning of the writing. The smooth flowing of the hieroglyphics that seemed to run from her fingers was almost hypnotic.

Her concentration was broken by someone in front of her getting up, bowing to the reader, and quietly making for the door. There was no doubt about it. It was Giles Imrie. She would have known him anywhere. The polite bending at the hips, the lean figure and face of Sir Bernard's nephew. Her pencil was no longer sliding over the page. Her concentration had gone.

He had come to Glasgow, presumably to work. He wasn't Scottish. Was he by any chance a reporter? Her brief impression of the other students as she came in had been that they were mostly young men. It would be an obvious place for them to come, the kind of pupil Jack Craven was angling for. The reader's voice was no longer soothing. He had a slight lisp. Perhaps that was why he had volunteered to read.

She closed her book, put it in her case, and, making her excuses, quietly left the room. Giles Imrie was in the foyer. He came towards her, smiling. She felt suddenly elated. 'I thought it was you,' she said to him.

'I decided to wait. I saw you coming in.' They smiled at each other in pleasure.

'Are you a reporter?' she asked.

'Very junior. I've just been appointed. My uncle knew the editor. I only slipped out for an hour. One of the chaps beside me knows this place. But what are you doing here? You seemed very experienced when I saw you. Pencil flying...'

She laughed. 'I teach in the evenings at a business college. I want to get a certificate for a higher speed ... at the Principal's request.'

'Well, anyhow, this is great!' She had never met anyone quite like him – his voice, his lean good looks, his general un-Scottish-ness. 'I could see you home if it's near. I'll get a cab. May I?' No Scotsman had ever said, 'May I?' to her.

'No, really. It's no distance. I'll nip down to Argyle Street and get a tram.'

'Do you live anywhere near Uncle Bernard's? Kelvinside?'

'No, that's up in the heights. I'm down in the depths. Or nearly. We're tucked in between Argyle Street and Sauchiehall Street. I could walk up there, or down to Argyle Street. It's six or half a dozen.'

He looked mystified. 'Well, whatever. Is it possible to get a cab?'

'Not immediately, I should think.' She had only once been in a cab, at Muriel's wedding. 'Please don't bother. I'm quite used to walking.'

He glanced at his watch. 'I'm due back any minute. What bad luck!' He smiled regretfully at her with, she thought, a beautiful all-consuming kind of smile.

They walked down the steps to the street and she said, 'Well, I'd better run.' Her feet seemed stuck to the pavement.

'Me too. But I can't let you go before you tell me when we can meet again. I'm off tomorrow evening. It's terribly short notice, but would that suit you?'

She hesitated because she couldn't believe this was happening. 'Well...'

'Do say yes.'

'Yes.' It was ridiculous, standing there grinning at each other. 'Where?'

'You say. You know Glasgow.'

'The Ca'd'oro? You can't miss it. It's on the corner of Union Street and Gordon Street.' That was a master stroke, she thought, pleased. We can go there if it's only coffee, or ... well, she would leave it to him.

'Perfect,' he said. 'I can find out back at the paper where it is. Seven o'clock?'

'Seven o'clock's fine.' She wasn't teaching

that evening. 'You'd better get off or you'll be late.'

'Yes, I'd better.' He touched her arm almost shyly. 'What luck!' he said. 'See you tomorrow, Miss Crichton.'

'Jess.'

'Jess. Mine's Giles.'

'Yes, I know. Cheerio, then.' She turned and left him standing, bareheaded. English girls wouldn't say 'Cheerio!' would they, she thought as she ran along Bothwell Street.

She saw him in her mind all the way home, lean, dark, white smile – so different from Lachlan who was broad and tall and strong. But *he* hadn't touched her heart like Giles, not in this peculiar, trembling way. Just as well, she thought, remembering Maureen.

Twenty-One

Her feeling of well-being after her encounter with Giles Imrie drove her out of bed early the following morning although she didn't have to go to work. But her mother's face decided her that she would keep quiet about it meantime.

'Read that!' She threw the letter she was holding across the table to Jess. Peggy, she thought, her spirits falling.

'Just to tell you,' she read out loud, 'that me and Noble got married last week. Our address is c/o Mackie, Mains Farm, Drumairn, Perthshire. You'll all be welcome to come and visit us any time. I'm happy, Mother. If I was you I would accept it. Maybe it's not what you'd have liked, but you've still two others who won't disappoint you. Peggy.' She handed the letter back. 'Well, that's what you wanted. We should go and see her, Mother. Let bygones be bygones.'

'You want me to go crawlin' there after how she's made me suffer?'

'You're going to be late.' She didn't want

213

any quarrelling.

'And don't you go either! You're the only one I can rely on now. She's always taken her own way, right from the time she let you get run over by that tram.' It was such a ridiculous remark that Jess burst out laughing.

'Oh, Mother!' She stopped herself. No quarrelling. It was going to be a good day.

Her mother was throwing on her coat. 'That shop! I get the heavy end, as usual. You mark my words, there'll be a wean on the way...' James came into the kitchen.

'Shouldn't you be away by this time?'

She looked in an agitated fashion at the clock. 'Aye ... Your sister's got married to that Noble! As if a hadn't enough to worry about ... A'll be late, but whose fault is that? Eh?' She went out, banging the door behind her.

'Does that make me an uncle?' James said. He must have heard his mother's remark. He sat down at the table in his pyjamas, his hair tousled, a warm smell of bed coming from him.

'Don't be daft, James!'

He was unperturbed. 'Ah, well. As long as Noble and Peggy are happy.' He began to butter a slice of bread. His nonchalance never ceased to amaze Jess.

'Since you're up, would you like breakfast?'

'Yes, please. Bacon and eggs. I like Noble. Oh, and the Grays have asked me to go for the weekend. She didn't give me a chance to tell her. Will you?'

'I'll be out. But I'll leave a note. She won't feel happy to come back to an empty house.'

When she was cooking, she turned and said to James, 'I'm quite excited. I'm going out tonight, to dinner, I think.'

'Dinner? That sounds posh. You look pleased enough. You should see your eyes!'

'What's wrong with my eyes?' But she felt a piercing kind of sweetness as she stood there. She composed her face before she turned to James with the heaped plate.

'I'll go up to town and buy Peggy a present.'

'I wish I could help, but no can do.' He began to eat. 'The only thing wrong with Noble is that he doesn't play rugby.'

'Watch it,' she said. 'You're becoming a snob.'

She went to Trérons in Sauchiehall Street when she had washed up, and bought some bedlinen for Peggy and Noble. You couldn't go wrong with bedlinen. And, because she was feeling happy, to Dolcis where she got herself a pair of high-heeled court shoes. The girl complimented her on her 'nice narrow feet'.

James had gone off to the Grays' and she had a bath in the afternoon then dressed herself carefully in a patterned black and green silk dress, the new shoes and her green coat with the chinchilla collar.

The girl she saw in the mirror was bright-eyed, flushed ... Or was it too much rouge? She nearly made herself late scrubbing it off. The finished product pleased her, especially when she wrapped the coat round her, feeling it slide on the silk underneath, and held it at her waist with one hand, *à la* Lady Elizabeth Bowes-Lyon.

At the last moment she remembered James' request and wrote a short note to their mother. *James is at the Grays' for the weekend. Don't worry, I packed a pair of fresh pyjamas for him. And I forgot to tell you I'm going out for the evening. I've left some supper for you in the larder.* She had a twinge of guilt at the thought of their mother coming back to an empty house, but soon dismissed it.

She walked to the tram stop, feeling free for the first time. For a long time she had worried about Ronnie Wilcox, but it was beginning to fade since her visit to the police station. Poor soul, she thought ... and I'm so happy. Lachlan would be glad she had taken his advice. Maybe some day she would write to him at his mother's address. Maybe...

She sailed along Sauchiehall Street once again on the top of the tram, thinking what a beautiful street it was, how happy she felt, as if she were at the beginning of something quite new, and that circumstances had been preparing her for this all her life. At the stop before Gordon Street she got up and ran downstairs, enjoying the clatter of her high heels, thinking, if he isn't there, my heart will break.

But he was. Smart and sleek at the arranged corner and coming forward to greet her as if he had been looking forward to this all *his* life.

'Did you come by Argyle Street or Sauchiehall Street?' he said, laughing.

'The tram from Charing Cross. I walked there because it takes a halfpenny off the fare.' She felt completely, beautifully natural, as if the tone had already been set.

'A true Scot. I thought we might go to the Rogano. I've been making enquiries. It's where the sharp guys take their molls.'

'It's one of our best restaurants,' she said. She had never been in it.

'Passable, then?'

'So passable that I've always passed it.' Where was this coming from?

'Are all Glasgow girls as jokey as you?'

'No, I'm quite original. It's no distance from here, the Rogano.'

'Well, supposing you lead me to it? You're the native here.'

'As long as I don't lose you on the way.' They had to dodge through the Saturday evening crowds along Gordon Street, then cross Buchanan Street to reach Royal Exchange Square. 'This is it,' she said.

'Well, that didn't tire us out. After you.' He held open the door.

It was very sober inside, with white tablecloths that couldn't have been bettered at Trérons, and napkins and menus of the same size. A waiter appeared and took her coat; another one led them to their table and asked them if they would like a drink before dinner. Giles looked at her smilingly over the wine list.

'Perhaps we ought to celebrate getting here. It was quite an arduous journey.' He pointed to something on the list, and the waiter nodded and said it was a very good choice.

'I should have asked if you liked champagne.' Giles looked consideringly at her.

'I've only had it at weddings,' she said.

'There's no law against having it at other times.'

The waiter looked satisfied and went away.

'You look ravishing,' Giles said, now turning his attention solely to her. He spoke quite a different language from the clerks in the office.

She flicked the silk collar of her dress. 'It's my mother you have to thank,' she said. 'She still buys our clothes. She thinks no one can tell good material better than her. You've to watch you don't buy something you could spit peas through.' She saw the amusement in his face.

'I get her point, but it wasn't the dress I was admiring, nice as it is. It was you.' She smiled, but said nothing. 'You don't seem to believe me.' She put her hand to her mouth to hide another smile. 'Don't you know how pretty you are, Jess?'

She shook her head. 'They don't say that much in Glasgow, at least not the clerks where I work.'

'Bad luck. And your hair. It's brown, but there are gleams of silver in it. Quite ravishing.'

'I used to be very fair. Then it went brown and stayed fair at the edges.' She touched her brow. 'I thought of dyeing it.'

'You mustn't. It's a bewitching colour, and dense.'

'Yes, I have to have it thinned.' She thought they had gone on long enough about her hair. Fortunately the waiter came back with the champagne in an ice bucket and went through the performance of taking it out, uncorking it, wrapping it like a baby in a white napkin, and pouring it carefully into large glasses. She'd seen it all in the pictures – Norma Shearer, she thought.

Giles lifted his glass and said, 'To you.' She lifted hers too, thinking, I've seen all this as well – they live on champagne in

Hollywood, but going along with it to please him. 'Is it all right?' he asked.

'Lovely,' she said. It was. Like velvet. 'I've been wondering,' she said, 'why you accepted a job in Glasgow? It can't be as nice as where you came from.'

'I'd better put you out of your misery...'

'I'm not in misery at all.' She didn't want him to think she was fishing. 'I'd just like to know.'

'Right. Lyndhurst in Sussex is my home.' His face became serious. 'Why I'm here ... You know my uncle's son, Roger, was killed in Spain?'

'Yes. I was very sorry. News gets around the office – although I don't gossip.'

'I'm sure you don't. Well, I admired Roger immensely. He was two years older than me. We both went to the same school, the same Cambridge college, and I did what he had done – took a journalism course in London when I came down. I copied him in everything – school, college, ski-ing ... Our two families always went to Zell am See.' He must have seen her perplexed look, for he added, 'In Austria. It was a tradition to go there for Christmas, for the celebration of St Nicholas. Have you ever seen it?' She shook her head. 'The men in the village dress up in goatskin costumes and wear devil masks, really medieval, and they hit anyone who gets in their way with beech twigs.' His eyes lit up. 'The scene beside the lake, over-looked by the Kutzsteinhorn, and the whole thing lit by torches...' He stopped. 'I'm sorry, I shouldn't go on, but we all had such good times, and now Roger's dead ... Well, I should be glad we had it, had him...' He stopped again.

She felt his sadness. 'You have the memory.' She would have liked to touch his hand.

'Yes, lovely memories. Well ... then I was offered a placement here in Glasgow after my course was finished. I didn't particularly want to come north, but Mother – she's Uncle Bernard's sister – was quite keen I should take it. I think she thought I might cheer them up a bit, so here I am.'

Jess was left with images in her mind, dancing figures, snow that sparkled under the lights from torches, a lake, an ice-capped mountain, and Roger, like an older Giles, but possibly fair instead of dark, who at least had those wonderful images too when he died. A violent death, unlike drowning...

'Your cousin would volunteer for Spain?'

'Yes. Typical Roger. Always a bit of a maverick, liked to be where the action was. I wouldn't mind doing the same thing.'

'You'll probably not have to go so far away.'

'Yes. Poor old Austria, with that man on

221

the rampage. What I'd really like to be is a war correspondent, hence the journalism thing. But, no, they'll whip me in for active service. I'm far too fit ... I say, you have to eat! Have you looked at the menu yet?' He smiled his swift smile. He was doing the ravishing now.

'No.' She lifted hers and was confused. She looked over it at Giles. 'It's difficult to choose.'

'What would you like if you were asked?'

'Smoked salmon,' she said. 'I've had it at staff dances and I really like it. Then roast duck with roast potatoes and green peas, then Pavlova. Do you know what Pavlova is? You get it at the Grosvenor.'

'Well, I'm sure this place will try to keep up.'

'What would you like best?'

'The same as you. I have a hearty appetite.'

'And you're so thin.'

'You could spit peas through me.' He grinned at her. 'Fortunately, we'll have them.'

She laughed. 'You like teasing me.'

'Because you're so sweet. And puzzling. Half of you's ... well, childlike, and the other half's quite sophisticated.'

'I'm working on myself.' She thought of Lachlan.

The waiter arrived, Houdini-like, pad in

222

hand. 'Sir?'

'We want smoked salmon, duck and Pavlova.' The waiter seemed to hesitate. 'Is that a problem?'

'Certainly not, sir.'

'And we'll need some claret.'

'Certainly, sir.'

'Do you think it's on the menu? The Pavlova?' Jess asked after the waiter had departed.

'It is now.' His eyes stayed on her, and she looked away, blushing.

'Have you lived in Glasgow all your life?' he asked, kindly.

It was an old chestnut. 'Not yet,' she said. They laughed together. She felt she had to tear her eyes away.

They had to sit back while a trolley was wheeled in with the duck and vegetables. She watched the waiter dismember the duck, put a portion on each plate, and set the plates in front of them. 'Palaver,' her mother would have called it, especially all those serving dishes with vegetables.

'I met someone when I was on holiday in Skye,' she said. She thought the laughter went out of his face and she said quickly, 'His fiancée is a psychologist, and he said that to really understand yourself you have to go back to your roots.'

'Know thyself, and all that? I've had a fairly unchequered past. Mundane, almost.

Same house since I was born, Father wasn't in the last war ... I mean, fighting. He was in the Diplomatic Service.'

'Neither was mine. It was a reserved occupation. He had a milk business.' She saw a query in his eyes. 'Wholesale and retail. He died before he was forty. We've moved three times. But there are lots of memories. Do you think when I finish remembering I will know myself? Be fully sophisticated?'

'Oh, I hope not. Besides, I don't think you are ever finished. Something has to fill your mind when you go to bed.'

'That's the time for memories. I think I'll have another roast potato.'

'So shall I. They're delicious.'

'At the Rogano with Giles.' It was like a title for a short story. The atmosphere was hushed; they were in their own world. She felt she had never liked anyone so much – in a different way from Lachlan, an exciting way. And herself growing prettier under his gaze, funnier, flirtier. She felt herself grow into what she would like to become – whole.

His background had been smoother than hers – his sister hadn't run away, his mother was softer. But she wouldn't have the guts her mother had, nor probably the temper and the occasional bitterness ... But then she hadn't lost a young husband. And then again, how could you tell what his mother had gone through? It was how you dealt with it.

When they came out of the Rogano she was ever so slightly inebriated, but very happy. She stopped when they were outside and said, 'That's the best evening I've ever had ... or one of the best.' She didn't want to overdo it.

'But you're not leaving me here, unless you're not fit to walk to my car?'

'You haven't got one.'

'Yes, I have. I fixed it up this morning. It's parked in the Square here. May I run you home?'

'Oh, there's no need. I can get the—'

'Certainly not. I've had enough of listening to how you cope with the Glasgow tramway system.' She allowed herself to be led to his hired car.

'But you'll have to direct me,' Giles said when he had turned into Renfield Street and was driving up its slope.

'It won't take you much out of your way,' she assured him.

'How do you know since you don't know where I'm staying?'

'That's true. Where?'

'West George Street. A private hotel there. It's quite comfortable. I like hotels.'

She wondered at him not staying with his aunt and uncle. 'Wouldn't you rather live in a house?' she asked him.

'Eventually, yes, when it's my own.' He gave her a brief glance. 'What age are you, Jess?' He had slowed down. 'I turn right here?'

'No, left. Into Sauchiehall Street. I'll direct you from here. I'm twenty-three.'

'So am I.'

'Will you stay on in Glasgow?'

'I don't know. I couldn't be a foreign correspondent here.'

'You could practise on us.' They were through Charing Cross and he was speeding along past the elegant Newton Terrace. 'Left again.' The elegant terrace was left behind. 'I'll tell you when to stop. Flat-fronted flats.' They had reached her close far too quickly. She looked up at the window of their front room and saw the curtain flicker. Sherlock Holmes, she thought.

'I would ask you up,' she said. 'But my mother tends to go to bed early.'

'Oh, that's all right. I know about mothers.' He had switched off the engine. The street was empty. Over there, against the wall, was where Ronnie Wilcox used to stand. She would see him there for a long time. She knew Giles had turned to her.

'Thank you very much,' she said. She remembered she had already said it at the Rogano. They looked at each other.

'Jess...' he said. She began to tremble, even her mouth trembled, a fine tremor. 'Am I going to be allowed to kiss you goodnight?'

'All right,' she said. She wanted him to kiss her. Very much she wanted him to kiss her. She felt his hands on her shoulders and knew he would feel the tremor and wonder why.

It wasn't a thank you kiss. It was something much more important, something like what she'd had with Lachlan – except that with him warmth had been the important part, comfort. This was far more. She lifted her head and looked at him.

'You're trembling,' he said.

'I know. I can't help it.'

'You're so sweet.' His voice broke. 'I can't believe anyone could be like this at your age, so untouched.'

'I never liked anyone touching me. Only one, but I *liked* him.' She came out of his arms. 'Excuse me. I have to calm down.'

'I can't believe it ... You're shaking.'

'I know. But it's not because I don't want you to touch me. I want you to touch me. I learned a lot in Skye. It changed me ... just changed me. I realised I'd grown up with the wrong attitudes, that I wasn't thinking straight.'

He didn't reply.

'What's wrong?' she said.

'I feel like a marauder.'

'A marauder!' She went into his arms again. 'You haven't got to feel like that. I was

227

only telling you about Lachlan so that you would know I had changed, that I'd got the hang of it.'

'Loving?'

'No, living.'

He kissed her. When he stopped she asked him to kiss her again. Lachlan was fading into the early morning mist.

'You are...' He looked at her in the darkness and she thought his mouth was beautiful even when he wasn't smiling. 'You'd better get up there.' She thought *his* voice was shaking. 'You are unique, do you know that? When are you going to the speed class again?'

'Monday,' she said. It was the nearest day to Saturday, and fortunately, she wasn't teaching that evening.

'I'll meet you at seven o'clock. That was when you came out the last time. Is that all right?'

'Yes.'

'I shan't be at the class as I'm working, but you'll see my car at the entrance. Perhaps there will be time for a coffee. At least, I'll see you. I have to see you.' He kissed her briefly, missing her mouth, got out of the car, and went round the other side to open the door for her. He shook hands formally when they were standing on the pavement. She had looked up and seen another flicker of the curtain. Just shaking hands, Mother.

'Good night, Jess,' he said. 'This has been wonderful.'

When she was running up the stairs she slipped and banged her shin on the edge of the stone steps. It brought tears to her eyes. And she had scuffed her new shoes.

Her mother was waiting in the lobby. 'Who was that you were out with?' she said. 'In a motor?' She couldn't have looked worse if it had been a hearse.

'Sir Bernard's nephew.' Jess bent down to dab at her bleeding shin with her handkerchief. 'Slipped.'

'Sir Bernard's nephew!' Her eyebrows shot up.

'It's still bleeding. I'll have to—'

'Well, you'd better stick in there.' Her mother had drawn herself up, a look of gratification on her face.

Seek the solace of your own room. She'd read that somewhere. 'I'm off to bed, then. Goodnight.'

'Aye, well, goodnight.' She was eyeing Jess as if she were awarding her ten out of ten.

Twenty-Two

She was too excited to sleep.

She thought of her family: James with the Gray brothers opposite the Park, Peggy with Noble in Perthshire – lying in his arms, most likely – their mother and herself, in the same house but apart in their thoughts. Was she happy for Jess, or envious? Their mother had been always a creature of moods. Jess thought of the rows there had been in 'the premises' after their father had died.

She hadn't had the gift of natural authority their father had, which kept the business running on oiled wheels. There were sackings when various employees had been given their 'books', recriminations, weeping.

Ted Murphy had been one of the worst. A big, overconfident Irishman recommended by the Gray brothers to run the wholesale part, he had been a disaster, ruining hundreds of gallons of milk by overheating it while fraternising with the girl employees – especially Susan. Jess remembered that denouement.

Their mother had opened the 'kist' to put in the day's takings, and found all the money gone. Peggy and Jess had stumbled on the scene, and stood there, petrified spectators. Susan was cowering before their mother, who was on her knees at the open chest.

'You dirty besom!' she was shouting. 'I warned you about being too familiar. wi' him. You've had him up here, haven't you?' Susan nodded miserably.

'He jist wanted—'

'I know what he jist wanted. To jump into bed wi' you. My bed, more than likely. An' you jist happened to tell him where I kept the key of the kist, didn't you? Well, he's hopped off to Donegal with all ma money, to his wife and kids, more than likely! Ach, you make me sick!'

Susan stayed on, nevertheless, possibly because their mother needed her to look after the house and James when Jess was at school. Peggy had been taken away 'on compassionate grounds' and was helping downstairs, a 'good wee worker', their mother often said. Jess was the handless one, only good as a nursemaid.

The last straw but one was the General Strike in 1926. Peggy came into our bedroom one night after me, saying, 'D'you hear the noise?'

'Yes,' I said. 'I've been listening.' The usual crowd of idle men under their window had grown bigger as more and more were sacked from Beardmore's Foundry. 'Mr Soutar, our geography teacher, told us to walk on the opposite side of Beardmore's entrance. "The temper of the men is turning ugly," he said.'

'Ma's worried. She's sent Susan to tell the Police about the row they're making. You'd better get your clothes on.'

'I never took them off.' I flung back the bedclothes to show her that I was fully dressed. I had been scared at the noise.

'C'mon, then, we'll go into the kitchen.'

Our mother was there with Susan, newly arrived and breathless.

'He says that they've got everything under control, and not to worry. They don't want to start anything up.' She was flushed and excited by her encounter with the police sergeant – 'anything in trousers', Mother often said of her.

'Jist a lot o' cowards,' she now said. 'What do they care if a'm alone here with three young ones? We could all be killed in our beds!'

Despite that she sent us back to bed because she was dog-tired. I remembered looking at her and thinking how flushed she was, how she liked excitement, even danger, and how different she was from our quiet father. I didn't know the word 'incompatible' then.

I must have gone to sleep because I was suddenly wakened by the door bursting open and our mother appearing in her nightgown, her hair down her back, James in her arms.

'Are you two up?' she shouted. 'Did you not hear that?' I dimly remembered there had been some sort of crash, which I had assured myself at the time was a dream. Peggy and I jumped out of bed. Mother was addressing an unseen audience.

'I sent Susan to the polis, didn't I? And weren't they told that I didny have a man in the house? And didn't they say not to worry? Frightened out of their lives to come near...' Peggy and I were at the window.

'There's a lot of policemen there now, Mammy!'

'Aye, now!' She had joined us. 'But did you two not hear the crash? It was our shop window, I'm sure it was...'

'Look at the policemen!' I said. James began to cry. 'They're hitting them wi' their sticks! The men are shouting, and falling down!'

'A man, Mammy! Fallin' down!' James' tears suddenly disappeared.

'Look at that one!' Peggy pointed. 'He's got a bottle!' I looked and saw the man, saw him raise the bottle and bring it smashing down on a policeman's bare head. He must have lost his helmet in the scuffle. Blood poured down over his face, shining blackly under the street lamp.

'It'll be us next!' Mother was wailing now, but there were no tears. 'Well, they can't say a didn't warn them ... We're all goin' to be murdered and nobody's goin' to stop it!'

There were whistles blowing, the sound of motors; two white vans drew up to the kerb and some policemen jumped out. They went about the crowd, flailing with their batons, then began to push men into the van by their coat collars. Some struggled and escaped. I saw one streak across the road, take a flying leap at the billboards – which must have been about eight feet high – grab the top and lever himself up, sit on the edge for a second then disappear out of sight.

'You two get dressed!' our mother commanded and went off, still carrying James. We hurried into our clothes, and were ready when she came back. I could never keep up with her swift changes of mood.

'A'm not going down there, but a'll be ready when they come up the stairs. A want to know about the damage ... Peggy, go into the kitchen and make us a cup o' tea. Here,' she said to me, 'you hold James.' I took him. His childish face was flushed and he was punching the air with his fists. 'Bad men!

Bad men!' he was shouting. A general strike was strong meat for a three-year-old.

A policeman came upstairs to the flat when the crowd seemed to have melted away. 'Your shop window's been broken, Mrs Crichton,' he said. 'But there's no more damage. We're having to barricade it right away until we get a new pane for it. If I were you I'd get to bed and get some sleep till the morning.' Nevertheless, she insisted on going downstairs with him to be shown the extent of the damage.

We sat in the kitchen drinking tea at two o'clock in the morning and looking furtively at each other. James had been put to bed, tired with all the excitement. We waited until our mother came back.

'A'm fed up wi' the whole thing,' she said, drinking the tea Peggy poured out for her. She sat glumly at the table and I thought, Why can't we put our arms round her, or something? We didn't know how to. Nobody spoke. I stared at my teacup.

'A'll not forget this for a long time,' Peggy said at last, as if she had to say something. And then, 'We'll away to our bed, Mammy.' She made a movement of her head towards me, and I got up and followed her out of the room.

'D'you think she'll be all right?' I asked Peggy as we were undressing.

'A don't know. Put out the light. A've to

235

get up at six the morrow. One thing sure, she'll not let me have a lie-in.'

The next day the Gray brothers arrived. Their mother said she had given their names to the Police. They were prompt as always.

'We're living in terrible times, Maggie,' Mr Thomas said. He was the usual spokesman. They were ushered into the parlour. Susan was banished.

'I've had enough of it, to tell you the truth,' she said. 'Not only last night, although that was bad enough. But getting the staff to work together is even worse, although I tire myself out trying to please them.' Peggy looked at Jess. How often had they over-heard her shouting at some unfortunate!

'You could always shut down the wholesale part and just keep the retail,' Mr Peter said. 'It's too much for you, Maggie.' His sympathy was wasted.

'Shut it down! A'd never get anything for the business if a sold it! No, a'll never do that!'

'Maggie's right.' Mr Thomas agreed.

It was settled after some talking that she would carry on meantime, but if there was one more incident, she warned them, that would be the end. There was a limit to what a body could stand.

They sampled the home-made scones

with a cup of tea – Peggy had got them from the kitchen – and got up to go.

'Still chirping like a wee canary?' Mr Thomas said to Jess, giving her a pat on the head and a shilling to James.

She wished Mr Thomas could have heard their canaries, who, far from chirping, made a deafening noise at times. But the Gray brothers were always entertained in the parlour, the corner room which made Jess think of being under the ocean because of the green carpet – the green-dyed sheepskin rugs reminding her of seaweed – and the conch shells on the mantelpiece.

The suggestion about selling part of the business seemed to give their mother a new impetus. 'The cheek of it,' she confided to them when the brothers had gone. 'Throw away money like that! It's all very well for them to talk, and them rolling in it. No, a'll carry on. But a can't take much more. Anything else will finish me. You lassies don't know what it's like to be left on your own without a man ... Clear away they dishes while a go down the stair and lock up.'

'It's a shame for her all the same, all on her own,' Jess said, lifting two cups.

'It's not for want o' tellin' us,' Peggy said. 'And get the tray from the kitchen. You'll be all day goin' back and forwards that way.' She's just like our mother, Jess thought, going to fetch it.

In the kitchen the two canaries were going through their full repertoire. Mr Thomas would have to get a better metaphor.

1927
The straw that broke the camel's back came the following year.

Although they had only been spectators the night of the General Strike, the evidence of its effect was all around them. The women soon found they couldn't feed their families on the dole. It showed in the scanty purchases they made – skimmed milk, day-old scones and pancakes sold at half-price. 'Give me jist one slice o' ham, missus.' The man of the household had to get his protein while the children starved.

Their mother refused 'tick' – a loan – from the beginning. But a fair amount of barter went on. She was offered a cabbage from their allotments for a loaf of bread, services of a joiner husband for a Saturday grocery order. One original version was the offer of Bobby, the son of a customer, to teach the girls ballroom dancing for a week's supply of milk. Somehow or other, in spite of poor genes, Bobby had turned out to be tall and slim and a 'smashin' wee dancer', his only passion in life. Much later, at dances in the Plaza and the Grosvenor, Jess thanked Bobby under her breath.

But the crisis came with Danny, one of the

milk-boys. A creamery worker had been given his books with the usual slanging match. Our mother's anger settled on Jess.

'It's high time you lent a hand. Look at your sister! You'll get up with Peggy in the mornin' and fill the milk-boy's cans before you go to school.'

Danny was undersized, a waif in ragged clothes which were obviously an elder brother's cast-offs, and she began giving him some milk each morning on the sly. His eyes were pathetic, too large for his small, white, generally unwashed face. He wrung her heart.

Surreptitiously she gave him an old pair of her boots, but the next day he was bare-footed as usual. 'You're a softie,' Peggy said. 'His mother would pawn them for a bottle o' whisky. She and her man would do anything for a drink.'

Dobbin was still with them, and Paddy, who was unemployable anywhere else and yet indispensable to their mother. He was a disaster, sullen and endlessly complaining about the boys spreading hay about the stables, about his poor pay, about the missus always shouting at him.

Often, when he was late, Jess would unlock the padlock of the stable door and Danny would help her to push it back on its runners so that Paddy could get out the cart quickly when he arrived and yoke Dobbin.

She gave the horse a wide berth because of its wicked yellow eyes.

One morning, earlier than usual, she was wakened by the ear-splitting squeal of wheels. She knew what it was at once – the sound of the heavy stable door being pushed back. Only Paddy and their mother kept the key. Theirs hung on a hook inside the back door, where she knew it could be found if Paddy were late.

Had he gone off last night and forgotten to lock it? Jess wondered. He was becoming more careless every day, drinking as heavily as his wages would allow. 'For two pins I'd have him out on his ear,' their mother often said, but it was difficult to find anyone around who knew about horses.

Jess dressed hurriedly – Peggy was in the bathroom – and she was putting on her shoes when she heard screaming and a heavy pounding, followed by a terrible high-pitched neighing and frenzied shouting. She rushed to the window and saw Dobbin, tail flying behind him, hairy fetlocks spread like wings, careering along the middle of the street. In spite of his size he looked as if he were flying, unhampered by his cart or Paddy's vicious whip. Jess heard Peggy come into the room behind her.

'Somebody's let Dobbin out, Peggy!' Jess wailed. 'Oh, what's going to happen?' Peggy joined her at the window and they both saw the horse, its head raised, its nostrils flaring, making for a group of milk-boys.

They leapt out of the way and Dobbin turned blindly after them. Jess thought she heard people laughing, but it quickly changed to frightened screams and shouting as they tried to get out of the way. She saw Danny trip and fall, then the huge hooves poised above him. Her hand went to her mouth. In slow motion, it seemed, one of the hooves crashed sickeningly down on Danny's head, crushing it into the pavement.

Jess turned to Peggy, distraught at the sight. Peggy was still looking. 'That bugger Paddy!' she said. 'He must have let the horse out!'

'I don't think he's there. It's wee Danny! Someone's opened the door!'

'Aye, maybe.' She turned quickly from the window. 'Don't look. Did he not tie the beast up in its stall?'

Jess shook her head, speechless.

'That auld devil's gone away last night without lockin' up, the lazy bugger!' Peggy's vocabulary had early become rich because she liked to fraternise with the workers, much to their mother's displeasure.

'Oh, shut up! Shut up!' Jess pushed her aside. She had to look again. 'It's Danny, the wee milk-boy with the bare feet. I'm goin' to tell Mammy.'

She rushed into her mother's room where she was sitting up, bleary-eyed. 'What's all the commotion?'

'Dobbin's out! He's rushed up the street and knocked down wee Danny. Oh, come on, come on, we'll have to get a doctor for him!' Her legs gave way and she collapsed on the bed, sobbing. Her mother pushed her aside and got out of bed.

'Rin for the doctor instead of lyin' there bubblin'. Go on! Rin!'

When she got downstairs and into the street, two men who had been passing were carrying Danny into the stable. She followed and saw them lay him on a pile of straw. One of the milk-boys who had followed said, his voice shaking, 'His head's all mangled.' Another one – they were all there – joined in. 'Aye mangled to a pulp. That horse just went mad.'

She couldn't go near, nor even look; she was trembling, speechless. Then she remembered she had to get the doctor and took to her heels, crying all the way. The maid, a local girl, was haughty at first, then bending near Jess said, 'Are you the wee lass frae the creamery!'

'Yes. Never mind. He's got to come right away. It's Danny! The horse has kicked him. It's a ... matter of life and death.' The phrase had been in her mind for years. It was the first time she'd used it.

But it was a matter only of death. The two men had thrown an old coat over Danny's body. The blood had even soaked through that.

Twenty-Three

Jess went to work on Monday morning, a shadow still across her mind. It wasn't the tragedy of Danny's death which had driven their mother from 'the premises', but the bad feeling it created around them.

In a way, Jess thought, walking quickly up St Vincent Street along with the other office workers, Danny's death had been the catalyst. There were rumours, overheard remarks, a general feeling of hostility; it became a class thing, capitalists versus the proletariat.

'They', the Crichtons, had never known hard times. They could help themselves to anything in their shop. While everybody around was scraping to exist, they were living in the lap of luxury.

And why was the door of the stable unlocked in the first place? You couldn't put the blame on an old employee like Paddy. He should have been pensioned off long ago and a smart young man put in his place. But *she* wouldn't pay proper wages – that was the real reason.

Danny's parents were the prime agitators. Paddy kept a low profile, but Mrs High-and-Mighty, they said, knew he had staggered off the night before, the worse for drink, without tying up the horse or locking the stable door. And probably had forgotten to feed that poor old horse, making him raging mad. But *she* hadn't bothered.

The Gray brothers stepped in again. Robert had been like a son to them; they would do what they could for his wife. The court case had not found our mother culpable, but she agreed with the Grays to give Danny's parents a sum of money in recompense for their son's death. 'They'll drink it all in a week,' she said, but she'd had enough.

Jess felt stupidly embarrassed when she went into Sir Bernard's room for dictation. 'Good morning, Miss Crichton,' he said. She thought he gave her a quizzical look.

Had Giles gone to them for dinner on Sunday? Consommé, roast beef, home-made ice cream: 'Just a simple meal, Giles,' Aunt Emma – or whatever it was – would say when they were drinking their claret. 'Lovely, Aunt,' Giles would answer, laughing. 'I took that pretty little secretary of yours out for dinner, Uncle. Just a joke, really.' Sir Bernard had bushy grey eyebrows. Would they have risen in astonishment and would Aunt Emma say, 'Do you think Mummy would like that, Giles?'

But when she looked at him now and saw the sad cast of his face, and remembered he had recently lost his son, she felt he might well have said, 'Now, now, Emma.'

He didn't know that she knew they all used to go to Zell am See in Austria before Christmas each year on family ski-ing holidays, and at night watch the processions round the torchlit lake with the snow-covered mountains in the background. For some stupid reason her eyes suddenly flooded with tears at the beauty of it, and she fumbled for her handkerchief as she was taking notes.

'Have you a cold, Miss Crichton?' he asked kindly.

'Perhaps,' she said. 'I was sitting in the sunshine on Sunday, but it gets chilly in September. You don't notice, and then a little wind creeps up.' But she saw he wasn't listening. He was turning over his papers.

'Take a letter to Graveson and Co. There's the address.' He placed the letter in front of her. 'You write shorthand very fast,' he said.

Yes, I go to speed classes to improve it and I met your nephew there. And we're meeting again tonight. 'Thank you,' she said. 'I'm attending speed classes.'

'I admire your diligence. "Dear Mr Graveson, Regarding your letter of the twenty-ninth..." '

Miss MacDuff raised her head when Jess put the finished letters on her desk, which meant she had something to say to her. 'I have a note from Sir Bernard, Jess. He recommends a salary increase for you. It's not usual so soon, but he seems very pleased with your work.'

'Thank you, Miss MacDuff.'

'Yes, I must admit I was surprised. It's usually left to me, but...'

Had Giles said laughingly, 'Look here, Uncle, she's a decent little thing and if you saw the place she lives in! You couldn't see your way to giving her some more of the ready?' She knew she was making him sound like Bertie Wooster when he was nothing like him, but she worried about it all the way to the speed class and during it.

He wouldn't turn up – he would have thought better of it. She had just filled in a lonely evening for him during which he had learned that her mother was a widow and must be in straightened circumstances.

That thought made her feel miserable. She worked hard. Her mother had worked hard, and was still working. She didn't need charity. Her mind was still churning when she went out of the building and into Bothwell Street. The car was there, and Giles got out of it quickly when he saw her.

'I was terrified I had missed you,' he said. The sight of him made her feel so full of joy that she forgot all her doubts. He had wanted to see her.

'No, I kept an eye on the clock in the room. I got up exactly at seven.' She couldn't stop looking at him. There was a look of tenderness in his eyes. How could she have made him sound like Bertie Wooster?

'I'm so glad because I've just an hour. Look, I'll leave the car here and we'll walk round the corner to that pub in...'

'West Nile Street.'

'Whatever. And have a quick drink.'

'I've never been in a pub.'

'You can have a coffee. They aren't dens of iniquity. I don't like sitting with you in a car here. They'll think I've picked you up.'

'No,' she said. 'There aren't prostitutes here, at least not at this time.'

'You're sweet,' he said. She was beginning to realise he said that whenever she flummoxed him ... though anyone who worked in Glasgow soon recognised prostitutes. As long as you weren't taken for one, that was the main thing. 'All right?' He had locked the car and smiled ravishingly at her. 'Take my arm, Jess,' he said. 'It's more friendly.' It was. She had to take two steps to his one, which made her feel small and protected.

'It's wonderful to see you again.' They were in the pub. He found a table, left her there and was back in a few minutes with a cup of coffee and a glass. He saw her looking. 'Gin and lime,' he said. He slipped behind the table opposite her. 'I thought of you all Sunday. What did you do?'

'I tidied up at home then sat in the Park. Kelvingrove Park. What did you do?'

'Oh, I was working.'

'I thought you might have been at your uncle's.' She sipped her coffee giving him a limpid look.

'No, I was sent on an assignment to the Gallowgate with another chap. What a place that is! You wouldn't like to live there.'

She was immediately light-hearted. He hadn't spilled the beans to his uncle and he thought she lived in a much better place than the Gallowgate. 'No, I wouldn't,' she said.

'I have to tell you something.' He looked at her over his glass. She still hadn't decided what colour his eyes were because of their shadowed darkness. 'I'm spellbound by you. All Sunday in darkest Gallowgate. I've never felt like this before. I kept visualising you all the time, that peculiarly beautiful hair, or beautifully peculiar hair, which makes your eyes look like the deepest blue gentian. It's your innocence and yet your smartness – your mind is sharp for a girl – and there's your sense of humour.' He shook his head. 'You're ... tantalising! When I think of all the young men who must work in that office of yours, I don't know how you've escaped being snapped up by this time, but thank God you haven't.'

'There are hundreds like me in Glasgow,' she said. 'Thousands. It's you being English that makes me seem different to you.'

'I don't believe it. Your difference is ... different.'

'It's not a good enough reason. You're implying that if you went to Edinburgh tomorrow you'd fall in love with a girl there because she'd be different.'

'Don't be too smart. What I'm trying to say is that I've fallen in love with you.' She looked at him, straight-faced, trying to subdue her mouth, which was trembling.

'It's too soon.' She overdid the straight-facedness.

'No, it isn't. You can fall in love immediately, but it's only real if it's reciprocated.' His smile seemed sad. 'Is it, Jess? Look at me.'

She wanted to be honest. 'I've thought of you a lot. All yesterday afternoon when I was sitting in the Park. Meeting you was like finding something special, like walking in the street and coming across a diamond lying in the gutter ... but not sure if it's meant for you, or if you should pick it up.

Too good to be true.'

'You're a poet,' he said.

'I think I'm out of my head,' she said.

'If you're out of your head on coffee, what would you be like on gin? Shall I get you some?'

'No, thanks. What time have you got to be back?'

He glanced at his watch. 'Oh, God, in half an hour – worse luck. I've just time to take you home. Have you finished? I'm sorry to hurry you like this.'

'Yes.' She felt she had made a fool of herself talking like that about diamonds. And yet it was how she felt. There was a need to talk to Giles differently from the way she did to the clerks. 'I didn't come up the Clyde on a bicycle' kind of thing. With him she seemed to be testing herself against her feelings, trying to be sincere because it was important to be honest with him.

'What would you like to do when I get some real time off?' he asked as they were driving back along Bothwell Street. She was glad he had taken it for granted that there would be a next time.

'Drive into the country and walk through fields,' she said without hesitating.

'Really?' It was the voice of someone who didn't regard that as any kind of a treat. 'Do you know some country around Glasgow where we could do that?'

'There's Balloch,' she said. She had seen its fields from the train and there was a loch which was pretty much the same as an Austrian lake.

He didn't question her choice. 'Let's go to Ballock, then,' he said. She let him off with that.

When they arrived at her close he stopped the car and took her in his arms, not giving her time to tremble. 'Jess, Jess...' he said, kissing her. It was only dusk but she didn't worry, and he held her so tightly that she couldn't look up at the curtains. She was completely happy, slightly breathless, but he did the talking. 'It's amazing how I feel about you. So quickly. I longed for you all yesterday. It hurt. Who could have thought I would fall in love when I came here? "Glasgow?" I said when I got the job. "Oh, well, it will be good experience." My God, it is!'

It was becoming serious, she thought. Her heart was thumping against her ribs, his voice was shaking. He wanted more assurances, more loving. She wanted him never to leave her.

'I want you, Jess,' he said.

Her heart stopped for a second. Her head spun. No one had ever said that to her before. Fleur, she thought, her head still spinning, she was going to do a Fleur...

Twenty-Four

James seemed highly delighted with his visit to the Grays, and brought back an invitation for the three of them to go on Sunday. This pleased their mother, and she was in an equable frame of mind as she dished up toad-in-the-hole, her star turn.

'You look tired, Jess,' she said, which proved she was in a good mood. And if hearing the words, 'I want you, Jess,' constantly in her mind tired her, then she was tired.

'They've got five bedrooms,' James said. 'I get the run of the two attic ones and the telescope.'

'They're built for the gentry, you see,' his mother informed him. 'For business, but they usually had a country house at Kilmacolm or maybe the coast.'

'Can you see the Park? And the river, James?' Jess asked. *I want you...*

'It's a lot for Mrs Bell to clean, and she's no' so young.'

I want you Jess, want you, want you. 'I might not be able to go on Sunday,' she said.

'How would you no' be able to go?' Her mother's face clouded over. She pushed away her toad-in-the-hole pettishly.

'I might be going to Ballock,' she said.

'Where the devil's that?'

Jess laughed sheepishly, knowing her face was red. 'I meant Balloch! It's how this ... friend I told you about pronounces it. I wasn't thinking. He talked about taking me in his car there on Sunday, but he'll let me know.'

'It's how they talk, Ma. The English. We had great talks.' James was still with the Gray brothers. 'About the War that's coming.'

'How do they know it's comin'?' Their mother's good humour had been destroyed.

'They know. They read the papers every morning so that they're in touch with world affairs. We get told about the War at school. About the camps.'

'Boy Scouts? I always wanted you to join but you wouldn't. Not even the Cubs.'

'They look stupid. But when it's the OTC ... No, what they were talking about was the concentration camps. Hitler set them up.'

'For people against the régime,' Jess said. 'People just minding their own business but they call them Enemies of the State, Jews, Communists...' She thought of Sir Bernard's son. He had been fighting on the side of the Communists against Franco. She would have to read more.

'A don't know why they'd want to shut up Jews.' Their mother was still peeved. 'Harmless lot o' people, and they can make the money! See, on the trams they're dripping with furs and jewels, but nice with it.'

'The man they put in charge of the camp is called Himmler. And the camp's called Buchenwald, pronounced with a vee,' James informed his mother.

She turned to Jess, still peeved. 'Well, you'd better find out from your boss's nephew if you can go on Sunday ... What's his name?'

'Giles.'

'Giles! That's what they call prisons. Jiles!' James and Jess burst into laughter. 'That's Barlinnie, Ma,' he said.

'J-A-I-L-S.' Jess spelled it.

'Aye, laugh at your own mother! Giles, jails, what's the difference? Anyhow, you'd better find out when you're goin' to Ballock.' She was not without a sense of humour.

I want you, Jess ... She was in a state of love as she walked through the city, Giles smiling at her, his dark hair, his dark eyes, everything dark about him. That was why his smile had seemed so white. She wasn't impatient. She was ... receptive.

She looked upwards and admired the

255

Victorian ebullience of the buildings, the occasional experiments with the Gothic, the sturdy Edwardian edifices, somewhat Germanic – or was that because she had been thinking of Hitler looming over the world?

She noticed she was usually walking uphill or downhill and wondered if Glasgow was like Rome, which she had read was a city built on seven hills. Everything delighted her, even the flick of the pleats of her new suit against her calves, the sensuous feel of her Milanese stockings.

She accepted another small box of fudge from Dorothy in the office but declined an invitation to her wee flat in Garnethill beside the art school.

'I'm teaching most nights, Dorothy, and then there's my boyfriend...' She saw the woman's regretful look at the fudge and thought she was behaving wilfully, unpredictably, like someone in love.

She behaved in the same way with Jack Craven, who said how about another visit to Danny Brown's? 'I'm sorry. I'll be busy.' For the first time she saw the humour die in his eyes.

She went on Monday and Wednesday to the speed class, but Giles wasn't there, nor was he waiting outside in his car. She didn't go on Friday because she felt she would have been making herself cheap if she did. Her feeling of happiness disappeared.

Instead of a delightful wilfulness when she thought of Dorothy and Jack Craven, she merely felt mean.

She said to James when she was giving him his breakfast on Friday morning, 'Would you knock at the Grays' door on your way home from school and tell them we'd be pleased to come on Sunday?'

'Okay. So you're not going to Ballock?' It didn't make her smile.

'Not this Sunday,' she said. Her face ached with holding back the tears.

'Mr Peter's talking about getting a telephone.' Her heart lifted a little. She felt sure that she had once told Giles calls weren't allowed in the office, and he would know they didn't have a telephone at home. Their mother regarded that as particularly outlandish.

They set off on Sunday along Argyle Street past the Tallys, which had been a favourite of Peggy's. Mario had introduced a note of winter sophistication with saucers of hot peas swimming in a broth liberally flavoured with salt, pepper and vinegar. Jess and James were more addicted to double nougats.

She thought how her mother hadn't mentioned Peggy all week. Had Mrs Thompson given her some good advice? 'Now, Mrs Crichton, if I were you I should accept the situation. Even if she's ... you know ...

nobody's going to care. I've even seen announcements in the paper, "To Mr and Mrs So-and-So, a boy. Premature," when everybody can count...'

The close where the Grays lived was tiled with a fleur-de-lys pattern of green on cream, and the stairs had a polished mahogany rail. There was only one door to each landing, which meant that counting the ground floor there were four tenants in the building, whereas in theirs there were eight. In the Gallowgate which Giles had deplored, because of the preponderance of 'single ends' – one room only – there would be as many as sixteen tenants.

Mrs Bell greeted them at the door and led them along the hall, which had an oak table laden with brass ornaments. 'The devil to clean,' their mother had once remarked.

'It's the Crichtons,' Mrs Bell said, ushering them into the sitting room, but Jess noticed she had a special word for James as she took their coats. 'Back again, James? I think you like it here.'

The brothers were on their feet. Thomas held out his hand first. 'Come away in, Maggie. And Jess.' And Peter, coming forward, said, 'You won't want to sit with us, James. Away up and have a look at the telescope. But, remember, wait till I'm there.'

It was a pleasant room, not like what she thought Sir Bernard's would be. She saw it as a minor stately home with high ceilings and long windows looking out on to a shaved lawn – they were always shaved. The Grays had leather-upholstered chairs and a sofa, tables with magazines and books, oil paintings of the Highlands, and a smell of tobacco. For some reason there was a lady's fan opened on the mantelpiece – faded white silk with an equally faded pattern of rosebuds and edged with lace. Jess thought it must be a relic of Mr Peter's.

'How's Peggy getting on?' Mr Thomas asked their mother when they were seated. 'James was telling us she's married. That was sudden.'

'Yes.' Her reply was masterly. 'Practically eloped, you might say. These young ones! She was always headstrong, Peggy, and there was never anyone else for her but Noble, a childhood sweetheart.'

'What does he do?' This was an inescapable question in Glasgow.

'He's helping his aunt with her farm in Drumairn in Perthshire – her right-hand man. She's provided them with a house, so that's a blessing.'

'Well, all's well that ends well. We'll have to see about a present. But how about you, Jess?'

'Oh, I'm still a working girl!'

'She's keeping company with her boss's nephew,' her mother said, and not looking at her, added, 'Titled.'

'Well, that's good news.' They both nodded. Mr Peter said, 'You should stick in
there.' She had thought better of Mr Peter.
He looked at his brother and then at her
mother. 'Mrs Bell will take a wee time to
make the tea.'

Mr Thomas nodded and took over. 'James
says you're a bit tired of the dairy, Maggie,
now that Peggy's away.'

'Yes, I admit to it.' She nodded. 'But it's
doing well just now. Although I say it myself
I've a good business head. Peggy couldny
push trade like me. You've got to entice
them in, notices of offers in the window –
every customer likes a bargain or what she
thinks is a bargain.'

'Yes, you learned that in the East End. A
grand business that, if only ... Well, we
mustn't question the ways of the Almighty.'

'I'm still a fairly young woman, and look
even younger than my age, so they tell me...'
She paused. The brothers only nodded
gravely. 'But I must admit I sometimes
wonder if running the shop is too much for
me. It's the turning out every mornin' that I
find the hardest, standing in the cold and
dark winter mornings waiting for a tram. It's
not easy.'

'You're right. Peter and I are lucky living
on our capital. But first we had to make it.
Now we make it work for us with the help of

the *Financial Times.*'

'Robert was good at that. Even when he was dead tired that pink paper was out and he was poring over it before he went to bed.'

'That was evident, when you think he was only under ten years in that business and yet he was able to leave you nicely provided for.'

'I wish he was here all the same.' She didn't meet Jess's eyes.

'Yes, you've had a hard time. Mrs Bell, now, she's an old woman compared with you, seventy on her next birthday. She suffers from varicose veins and she says standing on her feet cooking is the worst thing for them.'

'She should try standing behind a counter all day. Though a'm lucky there. I've still got a good pair of legs.' She stretched her ankles. The brothers studiously avoided looking. Mr Peter gave a nod to his brother. Thomas turned towards her.

'Now, Maggie, I want you to hear me out. This is something we'd like you to turn over in your mind. Peter and I are wedded to this flat, until we're carried out feet first.' She made a deprecating noise. 'All our possessions are here. We can't be parted from them, a lifetime of memories. Mrs Bell would like to retire any time now, and we would be willing to set her up in a wee place somewhere. She would like Helensburgh and we're not averse to that. Property keeps its value there. Now that Peggy's in her own nest, and Jess on her way to hers by all accounts, would you consider taking Mrs Bell's place, at your convenience ... and hers, of course?'

She looked at him and then at Jess with a flabbergasted expression. 'Well, that's a surprise! You never know what a day will bring! But it's worth thinking about. It's not a money-spinner, this shop, and it's a long road to go when the weather's bad. With the premises I was—'

'On the premises,' Jess said. Both men laughed.

'She's got a sense of humour like Robert,' Peter said. 'That quiet word when you least expect it.'

'Aye, you never knew what he was thinking,' she agreed.

'So you think the proposition worth thinking about?' Mr Thomas said. He was the one who got to the point.

'Aye, I do. It depends on a lot of things. James, Jess, the shop...'

'James would come with you, of course. He likes it here. He's free to come and stay any time even now. And as for Jess, she has her own future ahead of her. I don't think she wants to live at home any longer than she can help ... Don't get me wrong, Maggie, but you know what I mean.'

'Oh, Jess will marry well. She's always

been the bright one. She's not likely to throw herself away on just anybody. How about the shop? Would you be able to get rid of it for me, supposing I was coming here?'

'Yes, we sold it to you; we can take it off you. Don't let that get in the way of your decision.' She nodded, lips pursed, a businesswoman. She would run the brothers' house in the same way, Jess thought. Maybe they would teach her to read and understand the *Financial Times*.

'I must admit I'm sorely tempted. We'll see how Mrs Bell goes on...' Mrs Bell came in.

'The tea's ready,' she said, standing with her arms across her bosom. 'Is the fire all right?'

'Fine. Peter's just been stoking it.' Mr Thomas got up.

'And how's your health these days, Mrs Bell?' their mother said. 'Are your legs still giving you trouble?'

Twenty-Five

Everyone's life was being sorted out except hers, thought Jess.

But then she remembered how Giles' voice had trembled when he'd said he loved her. There would be an explanation. She would just have to wait.

She was her usual efficient self when she went to take dictation from Sir Bernard on Monday morning. 'Good morning, Miss Crichton. Please sit.'

She sat and watched his face for signs as he turned over his letters. *I'm worried about Giles, Sir Bernard. I haven't heard from him for a week. Have you seen him?* He raised his eyes and rested them on her consideringly. He's wondering how to·tell me. Her heart seemed to come to a stop, juddered; she was in a hiatus of suspense and fear.

'Take a letter to the Zeiss Foundation.' Her face had just been a convenient hitching post.

In the evening she walked up the hill to Sauchiehall Street and sat in La Scala Café,

264

ordered a coffee, left it untouched for half an hour, and then walked purposefully down to Bothwell Street. Jack Craven depended on her. She would go to her speed class.

The car was at the kerb when she came out of the building after an hour, and she went into his arms as he opened the door and came towards her. She hid her face in his shoulder and wept. She wept in Bothwell Street in full view of passing cars and people, who didn't seem to find it strange to see a girl weeping in a man's arms. Giles held her closely.

'My dearest darling.' He was laughing. 'This is terrible! It's all my fault too. Come into the car.' She let him shepherd her in and take his place at the wheel beside her.

'I'm sorry. Making a fool of myself.' She laughed shakily at him as she wiped her eyes. 'But, where were you?'

'I had to go home quickly. Mother had a relapse after an operation, a hysterectomy, and the old boy went off the rails. Summoned Harriet and me.'

'Is she all right now?'

'Yes. It was just a temporary rise in her temperature. She was cross at him summoning us. Harriet said he was like a thwarted Shakespearean actor being deprived of his deathbed scene.'

'He was worried.' Harriet sounded hard –

probably worked in London, dark hair, long legs, painted nails. 'I'm glad she's better.'

'Oh, yes, she's as tough as old boots. But there was no way I could have got in touch with you.' There was Uncle Bernard, she said as a joke to herself.

'I thought you had decided not to see me again.'

'That's the last thing.' He put an arm round her and looked steadily at her. 'I told you. I'm crazy about you. I want you.' They were both trembling.

He ran her home and said they would have to do something about it. 'I haven't any time off just now, but we must meet as soon as possible,' he said.

'There's Balloch. We talked about it.'

'Oh, yes, Ballock.' His smile ravished her, as always. 'I had forgotten you wanted green fields and locks.' Her love turned to tenderness at that.

As soon as they could arrange it there were the green fields and the lochs, the slender beech trees bordering it ... but while he seemed happy he wasn't enthusiastic.

There was the fun they had rowing – he was hopeless, whereas her many years of practice on Hogganfield Loch came in handy. And there was the added advantage that while rowing she could look at his dark handsome face, darker because of his white open-necked shirt.

She sang to him without any trace of shyness as she rowed, 'Oh, ye'll tak' the high road and I'll tak' the low road...' but when she came to the bit where it said, 'But me and my true love will never meet again...' her eyes filled with tears and she looked away over the water to hide them.

'You're tired of rowing on the lock,' he said. 'Let's go and have tea.'

'Yes, let's,' she said, to the manner born.

They had afternoon tea in the parlour of a lochside hotel, where the wee maid was rendered speechless by Giles – or his voice. The rest of the afternoon they spent lying on his raincoat under some bushes because the rain came on when they were walking and they had to find shelter.

They were soaked to the skin in soft Balloch rain, and in the car going back he took her hand while he was driving and said, 'Well, I've seen Lock Lomond.' She was unaccountably sad with frustrated passion and tried to rid her mind of the song.

She told him about the possibility of her mother becoming a housekeeper to the Grays, and he brightened and said in that case she must get a flat of her own in the city. She saw herself becoming like his sister, Harriet, hard – with a cigarette between her painted lips.

'You'd love London,' he said. 'I had to see a man there on my way back – an appointment my father had fixed up for me. The bustle and the excitement, especially at night with the lights and the theatre crowds...'

She'd thought Glasgow had all that.

Their meetings were scrappy due to the demands of their work, but when they had longer they drove into the country to hotels like the Bailie Nicol Jarvie – he called them pubs – which he quickly became familiar with. Money never seemed to be a problem ... his frustration was. She sensed it when they kissed, an impatience – kissing was not enough.

She realised that his temperament was not restful, he had a driving kind of energy which she saw in his work, his concentration on speed writing, on photography. He wanted to become a war correspondent, he wanted her ... She didn't know which was the more important.

She felt, for her, that she behaved in an abandoned fashion because of her love. Now she could understand Peggy and why she had moved out. How long would it take her to break with convention?

But in spite of Giles and her love for him, she sat and passed her two hundred words a minute speed certificate in November. Jack Craven gave her an increase in salary, but he didn't suggest a celebration. When she looked in the mirror she saw a girl in love, sometimes eyes which were black-ringed, a mouth which was supple and even seductive. Perhaps he saw the same.

Twenty-Six

When Giles met her outside the office one evening he kissed her in the street as usual – which still embarrassed her as being un-Scottish – and said, 'Jess,' touching her hair lovingly. 'I've only got two hours off. I was thinking...'

They were walking towards his car and she braced herself. *You said you would ask him. Do you not want us to see this marvel? Is it that we're not good enough for him?* 'Mother has asked me to bring you home for tea tonight, Giles.' He didn't reply until he had seated himself beside her.

'I had other plans. I want to be alone with you.' His wistful look nearly broke her heart.

'I've promised her, you see.' She thought of the plaice lying ready by this time, dipped in egg and orange-coloured breadcrumbs. When she looked at him again his face was sullen.

'I'm no good at that sort of thing,' he said. 'Mothers...'

'Don't worry. It doesn't commit you to

anything ... Just this once...' She leant against his shoulder, deliberately seductive. 'A short visit, that's all.'

'You're a siren,' he said, brightening. 'And I love you madly. All right. Just this once, and remember you'll have to make it up to me the next time.'

'I promise,' she said, dreading the whole business.

Her mother was dressed smartly: she had used Jess's lipstick, and her hair was Marcel waved. It struck her not for the first time what a personable woman she was. James was there, and he took Giles into the front room at their mother's request – 'Show him your school books' – while she and Jess went to the kitchen to cook the fish.

'I've dipped the fish in egg and bread-crumbs.'

'You said you would.'

'He's quite a nice-looking lad.' She set the frying pan on the hob. 'And that voice. It's like the man on the wireless.'

'I told you. He's English.'

'Are you sure he's no' puttin' it on?'

'No, he talks like that all the time.'

'I've got a bottle of tomato sauce there, or would he like HP sauce? Put them both on the table in case.'

'You don't put sauce bottles on the table. Have you a jug?'

'On the shelf there. We've always put them

271

on the table before.' She hated being corrected. 'I've got chips in the oven. Are you sure that's all right for your fancy English friend?'

'Mother. Have you a lemon?'

'Oh, aye. A know all about slices of lemon with fish. They give you that at Craig's in all their tea rooms. A'm not a fool, you know.'

'What do you think of him, Mother?'

'He's a gentleman, I'll say that. It would be a shot in the eye for Mrs Thompson if you got tied up wi' the likes o' him, not to mention the Grays. If you were getting engaged I can just see him being asked to the Mansions.' She turned, brandishing a knife. 'The fish is ready.'

'Put them on that plate, then, with the slices of lemon. I'll get the chips.'

'Are you sure you wouldn't like me to have a pipe band playing?' Jess laughed and gave her a playful push.

Giles pulled out a chair for their mother, saw her seated, and when served, was fulsome in his praise for the fish.

'Plaice,' she said. 'You can't beat it for flavour.'

'I'm told Glasgow is the best place for plaice,' he said, darting a laughing glance at James. They seemed to have got on well. She didn't see the joke.

'Aye, we have some fine fish restaurants, not to mention fish and chip shops, but

272

you'll not be acquainted with that kind o' thing.'

'Oh, yes, one of the office boys runs out for them when we're working. I'm told if they're wrapped in the *Sunday Post* they have a better flavour.'

'Aye, as long as you don't forget a good shake o' vinegar. Jess'll bring you some if you like.' She laughed as she spoke, and Jess, looking at her, thought, she misses male company. She used to enjoy Noble.

'Where do you stay?' she asked. Giles looked puzzled for a second. 'My hotel's in West George Street.'

'No, I mean in England.'

'Oh ... *live*! Lyndhurst in East Sussex. A one-horse place compared with Glasgow.'

'Oh, aye, I've never been there.' She had never even been out of Scotland. 'Is it nice?'

'I suppose so. One tends to leave home, of course.'

'Aye, an' get married. Peggy's husband is a farmer away in Perthshire. Nicely settled, she is. It's nice to get your girls settled.'

'I'm sure it is. Lovely fish. And your sauce ... delicious.'

'Jess put it in a jug. It looks better. What does your father work at?'

'He's a publisher in London.'

'Books and things?'

'Yes, mostly non-fiction.'

'Would you like to do that?'

'Eventually, yes. There's a place for me in the firm.'

'Would you like to do that, James?' She turned to Giles. 'You can learn to do anything at the Academy, Mr...' She hesitated.

'Call me Giles,' he said. 'Jess does.' He kept his face straight.

'Giles is going to be a war correspondent,' James told her. 'I'd like that better than books.'

Jess shook her head. 'No, you want something steady, James. Wars come and go.' She met Giles's eyes.

'She's right, you know,' said James.

'Yes, it's a point.' Giles considered his fork, raised it, speared a piece of plaice, and topped it with a chip.

He excused himself when they had finished, saying that his time was limited. He was profuse in his thanks, and Jess could see that her mother was impressed by him.

'You're welcome to come any time with Jess,' she said. 'She's a clever lass, you know.' Jess looked down.

In the dark lobby he held her close and kissed her. His mouth tasted of fried fish. Probably hers did as well. Still, the visit had been a success. 'Did I pass?' he asked her.

'Just hold me,' she said. 'Don't talk.'

Her mother suddenly appeared at the door of the kitchen. 'What was the name of that place you stay at, Mr ... Giles?'

274

'Lyndhurst, Mrs Crichton,' he called.

'My friend across the road's interested in places.' She went back into the kitchen. In a second or two they heard her shouting from there. 'Jess! Where did you put the fish slice?' Her allotted time was up.

'Goodnight, Mrs Crichton,' Giles called. 'Lovely meal.'

'He's not bad,' said her mother when Jess went into the kitchen and lifted a tea towel.

'You liked him, then?' It had been no good – both were frustrated. But Giles had played his part, been charming ... although she knew he wouldn't come again.

'Aye, he's gentry all right. Ma mother had gentry next door to them in the country, a real titled lady, but a fearful howthery creature, she was. She used to leg it over our fence at the back for a short cut to the road, and mother said the lace was all torn on her drawers. But you can aye tell gentry when you meet them. I always thought you would climb up the ladder. Had it in you. Just like your father, genteel, nothing common about him. Not like Peggy.'

'She's happy. And Noble's a fine young man. Sometimes I envy Peggy her life.'

'Never!' Her mother looked astonished as she rubbed briskly at the ashets which had held the chips. 'What for would you envy Peggy? She'll be trachled wi' bairns till she's past havin' them. An' Noble'll become a

275

boozer, mark my words.' Jess thought she might be right.

At Christmas Jess offered to take her and James to visit Peggy. Although her mother was childishly excited – she had never stayed in a hotel before – it didn't prevent her from commenting on the fact that Giles was going home.

'I thought he would have taken you with him to introduce you to his family. That's the usual thing.'

'He's interested in his career, Mother. I'm interested in mine. I might even do more work in the College. Mr Craven would like that. Giles's mind is occupied with the thought of a coming war. Do you never read the papers? There's more to life, you know, than our own petty concerns.' Her mother gave this odd creature she had spawned a look of disdain.

The journey to Perth was an eye-opener for the three of them. The panorama of mountains was different from the Clyde coast, far grander, far bleaker, although the stone houses in the towns were elegant, and the occasional castle lofty and turreted. The churches were spired and frequent. It was another world. 'It's different,' her mother said, nodding approval.

She got into conversation with a woman beside her, but it came to an end rather abruptly when the woman commiserated with her in having to live in such a dirty, smoky place as Glasgow. James, however, was lost in admiration. Some of the older boys at school went on to finish at Glenalmond, the Perthshire school, where there was ski-ing. The pupils were tougher there, he said, and wore the kilt. We're the same, Jess thought; his horizons are widening.

Peggy had a slight air of defiance when she opened the door, but seemed glad to see them. Noble was welcoming, because it was his nature – easy-going, secure in himself and his place in the world.

'Well, Mrs Crichton,' he said. 'How do you think Peggy's looking?' He had sat her down in front of a hot peat fire in the kitchen.

'When's the bairn due?' she asked, looking at her daughter.

'Early in the spring,' Peggy said, raising her chin.

'How have you been keeping, Peggy?' Jess asked her.

'Not bad. And a'm livin' the life of Riley here. Noble's handy, sets the fire going for me before I get up in the morning, chops wood, washes up after our meal at night. And I've got good neighbours not so far away.'

'Is the village near?'

'Only about a mile. Folks think nothing of walkin' there, or cycling, and you can always

277

get a lift from one of the farm wagons.'

'How about Noble's uncle and aunty?' their mother wanted to know.

'They're busy with their own affairs, but they've given Noble work and this cottage, even furnished it wi' a few bits from their own. You can't say fairer than that.'

'No, you can't.' Their mother looked around with grudging approval.

What touched Jess was how happy Peggy and Noble looked. If it had been a rushed marriage it had been a willing one on both sides. Their eyes met frequently and lovingly, and Noble was attentive to her wants. 'Let me, Peggy,' he would say, jumping up if she moved. They had been meant for each other since his pin-dropping days.

But Giles ... life with him would be different. If there ever was a life with him. But equally, she told herself, Peggy's life wouldn't satisfy you. How did this strange dichotomy arise between two daughters from the same parents?

Noble took James for a walk up the hillside and the three women settled round the fire. Peggy described the pleasures of her new life, the neighbourliness, the occasional visits to Perth for shopping. 'I'm settled for life here,' she said. The challenging, fiery look her sister used to wear had changed to a soft, satisfied contentment. 'It's what Noble and me want.'

Before they went away, their mother, as if to reassert herself, dropped her bombshell. 'James and me will be goin' to stay wi' the Grays soon. Mrs Bell wants to give up, and I'll take her place. There will be a young lass to help me, and James likes it there. He'll have the top flat. He's got Academy friends. What's the name of that one you like, James, the one that comes about the Mansions?'

'Jock.' But he doesn't bring him home, Jess thought. He's establishing a bachelor existence for himself and his friends in those airy attics overlooking the Park.

'What about you?' Peggy looked at Jess.

'Oh, Jess is goin' steady with her boss's nephew,' their mother answered. 'A don't think it will be long before they get spliced.' Peggy looked at Jess again.

'The boss's nephew?'

'Titled, the boss,' their mother added.

'A dare say. Well. Born lucky.' But Peggy's face was set in soft curves of contentment.

'Mother's jumping the gun as usual.' Jess felt she had to say it. 'Giles – that's his name – wants to be involved in the War when it comes. That's first with him.'

'She's always on about this.' Their mother looked impatient.

'She's right,' Peggy said, surprisingly. 'We've talked about it. Noble's lucky. He's registered as a farm labourer, so he'll be exempt, like munition workers and that.

Aye, he'll be all right.' She nodded.

If she's smug, she has a right to be, Jess thought later on as they filed down the garden path and through the gate set in the white picket fence to the taxi which was waiting to take them back to their hotel. When she looked back they were standing at the door waving, smiling, Noble's arm round his wife's shoulders.

The visit was judged a success by their mother as the three of them travelled back by train to Glasgow, bearing their spoil – a fresh chicken, a dozen eggs, and a pot of grease from the Christmas goose which had been Noble's aunt's gift, 'for your chest in winter'. 'They're still in the backwoods,' their mother commented. 'Has the aunty not heard o' kaolin poultice?'

At the Christmas dinner Noble, glass in hand, had given them a fine rendering of *The Lass o' Killiecrankie*, swaying dangerously until Peggy had told him to sit down.

'How did you enjoy yourself, James?' Jess asked him. The eyes he turned on her were those of a young man.

'Have you ever read that poem of Burns', *The Cotter's Saturday Night*?' She nodded.

'What has that to do with it?' their mother asked.

Twenty-Seven

1939

'It's so good to see you, Giles,' Jess said. She leant forward and touched his cheek. She had to reassure herself that he still existed.

'Christmas was miserable without you,' he said, with a little-boy dark gaze. 'Oh, we had the usual things, of course. Harriet with her new man – a different one every Christmas – and our annual Christmas walk through the woods. And calling on neighbours on the way home. But people were sombre. "Hitler's on the warpath now," everybody was saying. Harriet's friend said they were going to hand out bomb shelters in London any minute now. It quite upset Mother. Reminded her of the last one, I expect ... with Father away.'

'How is she?'

'Looking older, I thought, but fine. Said, why hadn't I brought you along.'

'Does she know about me?'

'Oh, yes, she always quizzes me about my

281

latest. How did you get on?'

'I enjoyed it.' His latest? 'They seem very happy. Peggy's pregnant. And Noble's exempted, being a farm worker.'

'They're lucky. No worries.' She waited. 'You know this is a temporary job on the paper?'

'Yes, I know.'

'Sometimes I think, if I got fixed up permanently somewhere, then you and I...' She heard distinctly her heart thumping, although they were in a busy cinema café, with music, people talking, the clatter of laden trays. 'But if I were a war correspondent, I'd be moving all over and it wouldn't be much fun for you...' The dark gaze was on her, brooding.

She was suddenly sick with love. It made her blurt out, 'If ... we were married?'

He looked doubtful. 'Look at Roger ... I mean, if you're a war correspondent you're likely to be killed, and then it's hard luck on the wife. A wasted death, Roger's, when you come to think of it, considering Franco's on the point of strutting into Barcelona.'

'People get killed in wars but it doesn't stop them marrying. My cousin, Nessie, has a boyfriend in the Territorials and he wants them to get married before it starts.'

'It sounds selfish to me. It's not that I don't want to. I'm absolutely crazy for you...' She had a wave of Fleur-like faintness

282

again, and thought, what am I pretending to myself for? He wants me but he doesn't want to get married.

'It's the very devil,' he said. His sad smile ravished her, and she was tongue-tied. 'I shall be glad when I'm old and withered and can't *feel*. Come on, let's get out of this place. Would you like to go to the cinema?'

'I don't mind,' she said, rising. 'Anything.' She felt a sick-making sadness because all she wanted was to be somewhere with Giles where they could be close and private.

They were passing a corner when he said, 'Down there is where my hotel is.'

'Bath Street?'

'No, nearer your office. West George Street.'

'Is it?' In spite of their Christmas expedition she still thought it quite exotic to stay in a hotel. 'What's it like?'

'It's all right. Mediocre, really. It's owned by the fearsome Miss Gallacher, who looks after her "gentlemen", as she calls them, fairly adequately. Except for me, they're mostly commercial travellers. Would you like to see it?'

Was this a plan? 'Wouldn't she mind?'

'I'm sure she wouldn't. Actually she's spending a few days with her sister in Tiny Brewick, she informed me. Is there another place called Large Brewick?'

'You're pulling my leg. It's Tighnabruich.'

She spelled it for him.

'Well, anyhow, if you've any qualms, she's not there. Just two maids – sisters, Annie and Lizzie, who aren't interested in me. They prefer commercial travellers.'

'All right, I'd like to see it. Then I can picture you.'

The hotel was tall and narrow, squeezed between some office buildings with a flight of steps leading up to a heavy black door graced with carriage lamps and an impressive brass knocker. Giles opened it with a key and they stepped into a narrow hall which was empty and dimly lit.

They went upstairs together. She walked quietly, but in any case the stairs were thickly carpeted. The walls were covered with dark maroon flock wallpaper, and the wall lights had maroon accordion pleated shades.

'When I leave I'm going to advise Miss Gallacher to change her decor. It's too brothel-like.' He ushered her into a large room at the top of the stairs with a bed occupying a good part of it, but leaving room for a sofa in front of a gas fire, which he lit. The curtains, heavy maroon velvet, were drawn, possibly by Annie or Lizzie.

'Let me help you off with your coat.' He was airy. 'Sit down, Jess.' They sat on the sofa. 'Well, this is my humble abode.' He smiled at her. 'How do you like it?'

'Cosy. As snug as a bug in a rug.' She trotted that out to amuse him.

'Would you like me to order coffee?'

'No, thanks. I'm not staying, Giles. It's just a wee look...' He took her in his arms.

'Just a wee look...' He kissed her, and, overcome with the sweetness of it, she put her hands on the back of his head.

'I missed you so much at Christmas. It hurt.'

'You're so sweet. What are we going to do about it? I missed you all the time.' He gently pushed her against the end of the sofa and they fell back together. They were lying askew. Her feet were still on the floor. 'I want you so badly, Jess.' His face was against hers. She felt one of his hands on her breast.

'I know.'

'I'm nearly falling off this damned sofa.' It was of the chaise longue variety. He pulled her to her feet, still holding her. 'Let's lie on the bed.'

'Do you think we should?'

'There's no law against it.' He was laughing at her.

'I'm only here for a minute. Supposing Annie—'

'Or Lizzie? They're busy themselves.'

'With Miss Gallacher being away in Tiny Brewick?' She was joking too, to hide the tremors running through her.

They lay stretched out, facing each other, and when she met his look he pulled a comical face. 'You aren't sinning against the Holy Ghost, you know. Don't feel guilty.'

'It's stupid, I know.' She tried to explain. 'The room is strange to me, and it's a hotel.'

'Forget it.' He sounded impatient and his kiss was now hard, fierce; his hands ran down her sides, under her skirt – everything he did she wanted him to do. A very demanding kind of tremor was now following one of his hands which had moved searchingly downwards. This tremor to end all tremors – demanding, impatient – frightened her so much with its intensity that she rolled away from him, panting. 'I'll have to go home,' she said.

He lay looking at her, unsmiling, then slowly got to his feet. 'Sternly Scottish Jess. Ah, well, if you must, you must.'

She walked shakily to the sofa and put on her coat. Mr Anderson, strangely, came to mind as she did so. It couldn't have been far from here. 'I feel stupid now.'

'Never mind. I'll take you home.'

'The big picture would have been over anyhow,' she said, clowning, but disappointed that he hadn't tried to persuade her to stay. She got up, buttoning her coat.

He came to where she was standing and held her loosely and without passion in his arms. 'Don't lie awake castigating yourself.'

He looked at her and sighed, a kind of 'is-it-worth-it' sigh. 'Right. Let's go.' He released her, and she felt discarded. In the car before she got out she turned to him.

'I'm sorry I behaved so stupidly.'

'It doesn't matter. Only don't think I planned it, luring you to my lair. It was a whim of the moment.' She kissed him, but his lips were cool.

Her mother was sitting in the kitchen having a last cup of tea. Jess thought she looked lonely. In books, especially in the Forsyte world, she would have put an arm round her and said, 'Darling Mummy. I'm so much in love, it frightens me...'

'Whit's wrang that you're in early?' said her mother. 'Has he ditched you?' She wished, as she poured herself a cup of tea from the pot, that she had allowed herself to be seduced.

In bed she thought about the evening. You made a fool of yourself, she thought, because your thought processes are like a badly knitted jumper. Best thing you could do is to rip it out and start all over again. Probably everyone has worked it out for themselves then gone ahead, even Miss MacDuff. She tried to imagine Miss Mac-Duff with her golden wig unbunned lying in bed with a man, but couldn't. Maybe the whole world's at it, she thought, and you're the simpleton.

Perhaps she imagined it in the days that followed, but Giles seemed cooler towards her. It might have been the general atmosphere. People looked grimmer, the papers were full of conjecture, Giles's mind was constantly on the coming war. He talked about it endlessly.

'You didn't waste much time saying goodnight the night,' her mother said to her one evening. She must have been behind the curtain. 'But don't think you can hoodwink me by running up the stairs two at a time when he's kept you oot till aw oors. Where were ye?'

'At the pictures. It was a long one. Then we had a late supper.' She felt weary, almost out of love.

'Whit was it called?'

They had in fact gone for a run southwards out of the city. Giles had taken a liking for speeding along country roads in the dark. They had got out and walked on the moors above Carmunnock and then lain on their backs in a hollow in the short turf to look at the stars. It was too cold for passion.

'Can you imagine these skies full of bombers?' he had said. 'I can almost hear their heavy drone. Roger said in a letter once how menacing it was. I'm sorry I won't get to Catalonia ... where he was.'

'Why?' She knew her voice was short. 'You

might not have been here if you had.'

'I wanted to avenge his death.' They were quiet after that.

'It was the new Walt Disney,' she now said to her mother, the lie tripping lightly from her lips. 'But we sat through almost twice because Giles wanted to see the *Pathetone News* again.'

'Funny, that.' And then quietly for her, she added, 'You're really going steady with Thingummy?' She could never say 'Giles' without laughing.

'Giles, Mother. Giles Imrie. It's quite an ordinary name. You've met him. And you liked him. Yes, I'm going steady. I hope. At least he's the only one I go out with, if that's what you mean by steady.'

'A like things in the open. You never know when a'm maybe going to the Grays, and movin' oot from here with James. Peggy's nicely settled noo.' She had evidently stopped worrying about Peggy. 'If a knew where a wis wi' you...'

'Do you want me to ask him what his intentions are?'

'It widny be a bad idea.'

'We've been over this before. His job is temporary. He might suddenly leave. Join up.' She was making Giles's excuses for him.

'Would he ask you to marry him, then?'

'Oh, I don't know, Mother! There's a war coming! You know that as well as I do!' She was angry because she was miserable.

'None o' your lip.' And then in a ladylike tone: 'Well, Mrs Thompson is impressed. She says she's seen the motor at the close, and once when she just happened to be looking out of the windy she was real struck by the way he helped you out. Well, he's the boss's nephew, a told her.' Jess smiled, shaking her head. In her own way her mother was trying to further her romance, God help her.

The inevitable declaration of war only made Giles even more single-minded about his plans. Although he was as loving, and as loveable, as ever, his free time was limited; he was busier than ever at work, and outside that he was concentrating on perfecting his photographic and reporting skills. Had it not been for his single-mindedness and constant talk about the War, Jess would have scarcely been aware of it – at least in Glasgow – except for a stringent blackout and the issue of gas masks.

And there was his new liking for driving hard out of the city with her and stopping for a drink at any outlying hotel they came upon. One evening he was unlucky in his choice of a stopping place, a garish roadside pub near Edinburgh full of noisy people who were there to drink rather than eat. The menu was mediocre and the service slipshod. What he preferred was an intimate atmosphere, subdued decor and lighting, quiet but efficient waiters.

They left early, and as he drove swiftly homewards, she kept quiet. She had a feeling of foreboding. He's fed up with Glasgow, she thought, perhaps of me. He'll be leaving soon, and I'll lose him. My heart will be broken.

He suddenly swerved off the main road and drove down a side road overhung by trees, which soon dwindled into little more than a path. He stopped and turned to her.

'I'm behaving badly. I was in a filthy temper when we left that place.'

'Never mind.' She went into his arms, thinking it wasn't only the place – it was the climate the War had created, of uncertainty, of restlessness, of an inability to see into the future.

They were suddenly kissing and fondling each other in a kind of desperation. Nothing mattered. Only the two of them now...

There was a sudden violent knocking at the car window on her side, and she turned, terror-stricken. She saw the face of a man peering in only a foot away from her. His mouth was flattened horribly against the glass, and she saw the shape of the words he was mouthing against it. 'Dirty f———s!'

'Jesus Christ!' It was Giles's voice, ugly, unfamiliar. 'I'll take the grin off that

291

bastard's face!' He was opening the door as he shouted.

'Don't go out!' She held on to his arm. 'Leave it!' She turned, still holding him, and saw the grinning face had gone. 'He isn't there now, Giles. Calm down.'

He didn't answer. He sat silently, his head bent, breathing quickly. After a time, still without speaking, he started up the car and drove along the lane until he found a farm gate, where he turned. In a few minutes he had gained the main road.

He scarcely spoke until they had reached Glasgow. Driving through the centre towards her flat he said quietly, 'That was horrible for you. Dirty...'

'Don't think about it.' It was true, though: she felt dirty. There was no future in speeding to sleazy hotels with him, sitting petting in his car. No future. He was desperate to get away, to be involved in the War, not marking time in Glasgow with her.

'I wouldn't have had it happen to you for the world.'

'I told you. It's not important,' she lied.

She heard him sigh. 'Not the best of evenings.' She bit her lip, her throat filling with tears. She turned to him.

'Goodnight, Giles,' she said, and kissed him on the cheek. 'I love you.' He took her hand, held it silently for a few seconds, then let her go.

'I've been waiting for you,' her mother said when she went into the kitchen. She looked excited. 'You'll never guess! Mrs Bell was givin' the attic a clean and she fell doon the stairs. She's broken her leg!'

'My goodness!' Jess sat down at the table. 'What an upset for them. Where is she?'

'She's been taken to the Western. The brothers want me to come right away and run the house for them until she's able to come back.'

'But what about ... here?' She kept her face straight in order not to show her delight.

'James will come with me.' Even her mother's diction had changed. 'He's nearer the Academy there and he likes it any roads ... but there's not enough room for you. Well, there's a limit.'

'I can quite easily stay here. Keep an eye on the house till you come back.' She hoped she sounded non-committal.

Her mother's brows were drawn together. 'Mrs Thompson would give you your tea, wash your sheets.' She always presumed Mrs Thompson was at her beck and call.

'You don't have to ask help from Mrs Thompson, or anybody for that matter. I'm perfectly capable. Besides, Mrs Bell will be back before long.'

'Aye, that's right. They bump them oot.

Well, I suppose you could stay here on your own for a week or so. I wouldn't have trusted Peggy, but after all...'

He's the boss's nephew, Jess finished for her silently.

'But, mind – no comin' in late or bringin' anybody back wi' you.'

'I wouldn't dream of it,' she said.

She was like a bird that had been let out of its cage. The freedom to do as she liked was so pleasurable that she didn't think of the other advantages immediately. But, of course, if she felt like inviting Giles to come up she would – her fingers had been crossed behind her back.

Nessie was waiting for her when she came out of the office the following day. 'Hello, Nessie!' she greeted her. 'It's been a long time.'

'I've been busy. Jess, we're getting married. Bob's been given married quarters at Maryhill Barracks! Will you be a bridesmaid? His sister's bein' the other one.'

'All right. But I thought you said you'd wait.'

'It's too good a chance to miss.' Jess thought she turned her chin away.

'Have you time for a coffee? Or better still, could you come home with me and have your tea?'

'Your mother wouldny like that. Her and Ma never got on.'

294

'She's gone to housekeep for the Grays ... you know, they were my father's friends. Their housekeeper has fallen and broken her leg. We could have a good chinwag.'

'Oh, that's different, then. Aye, that would be great. A've got a lot to tell you.'

They settled down at the kitchen table with a pile of fish and chips, a plate of bread and butter, and a large pot of tea.

'This isn't the kind of meal I have with Giles,' Jess said, and could have bitten out her tongue.

'Oh, aye. Where does he stay in Glasgow, then?'

'In a hotel. I think his parents must help him with it.'

'You've landed yourself well and no mistake. Has he proposed yet?'

'Every time I see him!' she joked. 'No, it isn't possible for the time being. He's mad keen on becoming a war correspondent. He'd have to go wherever they sent him.'

'So have soldiers.'

'Yes, that's true.'

'Ah, well, maybe he's no' the settlin' doon type. Just wants a good time wherever he is. Bob's the opposite.' She looked resigned rather than happy.

'Help yourself to more chips. Do you remember Skye, Nessie?'

'Aye, that was happiness, real happiness. But you've got to come back to real life in the end.'

'Lachlan was very wise. Know yourself, he said.'

'I know myself, and whit ma life's goin' to be like. But Skye, that was different. I'll never forget it, or Hamish.'

'Neither will I. What colour are you thinking of for the bridesmaids' dresses?'

'Chrissie, his sister, thought powder blue.'

'Powder blue? Would you not like, say, leaf green, very delicate, chiffon, maybe?'

'No, Chrissie wants powder blue. With rosebud trimming. And she's got the say. Her father's gettin' us the hall cheap in Possilpark for the reception.' Jess gave in.

'Peggy just had a registry office wedding in Perth. Did I tell you she's going to have a baby soon?'

'You didn't have to tell me. Still, she could have had a big bouquet to hold.' They laughed together.

'Maybe there will be a lot of big bouquets now that the War's on.' Jess got up to make some more tea.

Should one face the inevitable, or go on searching? Know yourself, Lachlan had said. He'd been lucky. He'd had a good teacher in Maureen.

Twenty-Eight

'Powder blue with rosebud trimmings,' she told Giles, laughing. She was describing Nessie's wedding to him, not liking herself too much. She had been cynical about the vulgarity of the speeches, the innuendos which had become coarser as the sparkling wine changed to whisky.

'Slightly different from this.' He touched a diamanté strap of her black chiffon dress.

'The complete ensemble.' She swung the silver evening bag he had given her by its chain. She knew her outfit was too expensive-looking for the firm's tennis club dance, the high-heeled silver slippers matching the enhanced silver gleam in her hair – the work of an expensive hairdresser.

At first Giles hadn't wanted to come. 'You're afraid your uncle might be there,' she had said.

He had been cross. 'What rubbish!'

And he had instantly recognised that his dinner jacket was out of place, although his sweet temper soon asserted itself. 'Come on, darling,' he said now. 'Let's dance.'

'All eyes are on you, Giles,' she said when they were on the floor. She knew that they were both overdressed, and that it was her fault. She was acutely aware of the glances, the slight smiles: she saw heads go together. Common sense had flown out of the window when she had bought the black chiffon dress. And there was the black satin underwear...

'It's you they're looking at, a *femme fatale.*' She was bent over his arm in a tango, and, looking up at him, she felt stupid. She should have told him. They should have gone straight to the flat.

'Let's sit down,' she said. 'I'm dizzy.'

They sat, and she smiled at him as she finished her wine. 'You can take me home in a minute.'

'Already?'

'I have a surprise for you.'

'I have one for you! I'd rather tell you when we're more private.'

'For me?' She felt a tinge of despair. 'Come on, then.' They got up and left as discreetly as they could. Everyone was dancing. 'They'll think you're taking me on to a nightclub,' she said, smiling at people who glanced at them.

In five minutes he had parked at her close. He turned and took her in his arms.

'My lovely sweet girl.' He put his cheek

against hers. 'This is going to break my heart.'

'Go on,' she said. She shivered. A black chiffon dress with diamanté straps was no comfort.

'I got an official letter...'

'Giving you the sack?' Anything to stop him.

'No, the other way round. It was a letter from a London paper offering me the job of war reporter.'

'You're taking it, of course.'

'I have to. It's what I've wanted. There was a little bit of wire-pulling, of course.'

'Of course.' She turned and put her face against him, put one arm round his neck. A heavy stone, so hurtful.

'You're crying.'

'It's the shock. I always knew that ... sooner or later...'

'I'm desolated too. It tears at my heart, the thought of not seeing you. But it isn't the end, and you know I've always wanted—'

'And there's a war on. Where's my bag?'

'Here.'

'Would you take the hankie out? It's silly.'

'I've got a better one. Let me dry your tears.' The crisp linen didn't mop very well, but his tenderness was all she wanted. A sweet boy, she thought, but he has to be a war correspondent like his cousin, and he can't see beyond that. Meantime, his arms were round her – he even smelled young.

'Would you like a coffee?' she said, sitting up.

He laughed. 'Have you got a flask or something?'

'No, I can make it upstairs.'

'Your mother?'

'She's housekeeping for the Gray brothers. She's taken James with her.'

'And you're in the flat alone?'

'That's it.'

He shook his head slowly. 'What a girl of surprises! A beautiful surprising girl in a black chiffon dress.' And black satin underwear.

'Give me my bag anyhow. My key's in it.'

They got out of the car.

Twenty-Nine

They walked into the close. It was dimly lit as usual – a gas lamp, fly-spotted on its glass sides.

When they got to the foot of the stairs she could see the dark well with a further flight downwards which led to the back yard, the haunt of beggars and cats. She had never dared to go down there at night. Peggy had often emptied the ashes in their bin at the foot of it without worrying.

A cheerful voice came from the darkness. 'Goodnight, Jess!' She couldn't see anyone, but recognised the voice. Nellie, who lived in the flat above theirs. She would be doing her 'winchin'', impervious of cat pee.

'Goodnight, Nellie,' she called, just as cheerfully. Of course, she thought, although she couldn't see Nellie, *she* could be seen under the lamp. And Giles.

'Just a neighbour,' she said to him. They walked up the stairs. Halfway up she turned to him, not stopping. 'Will you be going soon?'

'Yes, very soon. I've known for a week. I couldn't bear to tell you. I wondered if I should turn it down, but I couldn't...'

'It's what you wanted,' she said. 'Roger...'

'Yes, Roger.' That was the nub of it. They had reached her landing. She unlocked the door and said, 'Come in.' Giles followed her. She thought the lobby looked strange and unfamiliar, like a film set. 'I think I've some boiled ham...'

'Boiled ham?' He was incredulous.

'I meant for sandwiches. I don't know what I'm saying. With your coffee.'

'Bugger sandwiches.' He pulled her towards him. 'Jess, darling. Do you want me here? I'll go away.' Panic struck her.

'Don't go. I want you here. It's the shock.'

'I should have told you earlier. I was confused, miserable about leaving you, knowing that it was what I'd been waiting for, that I had to take it. You understand.'

'I understand,' she said. She turned away but he detained her with his hand.

'Jess, darling, you know I love you, always will. I'll never forget you, your sweetness ... but the time isn't right for us. I'm obsessed by the need to be involved...'

'You don't have to explain,' she said. 'There's something ahead for me too. I don't know what it is yet, but I know there's something...' – she thought of the word – 'fulfilling. I know myself now.' Lachlan would have been pleased to hear her say that.

He was leaning on one elbow looking down at her. They were lying on her bed. She saw a heap of black satin underwear on the counterpane. It didn't matter; its seductiveness. He was as naked as she was. 'My God, Jess,' he said.

'My God what?'

'You're so beautiful. Are you sure?'

'I'm sure.' She didn't even have to think about it.

This was the first time she had seen a man's body. James had been too young to count. The dark chest, the muscular arms – but not overly so. And the bits. She had read the various names for those bits in books, but had never known anyone intimately enough to share names. 'Tassel', she liked. But this was no tassel ... it was rearing like a signpost.

This is it, she thought, giving herself up. The surge of desire was like a great flood sweeping through her, carrying away the grief of knowing that the first was the last.

'I want...' she heard herself moan, and thought, so they *do* moan...

He had rolled away from her, fumbling, and she knew why. He wanted her to have no cause for worry. 'You're making sure that I won't get pregnant?' she said. He glanced at her with a raised eyebrow, as if he'd rather she wouldn't state the obvious.

She wasn't a bit embarrassed, only impatient. She wanted to say, 'Why are you taking so long?' She wanted to say, Hurry! Because this is our last chance, our first and last chance. While it lasts it will blot out the thought that I may never see you again.

She thought, how right Lachlan was. He said I needed to be loved. And loving and being loved, she saw now, was the first step to knowing oneself – like the clearing house, almost, for what lay ahead ... There was a loud bang in the lobby. She felt Giles go rigid beside her. His whole body ... or rather, the rest of his body. She moaned, a different kind of moan.

For some reason her mother had come home for something. Someone had told her that she was here with Giles. Mrs Thompson? No, she was a friend. Jess felt sick, faint, but not a Fleur-like faintness. One of horror.

There was no sound of footsteps. They waited, caught in the same position, their hips touching. He broke the silence with a harsh whisper. 'It's the wind. Just the wind.' The wind didn't penetrate up two flights of stairs. He didn't know that. He wasn't a flat dweller.

Suddenly galvanised, she leapt out of bed, snatched at an item of black satin – luckily it was a slip – pulled it over her head, and, tiptoeing to the door, stood listening behind it. No noise. He was right. It must have been the wind ... A sneaky wind it was to have penetrated up two flights of stairs.

She inched open the bedroom door. Still no noise. She stopped shaking. It couldn't have been her mother. She was incapable of coming into the house without making a noise. A dim light shining through the fanlight from the outside landing was enough to show her that the lobby was empty ... except for something lying behind the door – something which had been pushed through the letter box.

It was the flap that had banged ... not the door opening, as her guilty heart had thought. She tiptoed forward and saw what the object was, something like a large black snail: one of her silk gloves which she had tucked into her pocket. Nellie must have pushed it through. She would have found it lying on the staircase when she was going up to her flat.

She stared at the limp, innocent blackness of the glove and wanted to laugh. Instead she burst into tears, standing there, weeping and moaning.

She went back to the room and sat down on the bed beside Giles. He was half-dressed and sitting on the edge like an invalid contemplating his first steps. She leant against him, now laughing and moaning, laughing and moaning. He put his arm round her shoulders. 'So it *was* the wind?'

She shook her head and lifted up the glove in her hand. 'Turn round, Giles.' He did. She waggled it in front of him. 'Nellie must have pushed it through. I must have dropped it on the stairs.'

'No!' He looked at the glove as if he had never seen one before. 'What a sell!' he said like a schoolboy. He put his hand on her shoulders. 'Lie down. Lie down again with me until you feel better. We'll just lie quietly until you get over the shock.'

She lay down, full length, breathing quietly until her heart was steady. The relief, she thought, when I saw that glove!

And then, strangely, because she felt so relaxed, she found she was lying on that short turf in the early pearly morning, with Lachlan, the lip-lap licking of the water on her bare feet. *What you need is to be loved. You don't know how good it could be ...*

'Giles,' she said. She touched his shoulder, felt the soft poplin of his shirt, white with a narrow strip of blue.

'Yes?' He turned and looked steadily at her. She would have to do it all.

'Shall we start again?'

He lay down beside her and they exploded with laughter into each other's mouths. This needn't be serious, she thought. My God, it's the beginning, not the end of the world.

It was good, very good, but the after-love was even better. They lay quietly in each other's arms and they talked about their lives and about being in love and how necessary it was.

And she said she understood about his obsession, and he was lucky to know what it was, whereas she had still to find hers out ... but she had taken the first step and she was glad of that.

'I don't have to look backwards now,' she told him. 'It's like joined-up writing. I go on from here.'

'I'm the same,' he said, and boyishly added, 'I've led a pretty sheltered life, actually; the whole thing – school, Cambridge – has been a play with the same players. I'm ready for action now.' The University of Life, she thought sententiously, but thankfully didn't say it.

'Well, I'd better get off.' And putting a finger under the strap of her black satin slip he said, 'This is nice. Why haven't I seen it before?'

She watched him dress, pulling on his trousers, finding his shirt at the foot of the bed and pulling it over his head – it was already buttoned – making man-movements as he pushed and tucked. She loved him.

He was dressed, businesslike in his striped tie, his hair sleeked back with a swift glance at the mirror. 'I think I'll just push along to the hotel.'

'Yes.' No more tears. She got up and went to the door with him. Before she opened it he took her in his arms. They looked at each other before they kissed. 'It was good,' she said.

'The best. I'll write.'

She nodded. 'Good luck.'

'You too. Thanks,' he said. 'For everything.'

'Thanks,' she said.

He touched her face lightly, and she tried to memorise his – the dark eyes, the broad brow, the youthfulness. She doubted if she would ever know anyone so youthful again. Or so beautiful.

She stood listening to his confident footsteps as he ran downstairs, as light-footed as she felt. They were the same age – on the edge, ready. She still felt his touch on her cheek as she closed the door.

Thirty

'I might be able to take some more classes if you like, Jack,' Jess said a week later. 'I have more time on my hands now.' Jack Craven looked at her. She prayed he wouldn't make any snide remarks like, 'Has your boyfriend ditched you, then?' but knew he wouldn't. That was for counter clerks.

'That would be good,' he said. They had met in the corridor between classes. He seemed less relaxed than usual. 'As a matter of fact, Mr Jamieson is in charge of the staff arrangements now.' The pupils were streaming past, chattering as they went. 'A lot's been happening. Look, Jess, are you by any chance free tomorrow night?' He was tentative.

Tomorrow and every other night, she thought. But she had been glad of the empty house to go home to from the office each day. Her mother's presence would have crucified her. She had been able to fling herself on the bed she had lain on with Giles and weep her heart out.

She had wondered if Sir Bernard had guessed anything. He would know that Giles had left Glasgow, but his face had been impassive as he dictated. Since it had scarcely altered after his son's death, it was unlikely it would register any emotion for the demise of his nephew's affair with his secretary ... if he knew at all.

'Yes, I am, as a matter of fact,' she said.

'Danny Brown's, seven o'clock? Okay?' His eyes were lit up with his usual humorous smile. For the first time she noticed them – hazel, dark-lashed, unlike his sandy hair. Nothing dramatic about Jack Craven ... but likeable, there was no doubt about that.

'Great! Well, I'd better get on to my next class. These lads will be tearing the place down. Seven o'clock, then, tomorrow?' He looked pleased, almost wistfully pleased, she thought as she went to hers.

The following day – a Saturday – she made her face up carefully to go and see her mother at the Grays. It might be easier to tell her there that Giles had left Glasgow ... and her.

At the door she ran into James just going out. There was another boy with him.

'Hello, Jess!' He looked different, she thought, since he had left the flat – more grown-up; there was a glint of hair on his upper lip. 'This is Jock Craven. He's staying the weekend.'

'Hello, Jock.' She smiled at him. 'I know your father.' He had the same sandy hair and hazel eyes, but an air about him which was more insouciant.

'Hello,' he said. 'James asked me to stay here the weekend. I was glad. Dad had an engagement.'

'Had he? Well, don't let me keep you two.' She saw they were carrying dark green canvas bags. 'We're off to OTC practice,' James said. 'Great fun, isn't it, Jock?' Jock smiled and nodded like an elder brother. She thought he might be a year younger.

'Is Mother in?' she asked James.

'In, and in her element.' He grinned. 'Well, cheerio. We'd better be off.'

'Cheerio,' Jock repeated. He gave Jess a smile which lit up his eyes like his father's.

James was right about their mother. She had Mrs Bell just where she wanted her: propped up on a sofa. She greeted Jess in a queenly manner.

'You're just in time for a cup of tea. I was giving Mrs Bell one.'

'Thanks. I only dropped in for half an hour.'

'You're lookin' peely-wally. Are you no' feedin' yourself right?'

'Of course I am. How are you, Mrs Bell?'

'Getting along fine. Your mother's looking after me a treat.'

'I'm sure she is. Are Mr Thomas and Mr Peter not here?' Her mother answered for her.

'They've gone down to Helensburgh to sign the lease for Mrs Bell's bungalow. A nice wee place, it seems.'

'I'm pleased for you, Mrs Bell. You'll miss the Mansions all the same.'

'Aye, but the brothers will be left in capable hands.' She nodded to Jess's mother, who accepted the attribute as her due with a reciprocal nod.

'Only the best is good enough for them. I'll be back and forward to get ma things, Jess. Is there any *news*?' She made elaborate play with her eyebrows.

'News? About the War?' Her mother tut-tutted in annoyance.

'The War? That'll soon be over. No, you and...' She drew her eyebrows together, and her lips looked meaningful. She still couldn't say it.

'Giles? He's left Glasgow.' She had practised saying that. 'I won't see him again.' She lifted her cup and took a sip of tea.

There was a silence. Mrs Bell sipped hers, looking away. She was all right with her bungalow. She was staying out of this.

'What do you mean you won't be seeing him again?' Her face was bursting with scarcely concealed chagrin, as if all the boastful remarks she had made to Mrs Bell

312

about Giles were rising in her gorge to choke her.

'He's going to be a war correspondent. He can't make any plans for the future. There's a war on.'

'You don't have to tell me that! As long as it's over before James has to go. That's all a have to say on that!' She nodded to Mrs Bell, who nodded feebly back. She turned to Jess again. 'You and me will have a good talk when a come to get ma things.'

Jess got up. 'I have an appointment for tonight. I'd better go. Thanks for the tea.'

You can talk all you like when you come for your things, she thought as she went down the stairs with the mahogany bannister, but it won't alter facts. It's over, that bright, beautiful love affair. It's over.

Everyone was making plans; she, too, must look forwards, not back. Her family's lives had changed. James, if the War lasted a few years, would be most affected. Nothing would ever be the same again. How, she wondered, would it affect her?

'I should have asked you if this place suited you,' Jack Craven said as they sat opposite each other at the restaurant that evening.

'I've always liked it here.'

'I lived in France for seven years. I got a taste for their cuisine. But I gave up trying to find it in Glasgow. Try mentioning frogs'

313

legs to a Scotsman!'

'I didn't know you were there for so long.'

'Yes, I did a year's teaching at St Denis in the north of Paris and met my wife there, so I stayed on. Jock was born there.'

'Oh!' She hadn't known this. 'But you decided to come back, despite the cuisine?'

'Yes. My father became very ill, but Janette never liked it here, so she went back to Paris and met someone else. She's got a new family. Jock elected to stay with me, or maybe it was because of his granddad. They were great pals.' He smiled at her. 'Now you know everything about me.' Not quite, she thought.

'I met your son today. He's very like you.'

'Everyone says so. He and your brother are great friends. It was good of him to have Jock stay this weekend.'

'It was good of you to let him.'

'But I was meeting you.' He smiled easily – it was the natural arrangement of his features, she decided. 'So let's get on to something more important. What would you like to eat?'

'I never look at the menu.' She felt a sharp stab of agony. *Do you know what Pavlova is? You get it at the Grosvenor...* 'What about roast chicken if they have it?'

'They'll have roast chicken. They run about in their thousands around Glasgow. And vegetables?'

'Peas?' *You could spit peas through me* ...
That musical, un-Scottish voice – not so
sharp this time – the agony. And she'd ask
for lemon meringue tart, when it came to
the sweet.

'I'm dying to know why you said I was to
see Mr Jamieson,' she said when they were
tucking into their roast chicken. It was the
first food she had really tasted since Giles
had gone.

'I'm leaving. I've appointed Norman
Jamieson to be Deputy Head, so he'd better
get his hand in. *I'm* dying to know why you
want to take more classes. I understood you
were ... fully occupied.' She wondered if it
was a meaningful glance he gave her.

'I was, but ... circumstances have changed.' She couldn't go on.

'But you're working every day as well?' He
hadn't noticed her eyes filling up, or was
pretending not to notice.

'Yes.' She was all right now. And she could
rely on the wine loosening her tongue,
blunting the sharp edges of her grief. 'I'm ...
trying to work things out. I know I could be
running my department at the office fairly
soon, but I don't want that kind of commit-
ment meantime. And I thought, if I took on
more work with you I might decide to shift
my allegiance, if you'd have me full time ...
As I said, I'm just beginning to work things
out. There's the War. I expect it's making a

315

lot of us think.' She smiled at him. 'It's over to you now.'

'I feel the same. The War's made me think. I'm too old at thirty-six to be called up – at least for a long time – but too young to settle down to running a commercial college while it's on. I felt there was more I could do...'

She was curious. 'You're becoming restless, like me?' Thirty-six, she was thinking. He must have married very young.

'I imagine most people are having to review their lives just now. I've talked it over with Jock, and he agrees with me. I've been accepted at the Admiralty – "for the duration", as they say – so I'm going to London.'

She was surprised, almost envious. She remembered how when she had been studying she had been offered a place as a typist in the Admiralty and her mother had put her foot down. 'Nobody leaves this house till they're married.' Peggy had had the guts to do it, she thought now. 'What made you choose the Admiralty?'

'Sentiment. My father was a naval engineer, and I admired him as well as loved him. He sometimes had to sail with the warship he'd been working on for its trials. He'd tell me about it. Once he took me on one, when it was docked at the Clyde.'

'Didn't you want to become a naval engineer like him?'

'Sure, but sad to say I was a poor maths

scholar and took languages instead at the University. I bought the College with money I was left by him. It seemed a good idea at the time.' Was it because he had a wife and child to support? she wondered.

'Did you just *ask* to be accepted for the Admiralty?'

'Yes, I put it in my application. I had Civil Service qualifications. I don't know what I'll be doing. Teaching, I expect.'

'What about Jock?'

'Oh, he approves. He's going to board at the Academy. Personally I think it's a good time for me to hand him over. I wouldn't want a son who traipsed around with his dad at his age.' She nodded.

'I think you're right there. James has been saved from being a mother's boy in a different way. Two elderly bachelors who admired my father took him in hand. My mother will be housekeeping for them, but her dominance will be...' She laughed.

'Defused, somewhat?'

'Or diffused. Her plan was that I'd be getting married and she'd get rid of our flat, but that' – try saying it this time without your eyes filling up – 'isn't going to happen.' She took a sip of wine. She'd done it.

'Strange how things turn out.' His look was not pitying, simply interested. 'But maybe it gives you room to plan for yourself.'

They were now tackling the lemon meringue tart, but she wasn't going to be able to finish it. Still, she had managed the chicken. And the wine was good.

He said, 'About applying for more work, Jess ... of course I'd love to have you, but don't push yourself too hard. If you like to regard it as a jumping-off place, do so by all means. You might feel you want to be more involved, move around like me. Your mother and James will be taken care of by those two elderly bachelors you tell me about. You're free as air.'

'So I am.' She lifted her glass. 'Free as air!' she repeated.

They had coffee, and he took her home in a taxi. She didn't ask him up to the flat, and he made no suggestions. But he got out and walked to the close with her.

'It's a great time to be alive,' he said. 'Exciting, dangerous maybe, but ... great. I don't think you'd forgive yourself if you weren't helping in some way. And I say that even if it means losing one of the best teachers I've ever had.'

'Thanks.' She laughed because it was natural to laugh with him. 'And if I can, sort of, keep an eye on Jock in any way, I'll be glad to ... until I become involved.'

'That's a kind offer. I'll take you up on that.' They shook hands, and she felt the same warmth as she had felt with Lachlan.

She went up to the flat feeling inspired, which was a fine feeling.

She would never forget Giles. He had been part of her, part of a process, but now they were both moving on.

How strange, she thought later, that Jack Craven should be going to the Admiralty, where she could have gone long ago. It would be interesting to know if her name was still on their files...